Salvaje

by

Lee Roland

Angel of Death, Book II

Salvaje

COPYRIGHT © 2022 by Lee Roland

Cover Art by *Debbie Taylor*

The Wild Rose Press, Inc.
PO Box 708
Adams Basin, NY 14410-0708
Visit us at www.thewildrosepress.com

Publishing History
First Edition, 2022
Trade Paperback ISBN 978-1-5092-4158-3
Digital ISBN 978-1-5092-4159-0

Angel of Death, Book II
Published in the United States of America

Praise for Lee Roland

"If you enjoy urban fantasies with strong, not-so-nice, sarcastic heroines with killer instincts and a plethora of diverse supporting characters, give [Book I Huntress Rising] a try! I guarantee you won't be able to put it down."

~ *The Eclectic Review*

The faint pat of footsteps sounded like a distant voice. A figure approached through a path created by retreating vampires, werewolves, and humans. A woman with stick thin arms and legs sauntered barefoot across the plaza, bearing down upon Anson Sewell and Orion, the vampire prince. Dingy mouse colored hair, streaked with gray, twisted, fell into a single, untidy, waist-length braid. She'd drawn that braid forward across her shoulder where her thin bony hands clutched it like a lifeline. Dressed in rags, a mass of odd bead necklaces and other small trinkets on strings hung from her lean neck. A glint of more precious stones peeked through that tangled collection.

Every five or six feet she would stop and dance a few steps. She had the look of someone the unmerciful noonday sun had scorched to the bone, then cast away to live out her life in tierra sombra, the Shadowland. Even before I heard her wordless song and saw her wild, pale eyes, I knew she was mad.

How amazing. Orion and Anson bowed to her when she stopped in front of them. The lethal vampire and the werewolf made of fur, fangs, and claws, bowed before one old human woman.

Dedication

For Woody. I'm almost finished here, love.

Book 1—Huntress Rising

Huntress Rising is a post-apocalypse urban fantasy. It's primarily the chronicle of human beings who live, love, and fight to survive in a deadly future. A group of humans, vampires, and werewolves who care about their world and its inhabitants have stolen equipment that will destroy the last nuclear missiles in the world. With a vampire who desires to control and use those missiles in pursuit, they make a dangerous journey across the country to Salvaje, New Mexico.

Book II—Salvaje
Protagonists

Maat Ferris is not always a reliable narrator for her own life story. She is inconsistent in language, but ferocious when she protects those she cares for. At twelve, she saw werewolves slaughter her family, and that violence left her emotionally filled with blind hatred of the beasts. Her loving but unstable Uncle Jake adopted and trained her to be a ruthless, vengeful, monster killer. While she is a skillful and exceptionally successful hunter, catastrophe often follows her interactions with people. Brash and narcissistic, she often miscalculates and makes appalling personal and professional decisions. Her worst was an attempt to kill vampires in the ruins of New York City. That challenge resulted in Maat enduring horrific torture that would dominate her life.

Colonel Xavier is a taciturn, methodical soldier with a dangerous, volatile temper he keeps under control—most of the time. A werewolf slaughtered his wife and infant daughter, and he's desperate to protect his surviving son. With that son held hostage by the tyrant president, the soldier must obey atrocious orders at times. He maintains tight control, remaining in the background, waiting for a chance for him and his son to escape. Then along comes a certain brash, volatile woman who sets off that explosive temper in a volcanic blast of fire and fury.

Maat and Xavier's crew.

Ty Daniels. Xavier's son. Ty is a lovable, immature seventeen-year-old who thinks he's in love with Maat.

Ajax. Demolitions expert and Maat's longtime friend. He's fond of big booms and big women, particularly his twins—blonde Mary and the darker lovely Giselle.

Jacob. A werewolf who has, for some mysterious reason, pledged his life to protect Maat.

Cody. A young vampire who supplied blood to save Maat's life when she was dying in Memphis. She's come to accept him as one of her crew.

The pursuing villains

Ruelle San Nicolás. A malicious thousand-year-old vampire who has a complex relationship with Maat. He has remained part of her life for years after saving her from other vampires in New York.

Aaron Gannett. Tyrant and dictator of a fractured land. Gannett is under the vampire Ruelle's control, and his mind is growing increasingly unstable.

Others

Ray Heflin. Resident of Salvaje, tradesman, and Wagon Master of the west bound convoy carrying Maat and her crew.

Lowell Parr. Former vice president in Gannett's government. He deserted Gannett to flee west with Maat.

Sabrina. Gannett's wife. A werewolf herself, she helped in the plot to steal the equipment, though she knows it might cost her life.

Sable. Maat's dear friend who co-owned a Memphis brothel.

Anolia. Gentle loving leader of Avalon, the agricultural commune where Maat fled when she was barely able to function. Killed by werewolves in Huntress Rising.

Places

New Washington ~* ~ Capital of the United States

Memphis ~*~ City in ruins, destroyed when army chasing our heroes are attacked.

Salvaje ~*~ City that earned the name of Savage.

Agricultural Communes ~*~ Farmers and families gathered in fortified compounds for greater safety from werewolf attacks.

Avalon Ag Commune ~*~ Maat's home.

CLT—Century Life Tarmac ~*~ The incredibly durable but limited interstate network of roads built before the war. Local roads might go to ruin, but CLT remained.

Miscellaneous

Werewolves. Some no more than animals and others almost human. Super sensitive to silver, but a regular bullet to heart or brain will kill them. Some go crazy killing when they change from human to beast form.

Vampires are killers. Incredibly strong and fast, the only weapon against them is sunlight—or removing their heads if you got that close and lived. There are not that many of them in the world, thank God. And yes, consumption of vamp blood is a restorative for human injuries.

Prologue

My mother named me Maat, after the ancient Egyptian goddess of justice and order. If you greet me with some benign variation of, *Hello, Maat,* you will usually receive a benign reply. However, *I'm going to kill you, bitch,* or some equally discourteous salutation usually results in physical violence.

Justice and order. No one has ever accused me of any kind of order, but I've dealt a lot of justice in my time. I made my first werewolf kill when I was thirteen. Backed up by my crazy Uncle Jake, I hunted down a werewolf that had slaughtered a family of five at an agricultural commune.

Unfortunately, in the last few weeks, my experiences with werewolves have spun around so fast it's left me dizzy and struggling to stay sensible. If I planned to survive the next few weeks, I needed to reclaim control of my life.

By 2035, World War III and the plague they called the Devil's Dance had leveled all the large cities and killed most of the world's humans. The apocalypse arrived bearing all the unimaginable tragedy. That's when the werewolves and vampires came out of hiding and attacked. Now, in 2085, my country is an empty land where pockets of humans struggle to survive. Vamps are rare. Werewolves are not. And of course, we humans battle each other too, as we have since the first cave man bashed another's head in with a rock.

With dangerously low populations, the last thing we need is for a handful of nuclear weapons, reputed to be the last in existence, to fall into the hands of Aaron Gannett, President and Dictator of the United States. Feeling his tyrant's grip on the country slipping away, Gannett is desperate to score those weapons.

But it's not really Gannett who worries me so much. The so-called president has fallen under the spell of a powerful and malevolent vampire named Ruelle. Ruelle sees Gannett as a puppet, a shadow leader for his schemes of a grand empire. I've known Ruelle for years. He somehow managed to weave his life into mine. For some unarticulated reason, he hasn't killed me yet. I've seen some of his plans—and the horrific results when they failed.

In a spectacular offensive, this hunter and Colonel Xavier—formerly Gannett's Chief of Security—managed to steal the equipment that will allow destruction of the nukes. Racing west across the vast empty country, pursued by Ruelle and Gannett's army, we barely escaped an artillery bombardment in Memphis.

Our destination? Salvaje, New Mexico, where vampires, werewolves, and humans live in a cautious semi-peace. Or at least that's what people who are supposed to know tell me. My loved ones slaughtered by werewolves and my own torment by vampires has made me an indomitable cynic. Now, three werewolves, one of whom died after pledging me her life, have challenged my beliefs. Then there's the young vampire. I'm now in debt to him since he saved my life. I'm not comfortable with it yet, but I deal on a day-to-day and night-to-night experience.

Oh, and I'd received a major injury and died for a few minutes along the way. At least that's what they say after they brought me back. After that, my perception of the world around me and my psychic abilities have undergone a radical change. A far more intuitive person has emerged from my trauma. Every mile I traveled on this journey allowed me to experience new things. My perception of the extrasensory world widens with each passing day.

We'd crossed the lonely uninhabited land, surmounted flooding rainstorms, a blinding dust storm, attacks by bandits, and two major mechanical breakdowns. We also survived the ragged and raging personality issues of a hundred utterly miserable, heavily armed men and women.

Salvaje will welcome our purloined cargo. But will it also welcome a thief and liar like me? Then there's Xavier, at times called Gannett's Butcher because of his former role leading Gannett's security. Colonel Xavier and I have multiple enemies. And what about our crew? How will Salvaje deal with Jacob, a powerful eastern werewolf, a stranger? Then there's Cody, a vampire who looks young but isn't, and Ajax, a former militia man and demolitions expert with robust desires for ample women and devastating explosions.

It's hard to comprehend that only weeks ago Xavier and ex-vice president Parr had kidnapped me from Avalon, a place where I'd sought refuge from violence. My kidnappers then set me on this dubious and dangerous adventure. I'd suffered brutal trauma and excruciating pain. I'd wept guilty, bitter tears for my beautiful friend and surrogate mother as she died in my arms. And yes, I'd fallen in love. Me, Maat Athena Ferris—a.k.a. Suriel, the fierce, mystical Angel of Death, now raced along the most dangerous path of all. I desperately desired Colonel Xavier, a man who can match and surpass my propensity for violence. Surely, if I survived werewolves and vampires, I could survive a romantic adventure with one human.

Couldn't I?

Chapter One

Salvaje 2085 A.D.

Almost there! Salvaje, New Mexico, the terminus of our excruciating journey drew ever closer. We traveled 1,500 miles from New Washington according to Heflin, our convoy Wagon Master and long-time Salvaje resident.

Heflin had asked me to ride in the lead truck with him again. I suspect it was his misguided and doomed effort to control me by keeping me close. His misgivings about me and my loyalty had seemed to ease after my injuries in Memphis. For a brief time, my suffering had proved my allegiance to his cause—or at least tolerable commitment. His original mistrust rose again as we headed west and grows wider and deeper again every mile closer to Salvaje.

Most everyone I've dealt with has found one or more facets of my personality and deeds objectionable at various times. What can I say? I grew up and live ass-deep in a violent world. That world created and molded me—a savage uniquely worthy of living in this brutal time in history.

"About thirty miles until home." Heflin, who hadn't spoken for the last hour, kept his eyes focused on the road straight ahead. His white-knuckled hands gripped the steering wheel tight enough to make me think he feared it might come loose and fly out the window.

The sun rose at our backs and cast multi-colored shadows across the hills. Salvaje, and my future, lay ahead. It was greener in places than I expected, considering the desert land we'd traveled through earlier. Cattle and sheep dotted the distant slopes, though I couldn't see what they were eating. Armed cowboys guarded the treasured property. We'd left the almost indestructible CLT, Century Life Tarmac, hours ago. The CLT had been our constant path since leaving Memphis. The less permanent local-road asphalt under the tires now bore signs of recent repair and remained smooth.

In Salvaje, I'm told, vampires, werewolves, and humans live in peace by virtue of a pact, a set of laws called the Asha. My actual life experience with vamps and werewolves labeled such ideas as self-deluding. But here I am. And I'll play fair—if they will.

Heflin had told me the Asha forbids vampires taking human blood. Animal blood had to suffice, hence the herds we'd passed. They practiced careful breeding of the cattle and sheep for meat and blood. Vampires? Animal blood? I raised my eyebrows at that bit of information, but it was his town. I guess he would know. I had a brief vision of the only vampire I knew intimately sneering at animal blood and tossing it back in the face of whomever offered him such mortifying nourishment. Then, if human, the unlucky bearer of nourishment became dinner.

Guarded by the mercenaries we hired in Memphis, we'd driven through the last seven hundred miles of absolute wilderness. Drivers slept in shifts, and we slowed to a crawl after dark. We'd left the CLT interstate only once when Heflin guided the convoy around Oklahoma City rather than through it. He didn't say why. We stopped only for fueling from the tanker trucks or to allow the road crew to clean drifting sand off the pavement a couple of times.

"What's that?" I asked Heflin, noting multiple approaching vehicles ahead.

"Another convoy, heading east." He slowed the vehicle to a stop and turned to me. "Will you trust me and stay in the Turtle? I need all of you to walk softly right now. It's hard for me to bring this many people in, especially a new vamp and a were. Those groups have their own society and hierarchy. Jacob and Cody will have to deal with how things are run."

His face was serious. Serious enough to make me want to check my weapons.

"Okay," I agreed, albeit reluctantly. Now he'd made me uncomfortable. "It's your town."

He must have heard my uneasiness. "I understand, Maat. But I expect no problems."

Then why do I have to stay out of sight, Mr. Wagon Master? And no, I won't offer you trust when you've obviously decided I'm unworthy of yours.

Stay in the Turtle? The thick boxy vehicle would grow hotter by the minute. The approaching convoy stopped two-hundred feet from us. As Heflin climbed out and walked toward it, men poured from the back of the first truck. A troop carrier. These guys didn't have uniforms, but they held themselves like soldiers—tough, like Xavier's former troops.

My psychic senses perked up. Two werewolves, a male in fang and fur and a female in human form, walked among them. A man and a woman climbed out of the lead truck cab and met Heflin. The soldiers stayed behind the two. The pair greeted Heflin with hugs and back slaps of congratulations. Their man had brought home the prize. At a wave of Heflin's hand, Parr walked forward from behind my Turtle and joined them. More backslaps and handshakes. I think he wanted to put the former vice president ahead of Xavier in the hierarchy of the new people. I wouldn't have. While I liked the former vice president, in our ferocious world, the soldier Xavier should outrank a politician.

I could see the male werewolf, now, standing tall and furry among the soldiers. Big, but not as big as Jacob when he changed shape. I wondered if weres walked around blatantly naked in Salvaje, whether male or female.

The were shoved his aura out, searching our convoy. I'd never experienced such before. I'd always been the one searching. Was this another new psychic sense I'd acquired since my heart stopped and I'd *died* for long minutes in Little Rock? I didn't know what the werewolf wanted, but the pack on this convoy was *mine*.

When his search hit me, I pushed back.

Wow! I staggered him. *Oh, Maat, if you could have done that back when you hunted the beasts*. He snarled and made a stride in my direction, though I doubted he could see me. The soldiers grabbed him. He backed down. I had to shake my head in amazement. Grab a fuzzy were? These humans lived dangerously.

A significant cluster of soldiers fell into line and marched toward us, led by Heflin, Parr, and the man and woman he'd greeted. I don't like soldiers of any kind, especially when they advanced at me. Thank God the werewolf stayed behind.

Earlier in the morning, right after daylight, Heflin had stopped us and ordered the trucks carrying the mercenaries to the back of the convoy line. He had hired them in West Memphis to guard us on the dangerous trip across the country. They'd done a respectable job. He told them to be on alert for an attack from behind. But left no defense from these newly arrived troops, but obviously he'd planned it that way.

Plans made by a man who didn't like me? No, I knew better. I slipped out the Turtle's passenger door when his head turned and hurried back so I would be with my crew. Our Wagon Master had made what now seemed a deliberate action to keep me from joining them. Yes, we were dangerous, even with our vampire locked away from the sun. Damn it, though. We were supposed to be his allies, to work for him.

Jacob, Xavier, and Ty stood together by Ajax's truck in the middle of the convoy. Ajax and his corpulent twins, blonde Mary and dark Giselle, sat in the cab. Good. All my people together. Cody slept in his box safely tucked away in the truck Xavier had driven. My people. How odd to think those words. The lone hunter, Maat Ferris, had acquired a family.

Heflin, Lowell, and the man and woman he was leading passed us and continued the tour. Heflin's eyes widened when he saw me standing by the truck with Xavier and the others, but he said nothing. Most of the soldiers followed the four. Xavier, silent as usual, stared after them, eyes narrowed. He didn't like the situation either, but Heflin was leader here.

"What is it?" Jacob asked softly.

I shook my head. "Don't know. Heflin's acting

weird."

Ajax slid out of the truck and joined us. His dark skin stretched over corded muscles. Tall and lean, and ready to fight. "More worms." He sneered.

Ajax was right though—more were coming and moving closer. They spread out every six feet along the convoy, guns ready. They faced us, keeping us in place, not outward to guard us from attack.

The convoy meeting us rolled forward and passed by, headed east. It seemed like a regular run, except for three empty troop carriers bringing up the rear.

Heflin suddenly appeared, body tight and fists clenched. Not anger, but more obvious apprehension. He coughed and cleared his throat. "I must send the mercenaries I hired back to West Memphis now. We don't allow strangers into Salvaje. I didn't tell them that when I hired them. A few will object. It's happened before, though I'm paying them three times the regular rate." He rubbed a hand across his head visibly plucking a few of the thinning bleached hair. "The soldiers are to guarantee they go peacefully."

Sounded rational. Except for one thing. It was Xavier the soldier who stated the obvious. "The string of guards is for us, then. Why? All action is back there." He nodded toward the rear of the convoy.

"It's just procedure, Xavier. It happens to every convoy. We have to account for every truck, every person who reaches Salvaje."

Okay, but I had a warning for him. I wanted him to know I'd figured out what he was trying to accomplish. "Sounds reasonable. But Hef, you don't try to deliberately separate me from my pack again. I assure you I can cause you considerable grief all by myself. I don't require back-up."

He stared at me, then slowly nodded. He turned and stepped quickly toward the front.

Ty, like the teenager he was, had to say it. "We're your...pack?"

To my utter surprise, normally reticent Ajax answered him. "And what else would we be, boy? A gang? A mob? Oh, maybe a posse."

Ty grinned. "Yeah. Posse. I like that. But we gotta have a name."

Ajax offered Ferocious Few, Brute Bastards, but Jacob objected when Ty suggested Harrowing Hellhounds. Referring to werewolves as dogs seriously pissed them off according to him. We all broke into much needed laughter, especially when Mary suggested she, Giselle, and I could rightfully claim to be the Brothel Bunch. I had owned half of a house in Memphis, and they'd worked in a few, so it seemed appropriate.

A good break in tension, even if the soldiers around us stared. Xavier remained taciturn as usual, but he did smile occasionally now. What a change. I leaned against him. It so tempted me, his solid assurance in a world of so little comfort. We'd battled verbally and physically since we'd met until something changed in both of us and we realized we belonged with each other. We'd been together since West Memphis. No privacy on a convoy, so we weren't lovers yet.

Ajax eyed me. He'd stayed close to his truck and his women for most of the journey. We'd not had much time to talk. I was not acting like the Maat he'd known for so many years. He'd wait for me to speak. He's my most loyal friend and I'd trust him with my life.

Ajax and I had met at the energetic age of seventeen.

We both enlisted in the Army's now defunct Freak Squad, an official government outfit to fight werewolves. The officers deemed him, me, and Mac McKellen the scourge of the squad, surpassed only by the beasts we fought. Mac was my first love, my dearest love, although there was no way to compare him to Xavier. We were barely more than adolescents when weres killed him and left me with injuries so grave I'd never be able to bear children. Ajax and I had great adventures since then, though, not all lawful. We did not regard soldiers as friends.

Things moved along fast. Good thing, since every minute sent the sun higher in the sky and raised the temperature to oven hot. Within an hour—and without any gunfire —the mercenaries headed back in the east-bound convoy. It was a financially satisfactory deal for them, but after such a long, torturous journey I would have been looking forward to a bit of down time, too.

Heflin came back as the eastbound convoy left. His lined face relaxed a bit. "Just a little longer. We're waiting on someone."

Blonde Mary leaned out of the truck and grabbed Ajax by the hair. He grinned, but the grin faded as she whispered in his ear. She released him with a pat on the cheek. He sighed and said, "Maat...the girls...you know..."

I knew. I had to piss too. Men had bladders like gallon jugs, and they could go to the back of the truck. I have performed the pee at the back of the truck thing, but I preferred privacy when I dropped my pants for necessary functions. The land at the roadside had patches of high thin bushes where we could walk twenty feet and be out of sight. It would do.

"I'll take them, but you three," I said to Xavier, Jacob, and Ty, "no matter what, if Ajax moves, pin him to the ground. I doubt if I can take the girls to the bushes without shit-mouth trouble coming down. I'll deal with it, but he overreacts worse than me."

Ajax growled, but Jacob, Ty, and Xavier smiled. I removed my guns and gave them to Xavier. I doubted I'd get by the soldiers carrying them. The twins climbed out of the truck, and we started for the side of the road. Several soldiers quickly closed in a circle around us. *Oh, yes, we were the ones they guarded.*

I held my hands out, palms up. "Hey. The ladies and I are going to the bushes for a minute. You know…girl stuff."

Another soldier came. A tall, muscular man with a rough, craggy face, his cool blue eyes assessed the situation. After a moment he said, "Don't go far."

I nodded. I glanced back at the truck where Jacob and Xavier had Ajax by the arms, thereby keeping the situation from morphing into a catastrophe. Ajax's taut muscles stood out under his dark skin.

"Thank you," I said to the soldier. "I'm Maat Ferris."

"Sergeant Patterson. Hurry. Watch for snakes."

Okay. I could do snake watcher.

When we relieved ourselves and returned, the Sergeant's expression had changed. His deeply tanned face had softened. He smiled at Giselle and made sure she noticed him before he left us. I didn't blame him. Both of Ajax's women were certainly attractive, but darker Giselle's skin did shine under the noonday sun. Pretty porcelain Mary would fare better after dark. Giselle had returned Patterson's smile, but she turned where Ajax couldn't see.

I retrieved my guns and moved closer to Xavier. "You reckon these guys are as competent as your black shirts?" Black shirt. My name for his New Washington troops. Loyal every one of them. Loyal to him alone. Gannett had soldiers with brown uniforms who would never approach the black shirt's skill.

Xavier shrugged. "Could be. Rough around the edges, though. Discipline is slack. I certainly know more efficient ways to conduct this particular exchange operation."

I leaned closer to him. Ajax winked at me.

Five trucks left our stationary convoy, including the equipment truck Xavier and I retrieved from the mountains north of New Washington. They turned right at a crossroad just ahead of us and drove toward distant rocky peaks. The confirmation, the symbol of all that bitter pain, all the mournful dead, easily rolled away. Almost all of the soldiers went with them. Unfortunately, the strange weres were among the ones who remained.

Heflin rejoined us with the man and woman he'd escorted to the end of the convoy. He introduced the man, General Mylonas, to Xavier. The woman he called Council Member Stalt. He defined neither the general's army nor gave the council member a specific purview. He did not introduce the rest of us. I guess we weren't important.

The werewolf among the Salvaje troops gave a psychic challenge again. I didn't answer. I wanted him to back off. I knew he wouldn't.

"There's going to be a fight." I spoke as casually as I could.

"Maat?" Heflin's voice said his stress level went

critical.

"I've been challenged, Hef. One of your...*tame*...weres. He started it, and he's going to attack. You want me to stand here and let him kill me?"

"But why..." Heflin appeared shocked.

I drew my knife. "I don't know *why*. I know werewolves kill humans. It's what they do. You were once militia. You should know better. I will not psychoanalyze monsters. Everyone here stay back. Your Salvaje werewolves? Tame, my ass."

Chapter Two

Jacob, my werewolf whom I just insulted stepped up to me. "Let me face him for you."

"No. He's focused on me now. It's personal. Maybe he knows who I am."

Xavier reached for me. I held up my hand. "Only one. Not an army. I did this a long time before you showed up."

His mouth tightened, and his fists clenched, but he let me be. He wouldn't smother me. At least this time. I loved him more for that impeccable gift of freedom.

The were came racing down the road toward me. I moved farther into the open to set myself apart. Me, he had to come to me.

I let myself relax, then focused on the heavy pounding of his clawed feet, the grunts of rapid breathing. He made a low whining sound, neither a growl nor a roar. The soldiers around him shouted and ran after him. They couldn't catch him but, if they did, he'd tear them apart. With each breath his whine rose to the familiar insane, killing roar I knew so well.

In the past I'd have drawn the Rudra and shot him. High-impact silvers would blow massive holes in his body. It wouldn't work here. A single shot, and his armed companions would react instantly, without thought or reason. We'd all die. So, human with a silver knife against a were? Maat Ferris, the experienced hunter. *Yes, that was me.*

But everything had changed when I'd crossed the Mississippi River. New realities had shattered my perception of the psychic world and wiped away life-long held concepts. I could not only sense him, but I could experience him as if I were inside his head. Another facet of my kissing death in Little Rock.

His rage...mindless, animal, no fight involved. Just death and destruction. He'd gone insane when he'd changed shape. How could the people of Salvaje live with such among them? Foam dripped from his mouth and sprayed down his chest. He flung his arms up over his head in the oh so familiar werewolf attack form I knew. At least that remained the same.

Time slowed in my mind. His race toward me reduced to a swim through clear syrup. I waited until he came within ten feet, and then charged. Ducking under his upraised arms and clawed hands, I jammed the blade into his heart. Efficiency in action. I'd faced them before, but not like this.

Release the knife and step aside to let him fall. Mistake. Deadly mistake. As he came down, he suddenly twisted, grabbed, and dragged me with him. Dying, his foul mouth with its four-inch canines opened wide. He attached those deadly spikes into my arm, near my shoulder. My mind returned to the blind agony of the vampires' red-hot iron bar on my back when they'd captured me in New York. His weight crushed me to the pavement. The scream I heard was my own.

Monstrous pain, shrill, razor edged...on and on... Jacob jerked the were's body off me. Xavier had me in his arms. Blood sheeted my shirt. My arm felt like I had steel nails driven deep and anchored in bone. *Move, Maat! Get up!* I had to pretend the were's impact had only stunned me. I must not show weakness.

"Help me up," I demanded, cried, cursed, and struggled. "Fuck it! Damn! Damn! Son of a bitch. Get me on my feet. Now!"

Xavier and Ajax lifted me. They stayed close and supported me. The urgency in my voice made it imperative. I had to stand. With their help, I did. *Alpha bitch! Yes!* My men would catch me if I fell. Thank God, Jacob, my own werewolf, knew better than to change shape and fight. I couldn't imagine what would happen if he did. I fought the massive waves of pain and tried to freeze my face in an expression to pretend nothing was wrong. I utterly failed in pretense.

The Salvaje soldiers came, guns pointed—at us. All they needed was the slightest provocation, and we'd die. Then the second were, the female in human form approached. She stepped past the soldiers and slowly came to us.

She stared down at the beast. He lay on his back with my silver-bladed knife protruding from his chest. She raised her eyes to me. Her face had no expression. "Will you remove your silver knife so that I may take my mate home?"

Her mate. Oh, shit.

"Xavier?" I asked. "Will you..." I didn't have the strength. He left me in Ajax's hands and went to the body. He exposed his own hands to show he had no weapons. The knife made a soft sucking sound as he pulled it out. I'd heard the sound before, but this time it made me gag. As he returned to me, I had to ask the female were. "Why did your mate challenge me? He attacked. I swear, I didn't want to fight him."

She shook her head. "I don't know. He has not been right in his mind for weeks. But I had not thought this would happen." She frowned. "You are not responsible."

The female might not hold me responsible, but from the looks the soldiers gave me, I'd bet they did. Such an odd thing to see, comradeship between human and were. Yes, I had Jacob as a new werewolf model in my life, but we weren't soldiers. Ajax and Xavier drew me away as they gathered around the body of their fallen comrade.

I managed to keep a straight face until we reached Ajax's truck. "God damn it hurts." I clenched my teeth. Sweat soaked me, and my body shook. Ajax swooped me up in his arms and hauled me off the road into the bushes. He sat me down in the shade of a stunted tree and tore my shirtsleeve. Xavier was on his knees beside me. He couldn't mask his horror.

"Maat!" Ty shouted as he ran up.

Ajax jumped to his feet. He grabbed Ty by the shirt collar and shook him. "Shut up, damn it. Just fucking calm down." Ty's eyes popped open wide, and he choked. Ajax released him. He staggered back and landed on his ass.

Giselle came running up with a jug of water. Lowell and Heflin followed her. Great. An audience. Jacob was there, standing apart. Such a strange look on his face. Ajax washed the wounds on my shoulder. I turned away while he carefully prodded them.

"Son of a bitch," I cried and jerked away. "Damn, damn werewolves." I swiped my arm across my face, smearing tears and snot and mixing it with blood. "Damn, fucking shitting werewolves."

"She's okay." Relief filled Ajax's voice. *Okay* was

debatable. He grinned at the hovering crowd. He was right, but I had big deep holes poked in my arm. And I didn't like being off my feet. Excruciating pain I could deal with. On the ground having a crowd towering over me…no way.

"Help me up." I struggled to rise, so Ajax and Xavier lifted me to my feet. I could feel Xavier shaking, and I knew what would come next. Tears dripped from Ty's eyes.

"Why the hell didn't you shoot him?" Xavier's voice came out as a low snarl. I hadn't heard his voice heavy with emotion since Avalon.

"I'm crazy, Xavier. And stubborn. You knew that, so damn it, leave me alone." A deep sense of fatigue settled in with the pain. "What is wrong with you, Xavier? Soldier? You *know* better. A single, random shot around armed soldiers would start a fire fight we'd lose."

Xavier's face was as pale as I'd ever seen. Fear. Fear for me radiated from every inch of the man. Okay, I think I knew what was wrong with him. Maat Ferris had addled his mind. I tend to do it to most everyone at times. But this was a man I loved. Of course, I had to tell them. Ajax knew. My head drooped. I drew a couple of deep breaths. "Look. I won't go fuzzy on you. I'm immune to werewolf bites. Always have been."

Long seconds passed weighted by their stunned silence.

"Shit." Lowell broke the quiet and laughed. First time I'd ever heard him curse. "So that's why."

We all stared at him.

"Aaron knew you were immune." Lowell's voice rose in excitement. "He had to have known. When you were unconscious, he had the doctors take so many samples of blood, tissue, and skin, I was afraid they might injure you."

"Why?"

Lowell shrugged. "A cure for Sabrina. That's all it could be. Or a vaccine to prevent the disease in the first place. How did he find out you were immune?"

I shrugged and instantly regretted the movement. Not good with a wound like mine. I slipped my good arm around Ajax and hugged him. Ajax kept my secrets, and I kept his. "Oh, hell. Ruelle. God knows what I told that vampire on the way out of New York." Near death, delusional, I might have said anything.

"Why are you immune?" Heflin stepped closer, seriously interested now. "Do you know?"

"Not for sure. A werewolf bit my father before I was born. He survived, but before he changed shape for the first time, he and my mother conceived me. Then he left, went away so we wouldn't be in danger when he did change. He didn't come back. I guess he died. Mom told me about it because she was afraid, I'd be born a werewolf or turn into one when I grew older. It didn't happen, of course. That's impossible. You all know there is no such thing as a born were.

"The first time one of the hairy bastards bit me, I was going to kill myself. Then I got the crazy idea if I were a werewolf, I might could kill more of *them*. Months later, nothing happened. I was safe. Second time one bit me, again nothing. Except the wound took me down for weeks. Neither of my previous bites healed as fast as they should have." I stared at the throbbing holes in my arm. "Thought I could avoid a third."

Lowell surprised me. "Your conception. Is that why you can see in the dark? Sense weres? And vampires?"

He hadn't shown much interest in anything since Anolia died.

"I don't know, Lowell. I've *always* been able to see in the dark. Not details, but shades of gray. It's improved as I got older. I couldn't sense werewolves until after the attack when they killed my mother. Sensing vampires came after they finished with me in New York."

I had considered my odd conception might be the source of my ability to sneak up on weres without them sensing me. I had no way of knowing the truth about the whole thing.

"Guys, could we go now? My arm does hurt. And I think you all know you must keep my secret. Don't answer any questions."

The pain had dulled to a throb keeping time with my heartbeat. The ragged canine teeth wounds had started to swell. I needed to move. Lowell and Heflin turned and walked away, speaking in soft eager voices as they went. Jacob stepped in front of me. Ty closed in too, and I could feel Cody my young vampire stirring in his box, frantic, unable to come to me. Jacob leaned close and rubbed his face gently against mine. Ty had to touch me too. Poor Cody couldn't do anything, but I let him know I was okay. I'd have to consume some of his blood for healing. I couldn't go into an unknown and dangerous place with my arm in such debilitating pain. Now, here was a new and amazing facet of my life. Voluntarily asking for vampire blood to heal me. At least it would come from one of my own.

Xavier's shaking hand gripped my free arm and drew me close. Silent as usual, he held me tight, and I could feel his body trembling in waves.

Welcome to Salvaje, Maat.

Chapter Three

Salvaje, New Mexico

It was noon and Heflin said the temperature pushed upwards of a hundred and ten. The stark landscape around us seared our eyes as it sunbathed in brilliant light. Xavier, Lowell, Ty, and I crowded in Heflin's Turtle. Jacob, Ajax, Mary, and Giselle followed in the truck behind us. That truck also carried my demo man's precious, but volatile, chemicals. Good thing heat didn't affect Pulp and Powder. The truck with our stolen goods, the equipment to destroy the country's last viable nuclear missiles, had already peeled away from the convoy and on its way headed north by another road. Only Hef's cargo trucks, laden with supplies, followed behind us to the city.

We'd been traveling through residential and small-town ruins for miles. Hundreds of thousands of people must have lived here once. The low humidity kept these ruins in better condition than those in the east. Blowing dust storms made drifts of yellow sand and buried some of them. The road remained solid and well maintained. It wasn't long before we reached barren desert again. Heat rose in the distance, smearing the horizon in great chaotic waves.

We topped a hill, and Salvaje lay below. Salvaje was

not my concept of a city. It looked like a knob of rocks plunked down on wide, flat, and empty desert land. As we drew closer, I could only see a featureless 30-foot-high cream and brown wall divided sporadically by darker seams. Monolith structures of varying heights jutted up behind the barrier. Only the height and mass of the place distinguished it from the barren land around us. If not for that height, the color would make it invisible.

"Damn, Heflin. It's a fortress, not a city." I leaned over, trying to see more. The land outside the wall was as bare and open as the surrounding desert. They'd certainly see anyone approaching for miles.

Heflin laughed. His tension had drained the farther we moved away from the site of conflict on the road. "Fortress. Yes. Built in 2039. We're north of what was Albuquerque, between the mountains and the Rio Grande. There is an older section of wood buildings, but primarily the newer buildings here are constructed of a material called Murlex adobe. Flexible and almost indestructible. City's supposed to be self-sufficient. And defensible. The wall is six feet thick, and we can close every entry." He chuckled again. "The size inside the wall is the primary reason we limit the population. It helps keep the peace."

"And cstablishes a system of privilege for those admitted."

He didn't say anything to my assertion, so I presumed it was factual. Would the wall withstand the mid-range artillery lobbed at Memphis? Not likely. I expect the height and thickness gave the inhabitants an illusion and false sense of security.

I wondered where Gannett found the bigger guns, they used on Memphis. I'd seen old newspaper pictures of barges loaded with guns and tanks, scuttled in the Atlantic Ocean. That disease-born insane feat went on for a decade. Thirty gigantic guns and fifty tanks had lain hidden in Uncle Jake's underground abandoned military bunker. They went when he blew everything to hell in his splendid final stand. I pray I'll have the courage to uphold the family honor and leave this world in such a spectacular manner.

"Tierra Sombra." Heflin sounded reverent, like a pious man, head bowed, entering a cathedral.

"Shadowland." Xavier reached out and laid a hand on my shoulder. He'd barely spoken since he helped me out of Cody's box. I'd had to consume enough vile vampire blood to help my shoulder heal. Vampire blood is the foulest thing in the world to me, even from my own Cody. The vampires who captured me in New York forced their loathsome liquid down my throat so I could live for another night of torture. The only mercy I received was the fact they didn't bite me. Thank God, with all of my injuries, I'd never been bitten by a vampire.

We didn't know what we would face in Salvaje though, and I couldn't enter a strange city injured, unable to fight. Xavier hadn't allowed me out of his sight. He never stopped touching me, as if he thought I'd escape his grip and float away. He'd changed since the first time we met on the mountain at Avalon. His taciturn disposition had deepened. We remained opposites there. I lived on the surface, but his nature went far deeper than mine. But how did I know? He remained a stranger in so many ways.

"Shadowland," Heflin confirmed. "Almost everyone goes inside or underground during the day. In

Salvaje, we're all people of the night. I've told you all about the Asha, the laws. You'd all better take time to learn them. The Council, you'll hear more about them…us. We have representatives of the three…races. Humans, vamps, and weres."

"Races." My hand went to my aching arm. Cody's blood, as much as I could swallow, had helped it heal. It wasn't perfect. I needed rest. Cody was a young vampire though, and it wasn't as potent as if he'd been Ruelle— or Emanis. When I was her prisoner in New York, Emanis' blood had been like drinking raw lightning. I shivered at the memory. Her immediate boost let me rest until they heated the irons for another round of their torture Maat game. I survived. Emanis is dead. Happy ending. Right?

Heflin chuckled. "Races. Yes. Plenty of monsters in Salvaje, Maat. But they're monsters because of what they do, not what they look like."

I noted he used *they* and not we as he had earlier. I guess he held himself above the monsters. We all accepted his words without comment. Surprisingly, none of my crew spoke again of the attack on me or my injury. My explanation that I was immune to werewolf bites hadn't completely satisfied them, though. They would worry until enough time for proof had passed. I approved of their vigilance. It pleased me they cared so much.

Heflin continued his enlightenment. "The Council controls the soldiers you saw earlier. Salvaje does have a government of sorts. The Asha only protects major concepts. Soldiers protect but are not policemen. Below a certain level, it's anarchy. Anarchy keeps my bodyguard business going."

I gritted my teeth. "I don't remember anything about

anarchy during discussions in Tennessee. Or bodyguards."

Heflin ignored me. Xavier started to speak, but I could tell he restrained himself.

"Ah, here we are." Heflin's excitement rose.

We had come around and approached the city from the north rather than the east. He pointed to his left at the equivalent of a massive unpaved parking lot filled with vehicles. No fences, but a troop of soldiers like those who had met us stood guard. I hadn't seen it in my first glimpse of the city. We would be trapped inside the walls while all means of escape remained outside.

Heflin sounded joyful. "We don't have electricity. We do have solar charged batteries. And loads of sunshine." We left the truck in the parking lot, and he led us to a low, multi-wheeled, open vehicle. "This is called a wain. Battery powered."

Eight feet wide, the so-called wain had eight seats, two abreast, with minimal space for cargo. Constructed of a type of plastic, it appeared formed in one piece, and then plunked down on six wheels. The color of the desert prevailed there, too—unrelieved shades of beige and brown.

Heflin's workers loaded Cody's box on a low-sided open wagon, hitched to the back of the wain. Cody had told me the heat didn't bother him, but the jostling of loading and unloading must have been rough.

Workers had already started unloading boxes from Heflin's trucks into more of the open wains. Heflin assured Ajax his truck with Pulp and Powder would be well guarded. Our Wagon Master had enormous quantities of goods waiting in West Memphis after our spectacular crossing. The size of his organization amazed me. I suspected this walled city was far from self-sufficient.

"These wains are the only vehicles allowed in Salvaje," Heflin said as we climbed in. "Each one has to have a special permit. No traffic problems for us. We walk almost everywhere."

A bit of minor amusement. "You have no police, but you have a bureaucracy that issues vehicle permits?"

"Maat, Salvaje is like no place you've ever been in your life. I can guarantee you surprises."

He passed around bottles of water and told us to drink and went over symptoms of dehydration. "Always drink lots of water, even if you don't think or feel like you need to." He made fair-skinned Mary, who was already an alarming shade of pink, cover up completely with a light blanket. My own mouth had grown rough and sticky, so the liquid went down quick and smooth as a beer after a long day. Almost as smooth. I'm quite sure a beer would be just fine. The last I had? When Xavier and I sat in a Memphis brothel drinking from greasy glasses.

Rolling along at a walking speed, we headed for an arch cut in the city wall. We entered a fifty-foot-long tunnel. No truck would make it through there.

"There are two larger entries." Heflin continued to act as tour guide. "One on the south and the other on the west."

Salvaje had rounded shoulders. According to Heflin, they'd poured the Murlex adobe into molds that contained few sharp edges. The buildings all hunkered down with a bland, almost innocent appearance. One and two-story structures predominated, but the occasional three-story thrust up like a sentinel. The narrow streets, cut with narrower alleys created a maze, a labyrinth between buildings. In color, structures ranged from cream to butter yellow deepening to coffee brown. An occasional miniscule window broke a sheer wall. Windows would allow the incredible heat to seep in so the only viable thing would be small. They all appeared the same, except for height and color. The doors, carved with fanciful motifs, floral, animal, geometric, gave each house its individuality. Metal plaques mounted beside each arched wooden door distinguished one from another. Odd symbols on those plaques were familiar.

Heflin laughed. "Oh, yes, the plaques are addresses. No two alike. Vamps designed this city, that's their language. They have a separate language, did you know?"

Yes, I knew. Did Heflin know the plaques were not words but thousand-year-old symbols. Ruelle had shown me. He'd also told me his original name. I couldn't pronounce it.

Heflin went on. "Vampires came here in the 1800s when it was an ordinary town of frame buildings. A respectable wood craftsman makes a fortune here. Don't be deceived by the exterior. Rooms inside can be large since they don't require interior roof supports. Much of Salvaje is underground, too. I'll tell you more later." His voice deepened in a way that told me the *more later* involved significant information.

"Where is everybody," Ty suddenly asked. "It's deserted."

"Everyone is sleeping." Heflin chuckled. "Like *we* should be."

We rolled through silent, empty passages in what could be a dry valley of ancient tombs like I'd seen in my mother's collection of history books. No sidewalks, no shrubs, not a single leaf of green broke the monotony. No garbage, no trash littered the ground, either. Trash usually signified habitation. We did pass several wains like ours, but they carried or hauled cargo, not passengers. Heflin and the drivers of those wains acknowledged each other with a single wave of a hand.

Heflin's wrinkled face broke into a grin. Excitement filled his voice. "There it is." He nodded toward a three-story building. Colored like a patch of woodland mushrooms, it stood bland and nondescript as the others. "Home sweet home." His voice bubbled with pleasure.

Fancy iron rails ran up wide steps to a landing and a double door as ornate as anything I'd seen so far. We bypassed those, turned into an alley, then into a substantial covered bay at the back, where Heflin stopped the wain. The building was larger than it appeared at first. Temperature in the bay had to be twenty degrees cooler than outside.

A door from the building opened, and a lovely dark-haired woman stepped out. She clasped her hands as if in prayer. She came toward us, tall, slender, moving with a supple, erotic grace. Her long almond color dress matched the tones of the city and enhanced the beauty of dark eyes and honey-shaded skin.

She smiled. "Well, there you are. I'd almost given up." I heard relief in her warm voice. Heflin climbed out and marched toward her, obviously energized. When he got within five feet, she held up both hands. "No. Bathe first." She backed up several steps. The nostrils on her elegant nose widened.

"Damn, woman. Been on the road for a month now." He threw out his arms in protest, but the grin never left his face. "What do you expect?"

"I expect you to take a bath." She crossed her arms under ample breasts and stood firm.

Heflin grumbled. He turned to us, obviously not troubled by her rejection. He waved a hand at her. "This beautiful, but fastidious lady is my wife, Maureen."

Maureen's clear, intelligent eyes sparkled during the introductions. She seemed far younger than Heflin, but as she assessed us, I felt a keen wisdom that usually only came with age. She smiled at his introductions, accepting, but seemed not yet willing to offer more than a polite cautious welcome. I didn't blame her and suspected most who lived here in this guarded city would be the same.

"Maat, you, Mary, and Giselle come with me," Maureen said with a soft laugh. "We have a special bathing room for the ladies."

"I don't know how much good a bath will do," I told Maureen. I followed a discreet distance behind her, knowing I smelled as bad as her husband. "We don't have any clean clothes."

"Not a problem. I have clothes," she said.

"Big enough to fit us?" Mary giggled.

"Oh yes. Two of my girls are quite ample. Hef didn't tell you? He has his bodyguard business, and I run Paradox House. I employ twelve women, so I'm well supplied with feminine needs. I have to be out here."

Two thousand miles of aversity, and I wind up in a brothel. I had brief thoughts of the house I had owned with my friend Sable. The one crushed to pieces in poor doomed Memphis. I did wonder if Sable had crossed as many miles as I had the past few weeks. His journey from Memphis to Seattle had to be fraught with as much or more danger than mine to Salvaje.

At least it smelled better here. Most cities in the east had sewage disposal problems. In the list of important things, survival came before proper organized waste disposal.

Maureen led us through hallways and downstairs into passages, not constructed, but carved from solid rock. We entered a room lined with cream-colored tile. Shelves of stacked towels covered one wall, and benches stretched across the floor. On her orders, we stripped and piled our clothes by the door. I kept my guns and knife with me, but I left them on a bench as I entered the long rectangular shower room. It would easily hold a dozen women.

Soap and hot water. Ah, the fountains of heaven to wash away the stain of the journey.

Mary and Giselle squealed in delight, and I joined the celebration. Heavy steam billowed up and across the tile ceiling then condensed to glide down the walls. Fragrant soap leached the long, weary days on the road out of our bodies. It turned time to liquid and drew it, along with considerable dirt and body fluids, across terra cotta tiles into a drain.

"Where does the water come from?" I asked Maureen. The soft towel I used to dry my body soaked up moisture immediately. "Seems to be plenty."

"There is," she replied. "We don't waste it, though. We pipe cleaner drain water from the showers underground out to the farms for grazing land. There are farms to the west by the river where they can irrigate crops and maintain greenhouses in the winter. There's a separate waste disposal facility. This city had made great strides in sustainability and breaking from the power grid before the war."

She'd welcomed me when Heflin introduced us, but now she assessed me with a brothel madam's cautious eyes. Her words remained neutral, regardless of what she thought. "The City of Albuquerque completed a new poly-sealed snowmelt reservoir in the mountains to the west, right before the war began. We tap into it and do regular maintenance. It's survival for us. There's a solar unit on the roof for hot water."

Maureen pointed out large clay jars of oil and suggested we use it each time we showered. She combed my riot of curly hair and skillfully cut the worst of tangled knotted ends away. As Heflin had reminded us to drink water often, she stressed the effects of the dry climate and sun aging bare skin.

I sat on a bench while she salved and bandaged the almost healed werewolf bite on my arm. Her eyes widened a bit, and I suspected she recognized it for what it was. I'm sure she wanted to get Heflin's story on the strangers he brought home before she said too much. The green milky gunk she rubbed into the wounds eased the pain by half. Given Cody's vampire blood, by tomorrow I wouldn't feel it at all. She made no comment on my scarred back, where the vampires in New York had burned a crosshatch pattern marking me forever.

Our hostess led us to a room filled with racks and baskets of clothing, carefully sorted by type and size. Obviously, the fastidious Madam Maureen prized organization. She urged us to take extra. I found two pairs of jeans, a couple of shirts that almost fit me, and several pairs of socks. Mary and Giselle chattered, delighted with the comfortable, multi-colored robes like the one Maureen wore. "I'll have your other clothes laundered and your shoes cleaned," she promised as she led us back upstairs.

We entered a spacious room filled with brilliant woven rugs over a tile floor. Handcrafted wood couches and chairs decorated with woven multi-colored cushions filled it with a sense of welcome and comfort. A long dining table stretched across one end of the room.

I raised an eyebrow at Maureen. "This isn't…" It couldn't be a brothel.

"No. The Paradox is next door. There is a bar too, now fully stocked with beverages thanks to your convoy. This building is where Hef quarters and trains his bodyguards. This floor is living quarters, and the first floor is his training facility. He and I live upstairs on the third floor.

"Your rooms are at the end of the hall." Maureen smiled and nodded to the passage to my left. A brilliant crimson and black rug stretched the hallway's length, and paintings lined the walls.

Ajax stuck his head out of a doorway, and the twins ran to him. He winked at me as he closed the door behind them. At Maureen's direction, I walked on down the same hallway to the open door on my right. The room had two beds, and they'd placed Cody's box against the wall on one side. Ty sat on one bed. He gave a resigned shrug and smiled at me. I didn't see Jacob, but he was a grown werewolf and could take care of himself.

Xavier was suddenly there, his strong arms enfolding me. With the utmost care, he kissed my lips. A gentle teasing brush, no more. He led me into another room.

With the door closed and bolted behind him, Xavier came to stand in front of me. He, too, had obviously found a place to bathe and shave. I could see tiny bits of silver threading through his hair now. I had my guns in my arms along with the new clothes Maureen had given me, so I walked over and laid them on the rough, wood chest at the side of the room. Another smaller chest, carved with unidentifiable, but slightly familiar figures, sat against the opposite wall. Gentle afternoon light from a single tiny window cut high on the wall cast a cheerful, tawny glow over rugs, wall hangings, and bed covers on a bed easily large enough for two people. Again, shades of red, black, and yellow dominated. I wondered if Salvaje banned blue or green so not to remind residents how far they were from abundant water and vegetation.

Xavier stared at me with dark, heavy eyes. Eyes that seemed so expressive because the scarred face betrayed little of the man hidden inside. He wore only a pair of pants, and he, like all of us, had lost weight during the journey from New Washington. Still, he remained a powerful figure of a man.

He held out his hands. "I surrender."

"Who were you fighting?"

"Myself. I didn't want to love you any more than you wanted to love me. What if I lost you? Or you didn't want me. What if I'd killed you? You made me so angry. I kept trying to push you away. I couldn't. When I thought you'd died in Little Rock…"

He'd drawn a deep concern from my heart. There could be no secrets between us. We wouldn't survive secrets and lies. "This is a new world. We're mostly strangers."

Xavier didn't answer for a moment, then said, "Well, stranger. Let's get to know each other a little better."

He reached out and caught my shirt at my waist, and I lifted my arms as he drew it off over my head. He stared at my breasts, then his thumbs flicked across my nipples. I shivered. He took my hand, sat on the bed with me standing in front of him, pulled my pants down, and buried his face against my mound. I stared down at his dark hair, ran my fingers through the strands, pulled away from him, then stepped out of my pants.

I had gone to Avalon and found a haven from myself, my own agony. His coming, the first sight of him, the first moments in his presence, had drawn me back to a dangerous life. Avalon had given me rest, and he'd given me the vital strength to begin again.

Xavier stripped off his pants with a fierce urgency, and I watched him with eager eyes.

"Come," he said as he lay back on the bed.

I went to him, knelt beside him, and with our hands and mouths we explored each other's bodies. A surprised gasp, a strange, pleased whisper, told each of us when we'd reached a spot that would evoke glorious sensations. I'd always known I wasn't beautiful, but when I gazed into the mirror of his eyes, I knew he found something more substantial in me.

We weren't gentle with each other, for we were never gentle people. He pinched my nipples drawing both pain and pleasure, and my teeth carefully raked his cock, evoking a savage jubilant hiss from him. Blood roared in my ears as his hand worked between my legs. I felt so swollen—I wondered how I'd get him in.

With one quick, ruthless movement, he flipped me over onto my back and stretched my legs apart. "I can't wait," he choked. "Now."

I laughed as I dragged him down, and he plunged

into me. My hands skimmed down his back and over powerful rippling muscles. I twisted, wrapped my legs around him, and held on as we satisfied our hunger with pure glorious passion. This dangerous, beguiling man was my mate, one I could never have imagined.

Love and desire, built in New Washington and almost shattered over the rocks of our own stubbornness, had found us and joined us in ecstasy. Intense pleasure spread from my center, and I cried out in joy. Xavier shuddered and locked his hands in my hair. His body bucked and heaved, and we became one being. Then the love we'd both needed so much overwhelmed us and drove us over the edge.

Chapter Four

I woke wrapped in Xavier's arms. If it hadn't been for the insistent banging on the door, I'd have stayed there. "Go 'way." I couldn't get much force behind the words.

Xavier, now awake, rubbed his face against one of my breasts and grazed the nipple with his teeth. He rose on one elbow. I took the opportunity to run my hands down his incredible body.

"What do you want?" Xavier shouted.

Ajax's laughter boomed outside the door. "Heflin says we meet in ten minutes. He mentioned food, too."

Facing the inevitable, Xavier and I forced ourselves out of bed, maintaining body contact if possible. I had a concern I needed to voice. "Xavier?" I leaned against him. "I know he's your friend, but Heflin makes me uncomfortable at times."

"I saw. I don't understand. Such hostility. Maybe my fault. I told him in New Washington you and Ty were with me. A package. All or nothing. No one likes ultimatums. It's uncomfortable for me too. He had certain power over us in the convoy. He has it here in Salvaje. We can deal, though."

Oh, God, I loved this man. "Possibly he still doesn't trust me because of Ruelle. Do you? Trust me?"

"Yes."

I laid my hand on his chest. "Why? After all that's happened, why do you trust me?"

"Because you are, in word and deed, so elemental. You've never lied to me. You rarely hide your stronger emotions. Even with the vampire. You're just...Maat."

I didn't know what to say. *How rare. Maat Ferris speechless.*

I was seventeen when I lost my first love to monsters. I never dreamed I'd want, or have, someone like Xavier in my life again. I'd dedicated my existence to revenge, and I'd never developed a permanent, sexual relationship with anyone over the years. Sex was mostly relief after weeks of hunting. I'll admit Christopher at Avalon did soothe my soul. Rumors of my extravagant, erotic exploits mostly came from my association with Sable and my own big mouth. Once we dressed and armed ourselves, we found our boots outside the door, clean and scented like pine boughs. We delayed for a few passionate kisses before we headed out to join the group.

We were the last to arrive. Heflin waited there with the others. Ajax, Ty, Jacob, Lowell, and Cody, who had climbed out of his box at sundown to face his new world. Only Ajax's twins, Mary and Giselle were missing. He didn't complain so I figured they were okay. No one would have removed them against his will.

"Is everyone rested?" Heflin seemed way too bright and perky to suit me.

Ajax grinned. "Who could rest with all that howling going on?" I sighed. I'd have to take a little shit, I supposed. *So, I make a little noise when I come.* Xavier didn't complain.

"Probably an overstimulated werewolf, running through the streets," Heflin said with a straight face.

"Happens occasionally. Come on. It's eight o'clock. We'll eat first, talk a while, and then we have a night on the town."

We sat at the long hand-hewn wood table. I wanted to examine the paintings and brilliant red and gold textiles on the wall, but the smell of food was too distracting. An older man and woman, both with deep brown wrinkled skin and warm friendly smiles rolled in a cart filled with bowls of corn, rice, beans, and complementing slabs of beef and pork. They distributed them with a flair showing pride in their culinary creations. We didn't waste time when Heflin told us to dig in. Cody nibbled in tiny bites. He said he could taste some things other than blood. I knew Ruelle could not. He had told me he lost that gift hundreds of years ago.

It seemed an enormous meal at first, but time on the road left us famished for real food. I tried everything, all flavored with spices I'd never tasted in my life. Heflin said they came from Mexico. There was a trade route and a regular convoy. My world, once limited to the area around the Appalachian Mountains, grew wider every day.

Then they brought us steaming mugs of black, bitter liquid. Oh, God. Real, genuine coffee, not the false juice of the eastern mountain beans. I suddenly understood Uncle Jake's dreamy-eyed expression when he lamented the *good old days.*

When we finished, Heflin led us back to the couches and chairs. I was so full I could barely walk. I sat on a couch with Xavier, leaning against that big warm body I wanted so much. Ty started toward us. I know he wanted to sit by me, but Cody beat him to my side with vampire speed and grace.

Heflin went to a table near the wall and fiddled with a box. Music filled the room. A radio broadcast. I'd never heard one, other than the occasional army communication type. Heflin grinned, obviously enjoying our delight. "We have solar cell batteries and natural gas. There's a big booster antenna downtown in the city center."

The music ended abruptly with the words, "And now the news." Words redefined my life—again.

"Welcome to Radio Seattle, new capital of the free United States. This word just arrived by convoy from the east. The City of Memphis has fallen under the hammer of Dictator Gannett."

Memphis? I knew. We were there. My over-full, uneasy stomach ached at the words. The announcer went on. *Massacre of defending troops and civilians...destruction of the bridge...Memphis Army Base gone.* We had run from the thunderous bombardment. So heartbreaking, those dispassionate words. So, Avalon had once given me a sense of peace. The world had torn it from me. I survived. I would go on.

Estimates Gannett lost more than half his army, thousands of civilians fleeing city fired upon...Commander of the Memphis Base and soldiers fled down river.

Sable had made it out of town just in time.

Heflin turned the radio off. "Right now, men and women, technicians we have been freeing for over a year from Gannett's factories are unloading the equipment and preparing to open the vault that could rain nuclear hell on us. But there are separate compartments, electronic locks, and all we have is the equipment and a handful of technical guidebooks from before the war. It's going to take a few weeks."

Weeks? He was not paying attention to the right problems. "You know, Hef, Gannett may give up, but Ruelle will come. Gannett is a puppet, a front man. Ruelle's the one who wants to control the nukes. And he'll want pay-back for us stealing them."

"We're aware of that, Maat." Heflin's voice softened. "We've made mistakes. We knew about the truck and could have taken it years ago. Like idiots, feeling secure in our walled city in the desert, we didn't become alarmed until we learned Ruelle had the president under his control."

Xavier gripped my hand, his long, rough fingers entwined in mine. I had no doubt Ruelle's revenge on the thieves would include me. Curiosity nagged me about why the vampire hunted me down to do his thievery. I'd never known him to be so irrational. He was smart enough to make a better plan than the one I'd fumbled through. And he'd had time to wait for the most opportune moment. I wasn't a necessary actor in that drama as far as I could see.

"We have vampires here, too, Maat." Heflin's voice deepened. He sounded so smug, so sure of himself. "And vampires have helped us with this endeavor."

"Vampires. Helped you. Why?" I couldn't keep the derision out of my voice. What I knew of vampires wasn't everything, but my knowledge and experience surpassed anyone else in the room except Cody. It was deeply personal knowledge earned firsthand. Vampires were the most self-centered creatures on this earth, far surpassing humans in focus. They thought of little but entertaining themselves over the long years of existence. And blood. They thought about blood a lot. Why would

Salvaje be different?

Heflin shrugged as if a deadly facet of our survival was of no consequence. "I know you've had bad experiences with vampires and werewolves, Maat. I have too. But haven't you seen a more positive side to some of them now?"

He meant Cody and Jacob. A vampire too young and weak to be a threat, and a werewolf under orders from his pack leader to make sure I arrived in Salvaje alive. And Jacob didn't know why they'd made it so imperative. He'd simply pledged his life to defend me, and he kept my face turned west.

Heflin suddenly smiled. Not a pretty smile because it heightened my feeling our Wagon Master/employer harbored an intense dislike of me. He'd turned his animosity off and on since I'd met him. *A smile that suddenly said I'm going to cut you down, Maat Ferris.* Xavier sitting beside me frowned. I could feel his muscles, his whole body tighten in an automatic defense.

Heflin sat back and glared at me. "Now, Maat, about your personal vampire, why don't you tell us about the farm. Or maybe Cody will. He was in New York. I'll bet he knew."

My vampire? Ruelle, of course. His shadow would hover over me until I killed him—or he killed me.

Cody cringed. I don't know how a shifty asshole like Heflin knew about the farm. Yeah, it was that bad. A life shattering trauma outweighed even my torture in New York.

"True confession, right?" I gave him my nastiest look. "A little humiliation for Maat you think?"

He frowned, and his jaw went rigid. Had he expected something else? Yes, I would speak of what happened. After Avalon, baring my soul, after Anolia had taught me peace and forgiveness, I *could* speak of that time. Never forget, though. All the words in any language could not express the pain and horror of several events. I'd try, but it wouldn't make it easier.

"You should be more cautious, Hef. Some questions receive consequences, not answers. But I will enlighten you. After the disease and devastation, humans realized vampires were real, so they started to take defensive action. They got harder for vampires to catch. They fought back. So, what do vampires eat? Animal blood? Like *you say* they do here? I suppose they would. If there's nothing else. But if there are humans around, there won't ever be a *nothing else* situation for a vampire. How many missing persons in Salvaje?" I held up a finger. "But wait, you don't know, do you? No police force, no reports. And no grievances. No one spoke, so I went on.

"Unlike me, most humans were smart enough to stay away from New York." I assumed they all knew my story of capture and torture by the NY vampires. "When Ruelle first rescued me and took me away from the city, he had to carry me. He moved fast, but he could only go so far during a night. The morning after our escape, before daylight, he brought me to a place he called the farm." The muscles in my shoulders drew tight. Xavier, who held my hand, squeezed it gently. "The farm was a fenced compound, a collection of buildings, barracks, housing human beings. They'd had their brains deliberately damaged. And their food? The vamps brought in slug-like *things* living in the New York underground. And do not ask me what or where those sick things originally came from. I don't know. I don't

44

want to know."

For me some mysteries never required resolution. I gagged remembering but kept my fine dinner down. *See, I was a tough bitch.* "It was quite an operation, the farm. It had semi-intelligent overseers. And, of course, one crop. Human blood—vampire food. Haul their bounty to New York, dine at leisure. And they recycled. The remains after feeding went down to feed the fucking slugs."

Silence had settled around the room like a heavy blanket. I took that as encouragement to go on. "A number at the farm were vegetables…some like children…there were children, too. Pregnant women, the overseers did what they wanted, sick stuff. I was so weak, nearly dead, all I could do was watch."

I wet my lips and swallowed. "Ruelle took me from there to Ajax to heal. When I got better, Ajax and I went back to New York. We dropped a city block down on sleeping vampires. Then we went to the farm." I rubbed my hands over my face.

Ajax cleared his throat. I guess he felt he needed to shoulder some of the burden. His voice carried a deeper power than mine. "We lost our truck in the New York explosion. Had to cross the river and then walk. Super bad weather, so it took us ten days." There was none of the usual slangy, go to hell tone in his deep, tight voice. "Without vamps to bring the slugs from the sewers, the weakest starved, or the overseers killed and ate them."

My body shook then, a thick vibration that I know alarmed Xavier who suddenly laid an arm across my shoulder and held me tight. How could I speak of the horror? I'm a hunter. I'd walked through the aftermath of werewolf attacks. I'd seen and buried half eaten bodies. But at the farm there were living children dragging themselves along on broken limbs, blind, starving, eating their own fingers.

Ajax's voice deepened. "We saved what we could. The dying…we ended it for them."

The others, the vegetables, those so ill or maimed they would only live a few more days… By God's mercy, we located a safe full of drugs that Ajax was able to open. Part of the experiments in a farm laboratory. *Oh, God, that laboratory.*

And how did we decide? Did we take away those who could walk? Those we could feed, hunt game for. How would any of them survive if we left to come back with help? People had been avoiding the entire northeast, so it could be weeks. *And yes, we could have just walked away.* They'd all be dead soon enough.

I like to pretend the violence and torture in New York drove me to Avalon, but that was only part of it. I'd never considered myself a morally virtuous person. But to kill an innocent human being? An innocent, dying in horrific pain yes, but to do it…to use a needle full of poison? Or even a bullet when the poison ran out. Anolia had held me in her arms and wept with me when I spoke of the farm and what I did there—what I had to do.

I was born into a violent, war-torn world. I never questioned my part in perpetuating violence. Oh, I righteously killed to defend, but the rest of my life consisted of arrogant hostility. Xavier and Lowell had dragged me away from Avalon's peace against my will, yes. But I remember how relieved I'd been the night I'd strapped on my guns again and retaken my life of fury and death.

I finished the story. "We took the survivors to a

religious commune and gave the people running it what gold we had to care for them."

Heflin kept narrowed eyes on me. "My brother's daughter, my niece, leads that commune where you brought the survivors. She and others say you could have saved more. You should have gone to the farm first, before going to New York to punish the vampires for hurting you."

Oh, yes. My need for personal revenge triumphed over righteous acts. Selfish, selfish Maat. Guilt enough for a lifetime weighed on a soul.

I stared back at him. "Yes, we should have Short sighted, oh yes. We are not perfect."

Ajax surged to is feet. Corded muscles drew tight across his shoulders, fists clenched. "Your niece wasn't fucking there, Heflin. Neither were you. Get off your fucking throne and let God do the judging."

Heflin hunched over and spit out more words. "And yet, when Ruelle the vampire called, you went to him."

That was a lie. Ruelle had sent armed men for me. I'd have run away if I could.

I stood like Ajax to face Heflin. My relationship with Ruelle over the years had become part of the Angel of Death myth. Only the vampire and I knew the truth. "You listen, you son of a bitch. I've made many errors that will damn me, but I apologize for my life to no man. I realize the only reason you let me come here is that you want Xavier for something. Your choice. You can put me on the next convoy out." I shrugged to show my contempt. "If you require more, step outside. You fight, or you choose a champion. We'll settle everything in the street."

Something I never expected or wanted happened

then. Xavier stood and wrapped his arms around me. He gazed at Heflin. "What did I tell you about Maat, Hef? Back in New Washington. And you better believe that I know the road east, too."

Heflin rubbed his hands over his face. Whatever he'd wanted to achieve he'd failed. "No. No. I can't...Things here are too important. Please."

Heflin had chosen to deal with the immediate situation. He felt he needed Xavier enough to accept me and Ajax. He acknowledged such to Xavier with a nod of his head showing acceptance of the unchanging facts. "And I think what you said, Colonel, was something about her being a missing part of your soul."

I laid my face against Xavier's hard chest. "What a romantic. Dear God, love. You bounced me off a rock wall, chained me up in a helicopter, and tried to drown me. And that was only foreplay."

Xavier's arms tightened around me, and his breath whispered on my neck. Ajax didn't smile, but he winked, and I knew I and my pack were okay. Now, here is a thing. Xavier using his strength to protect me. I neither wanted nor needed that, but it was an excellent gift. He kept holding me as we sat back down on the couch.

Heflin studied the floor briefly. He looked up and when he spoke, he used a neutral almost clinical voice. "Maat, you, and Ajax warned my niece's commune where you took survivors about Ruelle."

"I did."

"Well, you described him. When Ruelle did arrive in New Washington, sniffing around Gannett, we realized we'd fucked up. We had to get that truck. So, Maat, Ajax, your actions, your information, triggered the events we've lived through these past weeks."

My thoughts went back to Christopher the silent Prophet of Avalon. I wonder what he would say—if I could persuade him to speak at all. I hadn't talked this much since I confessed my multitude of sins to Anolia. Might as well finish it.

"I met Ruelle for the first time in New York. I do not, nor have I ever known, why he aided me and remained in my life. I killed Emanis, that vampire in New Washington purely by luck. I'm not strong enough to kill Ruelle. I try not to piss him off, so he won't kill me. And I wait." I stared around the room, meeting each person's eyes in turn. "Ruelle conceived and carried out the plan of the farm. He bragged about it. I'm going to send him to hell someday. Fucking vampires. You Salvaje humans trust them if you want. I never will."

Cody started to rise. I grabbed him and held tight. "You don't have to be that way," I said. "While I live, I won't let you."

The young vampire relaxed against me, and I could feel his need for affection. I caught Ty's pout out of the corner of my eye and ignored him. Ty's life might have been hard, losing a number of people he loved, but it was nothing like Cody's. I cautioned myself, though. Cody might appear to be a boy, and I'm sure he felt like one at times. His life cut off, so young. But he could kill, probably had killed, to survive this long. I feared that eventually he would grow darker, living with death as he was bound to do.

All the words I'd spoken about Ruelle were true, as was my conviction that he needed to die. For all the knowledge of his evil, for all my threats, my genuine hatred, the emotions about Ruelle swirling in my heart were far more complex. Eventually, I'd have to deal with them. That's when I would kill him.

Heflin glanced at his watch. "Okay, time for lessons."

And just like that, he passed over many of the most traumatic events of my life. The information had seeped through the personal filters into the minds of every person there. We'd see how the game progressed.

"There are three bases of power in Salvaje." Heflin spoke like a schoolteacher. At least he didn't call them races again. "Werewolves, vampires, and humans. Humans control our little army because it balances things a bit. We keep the city closed to outsiders for a reason. Its limited physical size means it won't take much to tip our balance. The only way I could get you all here is as employees. Any problems with that?"

"As bodyguards?" I asked.

"Not Ty." Xavier spoke, firm voice, still the dad, still the power.

Ty glared at him and clenched his fists. "Why not? I've learned. I can—"

"No, not Ty." Heflin agreed. "Not right away. But I'll start him in training. That certainly won't hurt him. In the meantime, he can do other things." With the sulking boy dismissed he went on to stronger players. "Lowell will need work, too. Maybe he can unravel some of that shit out at the nuclear complex. Or at least encourage the people there."

"I'll most certainly try." Parr agreed as always, smooth as still water.

Ty grumbled, pouted, then settled down when Xavier glared at him.

"Money." Heflin held up coins. "Gold coins, two sizes, same as the east." He laid two on the table, one about an inch across and the other half that size. "And coppers." The copper coins were the same size as the smaller gold. "Your room and board are free here as long as you work for me, and I'll pay you the same as my other guards. Five full golds a week. That's the highest wage in the city. You can make a first-rate living in Salvaje."

"Unless you get killed in the line of duty." I had to point that out.

"Optimist." Heflin laughed. He wouldn't meet my eyes.

I shrugged. "Hey. I've crawled under a house full of sleeping werewolves to set a bomb for way less than five gold coins."

Xavier shifted beside me. What? Disturbed by my hunting tactics? I'd done worse to Gannett's troops at times. *My lover and I should get to know each other more before we, very cautiously, expressed any truer confessions.* He continued to hold me close, though. I so wanted to go make love to him again, talk to him, whisper private words in his ear.

Heflin stood and beckoned Jacob. They dragged a large box into the room. He outfitted each of us with sand-colored, hooded capes that fell a little below our knees, and clasped at the neck with an ornate metal pin. We all had to try on a few because each cape had to fit properly across the shoulders and around the body. Xavier's broad shoulders barely fit his, but Heflin said he'd order a larger one. A tailor made them to specification.

One side of the cape pulled and fastened back over my right shoulder, exposing my free arm and the Aries at my hip. It fell to cover the Rudra under my left arm and the knife on my left forearm. Sturdy material finely cut and sewn, it made my borrowed jeans and worn boots feel shabby. The hood folded back flat and had an attached face piece to draw over the mouth and nose.

"Dust storms this time of year." Heflin held up the three-inch flattened oval clasp that secured our garment at the neck. It displayed a simple, scalloped pattern etched into the metal. "Everyone wears capes like these, so you must learn to recognize the pins. They're symbols, and they may be the only way you can tell an enemy from a friend when the hood or mask is up."

While I had exceptional eyesight, the design would still allow anyone, enemy or friend, to come too close for my comfort.

Heflin finally looked at me. "It's also a matter of pride. My honor's involved, and I'd appreciate it if you remembered that."

I ignored him. Like I was going to run around his city attacking vampires and werewolves without provocation. I wouldn't. Not tonight anyway. My gut feeling. Provocation would come soon enough.

"We have to split up here," Heflin said. "I can't look after everyone at once, nor can I give the details you need to survive." Two rough looking men dressed in the capes joined us.

"This is Martin." He pointed at the shorter, darker-skinned man. "And this is Rollman." He nodded in the direction of the taller. "Ty, Ajax, and Lowell will go with them. Maat, Xavier, Jacob, and Cody can come with me."

I guess he was afraid one of us would wander off and make trouble for him. He kept me, Xavier, Cody, and Jacob, i.e., those he considered carrying the greatest propensity for violence, with him.

Ty protested a bit but went on when I called him a baby. Lowell could keep an eye on him. I wouldn't trust Ajax to do that. Too many things distracted Ajax—unless he was setting an explosive charge. Then his focus narrowed to his eyes and hands.

On the way out, Heflin led us through the main room of Maureen's domain. Talk about class. Sable my partner in the now crushed Memphis brothel, would have died for a house like the Paradox. Crystal chandeliers illuminated fine, bronze colored carpet and polished wood furniture. Conversation wasn't beer tavern loud, barely discernable over the clink of glasses. Waitresses dressed in black and white moved with swift precision between tables. Other women more colorfully and provocatively dressed wandered at a slower pace. A tight operation for a bar/brothel. Maureen the Madam, dressed like a queen, stood by the bar, and reigned over her kingdom. Sable would have also coveted her emerald satin gown and diamond earrings, too.

Mary waved at us from behind the bar, where she mixed drinks with the flare of a trained bartender. Her tip jar was over half full. She'd brushed and styled her soft blonde hair in a way that emphasized her pretty face. I surveyed the room and saw doe-eyed Giselle dealing cards at a gambling table. Gambling, oh yes, a poker game or two for me later. Giselle's fingers flashed in a quick, competent style, and the two men sitting across from her watched her as much as they watched the cards. I punched Ajax in the back to keep him moving. His girls would work, but neither was physically for sale. Maureen was supposed to make that clear. Ajax and I had discussed his proclivity for multiple partners more than once. I knew he was neither owner nor tyrant to his women. He could be fiercely jealous and over-protective, though.

Maureen's ladies gave us curious stares. I was happy to see no noticeably young girls among them, but I'd long since learned that houses didn't always put everything they offered on display. We passed through and exited into the blessedly cool Salvaje night.

Chapter Five

Windows weren't a major feature of Salvaje buildings, and I understood because of the heat. The deeper we went into the city there were terraces and small balconies overlooking the street. The owners had dragged out pots of colored flowers and stacked them along each protrusion to make it seem like walking in a hanging garden. Not verdant and lush as a jungle, but better than the bare walls.

The street was for pedestrians, not mechanical vehicles. No exhaust fumes, no foul smoke belching from tail pipes. Bright twelve-foot torches with shiny reflectors lighted the main way. Heflin caught me staring.

"Natural gas," he said.

The torches showed me why Heflin called Salvaje Shadowland. Brilliance flowed across the main streets, but in the alleys…shapes scuffled and scurried there. The stark empty corridors of noon transformed to smoky black holes between buildings.

There weren't many people about, but the number increased as we moved farther into the city. There were numerous capes identical to ours though a few strutted around in bright colorful garments. A few of the bejeweled royalty had men and women in beige capes following behind. I recognized Heflin's sigil on a few of the pins, but there were others, too. I needed to learn the pins and what they signified. I glanced at Xavier, and he winked. Yes, we might be following some pompous ass around soon.

"We're coming into the plaza," Heflin explained. "It's early, but I want us to have a good seat."

I'd always thought of plazas as square. This one consisted of a rectangular widening in the street to no more than 70 feet. Salvaje, for all the mystical whispering of its name, remained a small town. From what I'd seen, I could cross it on foot in a fast-paced hour. The sidewalk opened to twenty feet wide and elevated to a level six feet above the plaza floor. The rail on the street side made it look like one long veranda. Tables lined the railing in some areas.

The richly decorated doors made it an artist walk. More elevated torches topped with metal reflectors gave excellent visibility. As we progressed, I could see these buildings around the plaza had far more windows and balconies on the second story overlooking the plaza below. From the bright storefronts and open bars along the sidewalk, I'd say the plaza was a lively place.

Heflin halted near the plaza center. He had us wait while he went in a bar. He came back with men carrying tables and chairs. The way they deferred to him, obeyed him, I thought he might own the bar.

They placed two tables slightly apart, ends against the rail. Jacob and Cody sat at our table. I sat across from Heflin by the rail with Xavier directly behind me at the second table, so he too was next to the rail. Cody seemed uneasy since he woke, and the conversation about the evils of vampirism earlier hadn't helped. "You hungry?" I whispered in his ear. Heflin told me he would obtain calves' blood and leave it at the Paradox for him before morning.

He shook his head. "I'm okay. It's...can you feel them?"

"Vampires? Yes. Try to relax." I laid a hand on his shoulder. His fragile appearing boy's body quivered with a delicate vibration. Fear? Or excitement?

I could sense vampires and werewolves, but Cody and Jacob sitting so close blocked my senses. I couldn't pick out individual locations in any direction.

Cody might grow strong in a few hundred years, but by that time, and without guidance, a vampire like his master in New York might corrupt him beyond redemption. The potential was there, the darkness inside. I wondered if that darkness had grown in Ruelle, or if he was evil from the moment so incredibly long ago when he first tasted blood.

The plaza filled, not crowded, but men, women, and an occasional vampire or werewolf drifted in and out. Xavier, sitting at the next table had turned so he could talk to me. He'd been quiet since we left the Paradox, but that wasn't unusual. He seemed far more interested in our surroundings than me. I'd bet his soldier's mind was calculating how to defend, or perhaps attack this citadel in the desert. I wanted to touch him so badly, but I didn't know how he felt about public displays of affection.

"What is it?" I leaned into him. That wasn't too touchy, was it? I could whisper in his ear without the entire world listening. "What are you looking for. What do you see?"

"I see a trap. This whole city. If what we see is the entirety. All of this crammed into walls...Hef's dreaming if he thinks they would hold up against an attack. Surrounded by wide-open space there's no easy escape. He's suffering from false security, something he'd never fall for when we were in the militia. He even has more to protect here."

Yes, the soldier drawn conclusions about the defensibility of Salvaje. So I turned back and asked, "Heflin, what does Salvaje do? Why is it here? Someone tossed a dart at a map, marked a spot, and plunked it down here in the desert?"

"Not I." He chuckled, a low muffled sound in his throat. "Salvaje is pre-war, an absurd experiment in sustainability. It was a small town, abandoned until the vampires came."

"And they allowed humans and weres in?"

Heflin lifted a hand. A girl and a gray bearded man brought glasses and wine. "Yes. I think…" He paused and frowned. "Not to be philosophical, and only my opinion, but I think vampires and werewolves require humans around them to live. Not only to feed on, but a form of companionship, a reminder of what they once were. Possibly it was an experiment to see if the different races could live together."

"Whose experiment, Heflin? One like Ruelle's? Vampires in Salvaje have gathered their food supply close, treat them well?"

He shook his head and stared straight into my eyes. "I don't know. And I don't want to know. Salvaje functions. You may disagree, but there is an identifiable order, a way to live without the chaos of the east where humans remain on the edge, demanding that they rule all."

I thought for a moment. "If, as you say, vampires and werewolves want companionship to remind themselves of their lost humanity, it's a spectacular weakness. Properly exploited, it would make a powerful weapon for humans because humans don't need them." Sabrina and her pack lived carefully hidden among humans in New Washington. "Humans will battle for dominance, Heflin. That's how it's been since we came out of the trees. We kill anything that frightens us, not a live and let live culture. That's how we survived war and plague."

Heflin went back to my original question. "As for Salvaje's function, other than bizarre experimentation, you saw my convoy?"

"I rode in it, didn't I?"

"I'm not the only person in this city who runs trade routes. Salvaje is the largest trade junction in the west. The highway goes south around Albuquerque to hit I-25 then on down into Mexico. We have a transport corral with fuel and services west of town. It's a mile or so outside the walls. You'll see it eventually. *Temporary* offers rest for drivers and guards, a refueling and a distribution point. Goods come up from Mexico and Central America. There's no safe direct route to Seattle yet. You have to go back to West Memphis, north to St. Louis, then west through Utah. If we can clear that direct route, the west will grow."

I stared around me. Too much repetitiveness, too much conformity.

"Tonight, is *séptima noche.*" Heflin waved his hand at the street. "The seventh night. Another lesson for you. You know, like most civilized societies, we forbid violence."

I laughed to mock him. "And how is that working out for you? You rent bodyguards."

Heflin joined me in laughter for a change. "It works as you might expect. However, we've minimized collateral damage by ritualizing it as a sport. You'll see."

Men and women strolled by, and many acknowledged Heflin with a nod of a head, others stopped and greeted him. He didn't introduce us. Yes, we were .just employees Okay, so people stared at stoic Xavier who observed without making eye contact. He was a big man, unusual in looks and hard to miss. They dismissed the rest of us. That was fine. The less attention on Suriel, the Angel of Death from the east, the better. Everyone would know eventually, and things could change; or maybe no one would give a fuck and denounce it as a fairy tale.

I didn't need Cody to lean toward me to know more vampires were coming closer. I could hear them in my mind like the delicate tinkle of rain turned to ice—cold, sharp, and deadly. I forced myself to be still. If I could hear them, I'd bet they could hear me. After a moment, it passed, and it occurred to me that they had been sweeping the area looking for something—or someone. I glanced at Heflin and found his eyes on me.

I shrugged. "Vamps."

"Yes. They won't do anything without deliberate provocation."

"Neither will I." I hadn't provoked the scene on the road outside Salvaje, and it hadn't made a bit of difference. My arm had stopped hurting at least.

Ten vampires entered the plaza below. They strolled in like dancers, graceful, beautiful—male and female—each one made the bloodsuckers of New York look like worn, wooden puppets. All of these dressed in black, though they did decorate with gold jewelry at the wrists and necks. One stood out like a god. He moved with the same fluid elegance of his companions, but he had a vitality they couldn't match. His followers kept their distance, and at the same time gravitated toward him.

Cody gasped. He grabbed my arm.

"Heflin?" I didn't have to ask the question.

Heflin smiled. "That's Orion, Vampire Prince of Salvaje. He's not overly aggressive, but he's still dangerous. All vampires fear him. And so does anyone else who wants to live. Like I said, we live together...respectfully."

I heard the warning in his voice.

The vamps moved closer, and I got a better look at Orion. He seemed the opposite of Ruelle in every way possible. Dressed in black as befitted his kind, unlike blond Ruelle, long midnight silk hair fell to his waist in an ebony waterfall. It framed his pale, sculptured face. This vampire stood in another class so far above his followers as if he should be on a throne. Emanis and her vamps had given me immunity to their glamour, their compulsion. What would happen if I stared into Orion's eyes? I didn't want to find out.

A stir rippled through the crowd. The werewolves had arrived. I could feel them like a solid block wall. I counted twelve males and four females. At least they shouldn't sense me. My ability to walk among weres without detection should hold here. *Should. Maybe.*

As the vampires surrounded their prince, the weres surrounded one of their own. A sturdy, square-shouldered young man with hair as brown and curly as mine swaggered across the stone. These werewolves preferred all leather clothing. They didn't lack grace of sorts, but they strutted like really bad-asses ready for action.

"That's Anson Sewell," Heflin said. He leaned toward me, so he could speak quietly. "Abban Connor is the official leader of the Salvaje werewolves. He's at least three hundred years old. A crafty old bastard, and with no one fit to take his place if he died, he trained Anson as his heir. But lately there's trouble in paradise. Connor's weres, even the older ones, prefer the heir to him. The boy, he's smart, but he needs to grow up a little. He's too young, too reckless. Got too much power too soon."

The leaders of the two groups of non-humans acknowledged each other, then Orion, Anson Sewell, and their followers casually drifted toward us until they reached a point directly below the balcony. Something, some force, or gravity seemed to draw them together.

Heflin raised his hand and gestured to someone behind us. Two fingers, then three more. Moments later, two men brought clay jugs and cups to the table and set them in front of Jacob and Cody. Heflin must have decided to play the considerate host. Dear God, they were pouring blood into the cups.

Cody and Jacob turned to me for direction. This was not a social situation I believed they or I had ever encountered before. I didn't know what to do. I had my wine, but… "Heflin?"

"It's warmed calf's blood. Quite common. You'll find it served at banquets. Some humans like it, too."

It didn't feel proper. It made me incredibly uncomfortable, but this was Heflin's town. If he saw no harm…I nodded my agreement. Cody and Jacob were adults.

The pair each lifted a cup and carefully sipped the

thick, crimson liquid.

Cody smiled and sighed. "It's good."

Jacob remained non-committal. I'm sure he preferred his blood accompanied by raw still twitching meat. It took about thirty seconds to realize the magnitude of my mistake. Blood triggered a psychic response from them to me. Their bodies absorbed the nourishment, and it solidified their psychic link. Another post-dying aspect came forth, and I had no control as it broadcast our presence out to the world.

Werewolves are not as sensitive as vampires, but every vampire around us with any degree of power suddenly became aware of an alien vibration in their midst. A minor vibration, but if I could feel it, they could too.

"Don't drink," I hissed under my breath. Cody had the strongest psychic link to me. I grabbed his hand. He reached across the table and grasped Jacob's hand for physical contact. I used the link through Cody to draw them close to me. Xavier, sitting beside me, stiffened. He didn't understand but didn't question.

"Be still. Let it pass."

Vamps and weres are exceptional, and have the unique skill to remain motionless, mind and body, in a way humans did not. Maybe I could use my humanity to camouflage them, mix them with the masses surrounding us.

I opened my senses, dropped all my mental shields. Salvaje crashed in. The weaving scents of pine and sage and others more alien. Millions of stars easily visible above the steady glowing gas torches—I absorbed it, tried to become a part of this place.

It wasn't working. I felt a hum of vampire power

that skimmed my mind. Searching, like a light on a tower…searching…for me. Coming closer… Heflin be damned, I would fight if necessary. The search wavered.

It faded away as the crowd fell silent. That silence flowed like a wave from the far side of the plaza, moving swiftly as voices stilled. Were, vamp, and human alike fell back and cleared a path across the plaza floor. Heflin muttered a curse under his breath. The crowd below backed away leaving Orion and Anson Sewell standing together.

The pat of footsteps sounded faint, but soon a figure approached through a path created by retreating vampires, werewolves, and humans.

"Elspeth!" Heflin said the name like a curse.

A woman with stick thin arms and legs sauntered barefoot across the plaza, bearing down upon Anson Sewell and Orion, the vampire prince. Dingy mouse colored hair, streaked with gray, twisted, fell into a single, untidy, waist-length braid. She'd drawn that braid forward across her shoulder where her thin bony hands clutched it like a lifeline. Dressed in rags, a mass of odd bead necklaces and other small trinkets on strings hung from her lean neck. A glint of more precious stones peeked through that tangled collection.

Every five or six feet she would stop and dance a few steps. She had the look of someone the unmerciful noonday sun had scorched to the bone, then cast away to live out her life in tierra sombra, the Shadowland. Even before I heard her wordless song and saw her wild, pale eyes, I knew she was mad.

How amazing. Orion and Anson bowed to her when she stopped in front of them. The lethal vampire and the werewolf made of fur, fangs, and claws, bowed before one old human woman.

The woman giggled. "Elspeth knows something." Her voice rasped like sandpaper across wood, but from our vantage point directly above her, her words sounded clear. Her head bobbed up and down. She spoke of herself in third person as if telling a story. "Elspeth knows. Give her a present, and Elspeth will tell." She held out a filthy hand to each of them.

Orion immediately lifted a thick, gold necklace from his neck and draped it across her palm. Anson Sewell quickly removed a bracelet from his pocket. Diamonds sparkled in the torchlight as he placed it in Elspeth's other hand. Wow! Both had to have come prepared for such a demand. Who the hell was this woman?

Elspeth stared at the jewelry. Slowly, with a haughty smile, she turned her hands and released the gifts. They landed on the plaza floor with a flat, dead sound of hollow bones.

"Not enough." Arrogance tinted Elspeth's voice.

I didn't think it could get quieter, but it did.

Anson stepped back, rigid with anger.

Orion bowed again. "Lady, will you tell us how we may honor you?" His rich, velvet voice matched his physical beauty. Oh, that voice. An angel's song could come from his lips.

Elspeth giggled. Then she eased up to him. "Pretty, pretty vampire. Give us a kiss."

With no hesitation, Orion bent down and gently kissed her on the mouth. A genuine kiss. Not a lover's kiss, but not the hurried kiss of a friend. What would his lips taste like? Surely not the moldy grave of Ruelle's mouth.

When he stepped back, Elspeth patted him on the

chest. "Sweet, sweet." She turned to Anson and studied him.

"Tell me what you want," he said. He didn't look happy.

Elspeth smiled what I'd swear was an evil smile. "A favor. A small favor." She giggled. "Or not so small. Maybe."

Anson frowned. "What favor?"

"Elspeth will tell when time comes." She crossed her arms over her thin chest.

"Very well, Elspeth." Anson sounded as if he was a prisoner learning he had received a death sentence. "You may have any favor that is within my power to give you."

What a hell of a combination—a beautiful, breathtaking vampire, a strapping young werewolf, and an old woman with incredible power—who might or might not be—insane. Is that how Salvaje worked?

Elspeth giggled. "Tell you. Elspeth tell you." She paused, an egotistical queen projecting a specific dramatic effect. "Angel has come. Now. Angel is here." Once again, her head bobbed up and down to emphasize her words. She leaned closer to them. "Be afraid, nightwalker. Be afraid, young wolf. Death is near."

Elspeth suddenly threw her arms up, whooped, and danced around in a circle. Then she bent and scooped up the priceless necklace and bracelet she'd rejected earlier. She rushed from the plaza in a weird slow motion, pumping her arms and stepping high to prance like a pony into the night.

Life and noise whispered slowly. Orion and Anson didn't speak again. The vamps and weres moved off in different directions. They didn't go far though, and they joined us on the balcony sidewalk overlooking the plaza, but at a reasonable distance.

I looked to Heflin for an explanation. He blew out a heavy breath of air. His voice sounded deeper than usual. "That little scene was…interesting. I can't explain it. I can't explain Elspeth."

What a disturbing little show. Xavier had his hand on my shoulder, silently asking for peace. "Well, Heflin, what are my options? Should I get a sign with wings and a target and hold it in front of me? Or hang it over my back? You know, get it over with quickly. Or should I carry extra ammo and make a preemptive strike?"

Heflin frowned. "Everything Elspeth says is true, or it always has been. She's a mystic, a prophet of sorts. Things happen when she speaks, but seldom the way you think they will—or the way you fear."

"And you seemed like such a practical, level-headed person. Prophets, omens, sacraments, doctrine, and dogma." Was Elspeth like Christopher, the Prophet of Avalon? He refused to speak because his predictions always came true. He'd allowed Anolia to leave Avalon, knowing she would return in a coffin. I'm not sure I would ever forgive him for that.

Heflin's expression turned deathly serious. "Let me warn you. If she ever approaches you, do your best to be careful, be polite. Give her what she asks for if you can. She asked for and received my wedding ring once. Don't think *that* didn't cost me when I got home."

"I see you got it back." I nodded at his hand.

"Not I." Heflin chuckled. "My dear wife, who is utterly fearless, went to Elspeth and demanded its return. Elspeth gave it to her, but when Maureen came back to the Paradox, she gave the kitchen help orders that they were to feed Elspeth if she came and wanted food."

"What happens if we don't give her what she demands?" Xavier asked.

"Nothing directly. I don't know if she has that kind of power. But the weres and vamps fear her. Don't show her any disrespect. You saw them, how they bowed to her. I know, Maat." He held up a hand. "For you, the Angel of Death is a fabrication, an advertising tool. Something to up your reputation and employment as a hunter." He gazed around the plaza then turned back to me shaking his head. "Salvaje is isolated. More than ground, more than distance, separate east and west here. We're steeped in a mystic world. We thrive on superstition."

Okay, warning received. Most certainly I'd run into Elspeth eventually. Her arrival had broken the vampire's search for us and came at too convenient a moment to be chance. Her pronouncement that the Angel had arrived spoke for itself. I hadn't invented that title, but I had made use of it, taking great delight in spreading its message. I didn't know if it preceded me or followed me here. Even though he hated his gift, Brother Christopher had taught me not to ignore such fortuitous events, even if I refused to acknowledge that the universe had already written the future. I needed to adjust my attitude...maybe.

Chapter Six.

Noche de Lucha, Fight Night, as Heflin called it, turned out to be a series of battles. Hand-to-hand for humans, claw to claw for weres, and they declared the last standing werewolf or man the winner. The barbaric pounding and clawing left no unbloodied fighter.

"It's the best way for men and beasts to express their violent natures." Heflin was far too cheerful to suit me. "No fatalities. Most of the time. There are referees. Extracurricular bouts in private locations occur occasionally. Not our business—if no one complains. Our business is protecting spectators."

The weres fought on the far side of the plaza, but we had excellent visibility. Bloody howling, tearing battles, I could barely stand to watch. Ajax cursed and went inside the bar to get drunk. This was much too close to the constant fighting, suffering, and loss he and I had endured all our lives. We'd witnessed too many loved ones torn apart. Even knowledge of another kind of were such events produced horrific memories. Only Xavier's proximity kept me seated or I would have joined him.

The battles between men here were not much better, but they were at least familiar. It seems Heflin and I had widely different opinions on what constituted a civilized society. The vampires remained aloof, indifferent, obviously above participating in such violent spectator sports. They were not, however above betting of such contests.

Cheers, jeers, a considerable exchange of money, wagers considering odds on each combatant. Copious consumption of beer, wine, and warm calves' blood accompanied the bizarre circus. They'd set up the main arena for humans just below us.

I scanned the area around us and found Lowell, Ty, and Heflin's other bodyguards, Rollman and Martin, sitting not far away. During my younger days, and since it only involved humans, I'd be down there at ringside, drinking, wagering, and enjoying the entertainment. When I was a kid, Uncle Jake lied to Aunt Nell and spirited me away into town. I had a bar-side seat to a handful of spectacular battles. I loved watching a couple of stupid men pound the shit out of each other. Uncle Jake taught me to learn the body language of the fighters, so I became super good at choosing a winner. That was before time and relentless violence so drastically altered my life.

Xavier, however, took a keen interest in the current human champion strutting around the arena boasting and issuing challenges. I think in his life, first in the militia and later as Gannett's Chief of Security, he acquired fighting skills. Duty bound, it had left little room for such activities for fun. He caught me watching him. He sipped his wine and gave me a grin, his eyes sparkling. "I could take him."

"Sure." I laughed then sneered at him. "But don't expect me to wipe your ass if he breaks both your arms."

Xavier kept his eyes focused on the fights. Unlike living with the turbulence that had stalked a hunter, mercenary, and thief like me, the solder in him planned his battles.

"Heflin?" Xavier tossed the question to him.

"I wish someone would take the bigheaded bastard down. He wins all the time. I know you could but..." Heflin eyed me, not Xavier.

I said nothing and looked the other way. I wouldn't let my love cripple Xavier. He had to be an honest judge of his own strength and skill. Having found the love I'd been waiting for all my life...ah, so difficult. I ask for freedom for myself without a clue how to give freedom to someone I cared for.

"So. Last man standing?" Keen excitement filled Xavier's voice. "If I win, do I have to keep fighting until someone beats me?"

Heflin nodded. "But only a couple of hours. It's almost midnight—you have to hold out until two. You want to?" Xavier's excitement had infected him.

Xavier grinned. He looked happier than I'd ever seen him in public. Had escaping Gannett and New Washington freed something inside? Something more than the tight-assed soldier persona?

Heflin turned in his chair and gazed at the area where Lowell and the others sat. He gestured with his hand, and Rollman rose, came to us, and crouched by Heflin's chair. Quick instructions and Xavier followed the man away. He had laid a hand on my shoulder, but he didn't look back. It wasn't long before a ripple ran through the crowd. *A challenge, someone new, a stranger, walked among them. Figure the odds, make your bets.*

"How much will you wager on him, Maat?" Heflin asked.

"How about the good old-fashioned eye for an eye."

He shifted in his seat, an uneasy look on his face. Did he perceive a threat?

"You should have more faith in him." He smiled, but it quickly faded.

"I've got faith—and plans for his uninjured body."

Ty slipped into the Xavier-vacated seat. "What's happening?"

"Your father's having a disturbing mid-life crisis. He's going to challenge the neighborhood bully."

Ty gazed over the rail. Xavier and Heflin's bodyguard had reached the arena. He grinned. "Wish I had money to bet on him." He stood. "Let me sit there, Maat. You can sit on my lap."

I grumbled, but I did as he asked. He could see perfectly well from where he was, but I humored him. I settled down, wrapped an arm around his shoulder, and rested my cheek against his head. How did a solitary individual like me suddenly wind up with so many people to love?

I did admire Xavier's impressive body as he stripped to the waist. He was pushing 40, just as I would hit 30 soon. It didn't show on him, but of course the scar on his face made him look so fierce. I wasn't the only admirer from the comments I heard around me. No, I wasn't jealous. The growing urge to slap a couple of female mouths shut was only a reaction to the night's moderately harrowing events.

The bully gave Xavier a reasonable fight. He landed one blow to Xavier's hip that almost guaranteed I'd be the one on top tonight if I planned to have sex when we returned to our room. Xavier put him down shortly after that.

Only one challenger came after that—a big one,

easily Xavier's size. Xavier danced around him, caught his wrist, twisted his arm out of the socket and kicked him in the kidneys. End of fight. Xavier didn't strut. Not his style. He simply waited quietly, arms crossed, staring straight ahead. Did anyone else want to try? No one did. Not much later, they disassembled the arena.

We stood and watched as Xavier made his way back toward us.

"Look at that shit, will you." I shook my head and drained the last of the wine. Men and women alike cheered and crowded around to fawn over Xavier like a hero. One vampire even spoke to him. And he was oh so gracious, smiling, shaking hands. "How long you reckon it'll take us to shrink *his* head?" I had to ask.

"Not long," Heflin drained his wine cup. "I think he's in trouble."

More prophetic words. When Xavier returned, I stood to meet him. He grabbed me, locked his fingers in my hair and kissed me, long and hard. God, was this the man who made me a prisoner at Avalon? The one who threw me into a rock wall? The celebrated winner draped one arm around my shoulders, drew me close, and kept me that way as we walked back to the Paradox. After a few moments, I realized he had to use me as a brace to keep from falling. The alpha male refused to acknowledge pain in front of the adoring crowd.

I didn't have sex that day, or the next three days since Xavier's hip swelled until the slightest movement brought agony. Nothing broken according to the doctor Maureen brought in, only contusions followed by ferocious bruising. He inexplicitly refused Cody's offer of vampire blood to help him heal. We drugged him, and I slept through the day across the hall in the room with

Ty and Cody, so I wouldn't disturb him. Both doors stood open, and I could hear him if he needed me.

****

With Xavier only moderately drugged, Heflin called us all down to the main floor below our bedrooms. That floor included an exercise and weight room, practice fighting mats, and a stocked kitchen for daily meals. Our employment arrangement? Room and board, and five golds a week—a sweet deal. Right? But after the time on the road and only two days—two lousy days—in Salvaje, my skin felt like parchment paper, despite soaking it in oil after showers. The inside of my nose bled, and sand rubbed me raw everywhere, including sensitive body folds. Salvaje went to the top of my list of miserable places to stay for more than a night or so. I decided to make it my goal to leave as soon as possible. I'd done my part to save my world from the nukes, now let me go. But where would I go? And who would go with me?

No chains bound me to the man in my bed, the one who had so ferociously upended my life. But could I persuade steady soldier to join me in wandering as I'd been so inclined most of my life? Did I want to? How odd contemplating abandonment of the reckless, turbulent life I'd known for so long. At least Avalon had taught me how to let go.

We crowded around a sizable square table with a scale rendering of Salvaje. "No street markers in Salvaje, but there are numbers on the corners of buildings. Memorize this layout." Heflin pointed out the Paradox's location and the main plaza for reference points. "This is Casa Salvaje, the council meeting house. What little we have in the way of government is there." He noted a round building to the north. "And this is Lycos, the werewolves' main den. Most of them live close around" He pointed to a group of buildings west of Casa Salvaje.

"The Vamps stay to the south in a completely underground complex. Don't know how big or even how many there are. They keep to themselves. Never been there, don't want to go."

"What's this?" I pointed to a section of crosshatched lines.

"That's Timber City. Part of the original Salvaje's frame buildings. It was supposed to be torn down after the wall went up, but the vamps objected. Don't know why. It'll collapse eventually."

At his direction, we caught the edges of the table and lifted it off to expose another model like the first. Only underground. "This is not accurate. These tunnels once cut through the rock as an exact model of the major streets above. They were separate from the storm drains. Convenient, planned modeling so anyone could use them. Since construction, stupid assholes have blocked tunnels, cut into the storm drains. God knows what else. It's a maze, a deadly labyrinth now. The vamps and weres use them, but don't you go down there unless it's an emergency." He pointed to a curled symbol on the model. "If you see this symbol carved over a street-level door, it's an entrance to the underground."

"Interesting," Parr said. "Why were they constructed?"

"Mostly for daytime egress from one place to another." Heflin shrugged. "The deeper ones, several are huge, may have been bomb shelters. I've tried to find the original plans but no luck yet. Despite what it looks like here, it does rain. The water will fill particular tunnels and sweep away anything not anchored."

We set the model of the upper city back in place and began memorizing the street layout of Salvaje. Heflin quizzed us, to emphasize the consequences of getting lost—or trapped at a dead end.

Salvaje's social structure was the strangest thing I'd ever seen. It had the usual gold coin hierarchy, and the rich were always at the top. The collection and distribution of coins came from limited, but lively, commerce mostly involving convoys moving goods from Mexico and sending it east. The only part of that commerce within the city walls involved retail establishments. Workers ferried that merchandise on the multi-wheeled wains. People walked mostly. They didn't ride. I did ask Heflin about Salvaje's human leaders.

"There are three. Council Member Stalt, you met her on the road, Jamil Turlington, and myself are the human reps. We're elected. Frankly, it's a job few want. I don't want it either, but I'm scared of others that do. The vamps and weres occasionally send a rep, but rarely take part in government. They obey the Asha and keep to themselves mainly. But they reap the benefits of living here in semi-peace."

I was on that one. "Benefits? You mean no hunters, right? And gory fights on the plaza for entertainment. Salvaje monsters have their meals, their humans, well trained." He jumped up and marched out.

Pissed off, oh yes. I do have that effect on people. Life and experience skewed my emotions, but my memories are clear. I believed in my heart and soul that the fundamental nature of devious vampires and single-minded werewolves required flesh and blood. For me, it was simply a matter of finding a target and taking aim.

Xavier and I attended one of the Council meetings. Despite Heflin's statement about no involvement two vamps and three weres did attend. They didn't speak, but a werewolf, a solemn woman with silver hair, took notes. The biggest business that night involved the battle over whether to fund a program to clear and repair roads to the North to easily reach Seattle.

Information I received confirmed the rumors in the east that California would remain uninhabitable for three or four human lifetimes. Most people in New York died of the plague, but according to Aunt Nell's books, the government killed California with a line of bombs, trying to stop the disease. I wonder what the history books will say about us, the survivors.

The Paradox was one of four brothels in town, and a small independent tavern anchored on several blocks. Since they didn't allow many strangers in the city, lively competition ensued for the permanent resident's patronage. I located a gun and ammo store, a bookstore that loaned out the limited number of books like a library, and a leather and boot repair shop. Heflin did insist that as his employee I needed new jeans and better shirts. They were available, but I balked at the cost, ten times that in the east. He handed me two extra gold coins. He always had plenty of those. He regularly tossed them at his problems. Whether gold resolved those difficulties was something he didn't talk about.

I did observe that weres and humans mixed on a social basis in specific ways, but unlike my attacker on the road, the weres remained in human shape. One thing Hef forgot to mention in his description of Salvaje. No children. When I asked him about it, he shrugged. "We don't allow children in Salvaje. We can't provide a safe environment. No one can bring them in, and children who might be born here and their parents must leave within a reasonable time. You know that employment agreement you signed for me? The one you didn't read? You promised not to get pregnant."

No, I hadn't read the contract. Not that I'd ever have children. I wouldn't have wanted to raise a family in Salvaje, anyway. But families occasionally acted as a buffer against chaos and provided a semblance of order, a progression in life. It was easier to define right and wrong with the lives of children at stake. Humans had children. Vamps and werewolves did not. I had no idea how that factored into the rules and regulations of the Asha. It certainly favored the monsters by keeping human populations level. I didn't know how vampires reproduced. Ruelle wouldn't speak of the act, but he did say it was easier than weres. Sabrina had told me most werewolves died in the first change of shape. With children and the need to protect them, humans could easily outnumber the monsters in a few short years.

Heflin and others had pushed the idea of public fights as a method to ease tension. As usual, he hadn't told us everything. He'd made a tiny mention of private battles. Contests, he called them. Extracurricular was his word. My fights had always been for survival or an impulsive moment of rage. Here, the so-called private fights were orchestrated combat and did have strict rules. Nevertheless, after I started work, I'd watched men and weres die bloody deaths. Oh, no one forced them to fight. No one complained—I'm told. I hated it.

Bodyguard? Who did I protect? Humans. The only species that required protection. I guarded the backs of trained fighters, the sponsors of fighters, and the winners of wagering, the blood money laid down. There were no banks, so a person carried their winnings away, walking through the streets with heavy gold coins. Those jobs weren't my only duty but were the most dangerous. And Heflin didn't mention really significant orgies. I threw up the first time.

By the end of the first week, Xavier was up and moving around and I was back in his bed, which made me happier. When he wasn't working as a guard like me, we were both using Heflin's excellent training facility on the first floor. Ty went to work for Maureen as general handyman and janitor. It left him with little free time, so maybe he wouldn't get in trouble. Lowell and Heflin spent a good bit of their time together discussing Salvaje politics until they left for the missile complex. They'd show up occasionally, then leave again.

Ajax and his truckload of Pulp and Powder disappeared sometime during the week, too. He didn't say where he was going, but he asked me to look out for Mary and Giselle while he was away. I agreed, but I informed him I wasn't his harem custodian. I would only protect against harm, not keep them caged. They could act as they pleased. He grumbled but knew it was right.

Once before Heflin and Lowell left, I asked how work progressed on the missile complex.

"Three weeks," Heflin said. "Maybe less. We open the main missile complex, then each of five vaults that contain the controls for the missiles. Going to blow the smaller vaults. No chance a new president will come along a few years from now and figure out a way to rewire."

"And then?"

"The world goes on without the threat of nuclear terrorism—for a while."

"What if you set one off accidentally while you're fiddling with things?"

Heflin's mouth twisted in a wry smile. "Depends on where the actual missiles are, and if they're pre-programmed for specific targets. The silos are probably within a hundred miles, so if one blows inside the silo, we might see it. If a missile goes up…depends on where it lands."

Depends? New Washington, Chicago, Seattle, or would it wipe out an unsuspecting, struggling population on the other side of the world?

We listened to the magic radio every evening. It told us of elections, sports events, crimes committed and punished, entertainment—Seattle, the new cradle of civilization. It sounded accurate , but I worried about Sable. Would Seattle have room for a transvestite brothel proprietor and his odd following? My physical and emotional discomfort grew with each day here in this desert. Maybe I could persuade Xavier and the others to check out this so-called jewel of the northwest. I wasn't ready to settle in one place.

Chapter Seven

One of my first jobs for Heflin consisted of following an obese, flatulent merchant, carousing and weaving his way from brothel to brothel. He began at Maureen's and worked his way down to the lowest class house. He'd insisted I watch the festivities. Heflin warned me not to eat anything before I left. Said the ass banger would complain if I puked on him.

My next few jobs involved fights, protecting an unsavory manager and several gravely injured humans. The human's managers were known to violently cut losers from their lineup rather than aid them, but I refused to allow that on my watch. I escorted a few to safety. To my surprise, Heflin didn't object. The next three tasks involved gamblers with significant wins.

Xavier had recovered from his mid-life crisis injury and was working, too. I had several thieves challenge me, I guess because I was a woman. I taught them better. And Xavier? He walked around like he owned the place. No one challenged him.

Heflin often teamed me with Carmita, his only other female bodyguard. She was an ill-tempered, six-foot, two hundred fifty-pound Amazon who had run away from her sheep-herding family when they tried to force her to marry an old man. She asked Maureen for a job at the Paradox, but Maureen wisely passed her on to Heflin to train as a bodyguard. We tested each other on the practice floor and developed a certain mutual respect. Carmita was stronger, heavier, but I moved faster, so I dropped her a couple of times. I did like her. I respected her.

Our last job was guarding a human who visited a private banquet and subsequent orgy. Sable's shows inured me to the vulgarities of visual sexual stimulation, but only on a human level. Seeing a werewolf in full fur fucking a woman disturbed me. The woman started the show with the false seduction routine. The werewolf tried to be easy on her; I'll give him credit for that. Agony filled her eyes, and after a while she stopped pretending any pleasure. The audience didn't care. Fear and pain were always good bets when it came to entertainment here, more than any place I'd ever been. Artillery-wasted Memphis had once been a dirty carcass of a city. This was far worse. Probably because it was so neat and clean, so civilized on the surface. *Salvaje had a black heart, though, no matter how pretty its face.*

I hated it. I hated Salvaje, and I hated the ritualized violence. I could take sudden involvement, a fight for my life, but this city made it a discordant symphony. Heaven and hell were accurate human analogies for Avalon and Salvaje. A lot of nights I watched obscenities and I swore I was leaving on the next convoy east. The growing stack of gold coins from my salary and tips would make it an easy passage.

I asked Xavier what he wanted. He was the reason I didn't jump in a convoy and leave. His answer? "I love you, Maat. If you go, I'll go with you. But is it possible for you to tolerate it until I fulfill my commitment to set up a training program for Salvaje's army?"

"So why the hell are you working for Heflin. Not training the army?"

"General Mylonas has control issues. I've given them an ultimatum. And a deadline. We'll see."

****

Ty ambushed me as I walked through the Paradox early one evening, on my way to meet Carmita and cover a gambler at a private game. He grabbed me and held me tight in arms growing more muscular as each day passed. Xavier had to work two fights, back-to-back, so he'd already left.

"Hey!" I whacked his chest with my fists, and he laughed as he released me.

"Come on," he said. He grabbed my hand and dragged me to the bar. He reached over and snagged a ring with keys from under the edge. "I want to show you something."

"Okay. Make it quick. I have a meet up."

Few visited the Paradox this early in the evening. A couple of men sat with two of the girls, several more at the bar, and trouble brewed at the blackjack table.

Ajax had been gone three weeks. Giselle dealt cards from her usual place, carefully watched by her most steadfast customer. Sergeant Patterson, the soldier who found her so attractive the day we arrived in Salvaje, had become a regular. He drank slowly and played an occasional game I'd bet he couldn't afford on a soldier's pay. There was no such thing as a cheap drink in Salvaje. If others crowded the table, Patterson left. He and Giselle didn't talk much, but he'd reach out and touch her hand occasionally. They might meet other places. I didn't know. Mary smirked from behind the bar. Maybe the twins' relationship wasn't as cordial as it appeared.

Ty led me out of the bar into a hallway where he unlocked a door. He lifted an odd-looking cylinder from a nearby shelf. "Look at this," he said, "it's so interesting." He pressed a small lever on the cylinder, and a three-inch flame instantly flickered from one end. "They call it a fire stick. Uses natural gas. They have a bunch of them." He used the fire stick to light a lantern, and with him leading the way, we walked downstairs into the cool depths of a cellar, where racks of bottles lined the walls.

"There's five hundred and seventeen bottles of wine down here," Ty said. "I know because I did an inventory for Maureen. Two hundred and twelve kegs of beer in another room down the hall."

"I'm impressed. There isn't—wasn't—this much stuff in all of Memphis."

"Yeah. Maureen says Heflin brings it from a secret place in Mexico." He hooked the lantern into a holder on the wall. "You don't like it here, do you?

"Is it that obvious? Ty, my nostrils are dry sand craters, and my skin feels like I'm a lizard. What the hell? You dragged me down here to ask if I was happy."

"Yeah. I wondered if we might be leaving."

"No, not leaving yet. I hate it, but not yet."

He nodded, accepting my words. Salvaje was maturing the boy at an alarming pace. He selected a bottle of wine and we laughed as we climbed the stairs.

Ty turned off the lantern and set it back on the shelf next to the fire stick and a hatchet. He threw his arm around my shoulders and hugged me close as we went back into the bar room.

We arrived just in time to see Sergeant Patterson go airborne and smack into a table, sending patrons, girls, and drinks crashing to the floor.

Ajax had returned.

Maureen and two of Heflin's bodyguards, who acted as bouncers, came running. I headed for Ajax, but Giselle beat me there. The quiet, sweet-natured twin screamed and pounded Ajax's chest with her fists. He backed away—eyes wide with shock.

The bouncers avoided the pair and helped Sergeant Patterson to his feet. He appeared stunned, but not injured, so I moved closer to Ajax and Giselle. It was none of my business...well, yes, it was. Ajax was one of mine.

"How dare you?" Giselle had stopped hitting Ajax, but she shook her fist at him. "I'm just one of a pair of warm bodies you fuck." The fight went out of her then, and her round shoulders slumped. "You have all of me. I get nothing from you in return but the kindness and protection you'd give to any woman you kept. Then when someone else wants me—only me—you act like he's a thief after your property."

Ajax stood there staring at her. Since I knew him so well, I could tell she'd hurt his feelings. He genuinely cared for Giselle and Mary—as much as he could but couldn't understand why that wasn't enough.

Ajax held out a hand to her. "Come on Zell. You know I—"

"Giselle!" Patterson surged toward us.

Ajax jumped at him, but I threw myself against my demo man. Giselle did the same for Patterson. Maureen had arrived, and her bouncers started to wade in to end the violence but stopped when she held up a hand. She had a look of intense fascination on her face. Like most of her kind, she had a keen interest in human interactions.

Part of the Madam's survival guide I suppose.

When everyone stilled, Patterson caught Giselle by the hands. "Come on with me," he pleaded. "Be my woman. Marry me."

Ajax drew deep breaths, and his muscles tensed into hard knots as I stood there. I wasn't sure if I could hold him, but Ty joined me. I left Ty with him and went to Giselle.

"What do *you* want, Giselle?"

Giselle laid her hand on Patterson's cheek. She stared in his eyes. "I want to be with you." He sighed in relief. "Wait here," she said to him. She left him and went to Ajax.

"You've been so good to me, Ajax. You saved my life, getting me out of Memphis. I care for you, and I do thank you. But hopefully someday you'll know what it's like to want to be the only one. I hope, when it happens, that one woman wants you the same way. "She kissed him on the cheek.

Giselle turned and went back to Patterson, who opened his arms to her.

"You want me to help you get your things?" I asked her.

"What things? All the clothes are Maureen's. I left Cincinnati with just what I was wearing, and I left Memphis the same way." She smiled at Patterson, and then sobered. "Memphis…not here…I worked in a house…you have to know."

Patterson laid gentle fingers across her lips. "Every day is new. Let's go home."

He led her away, and I grabbed Ajax by the arm. "Come on. I'm heading for a job, but you need to get drunk. After you settle up with Maureen for her furniture."

"Not a bad idea." I could feel him shake. "I'll never figure it out. Being drunk's not enough. I got to go out again tomorrow anyway."

As we left the Paradox, I caught a glimpse of Mary, whom everyone had ignored during the whole fracas. Mary stared at Ajax with hungry eyes, and I knew she wasn't unhappy. Giselle was gone, and she might have him to herself for a while, but I'd bet it wouldn't be long before another one of Ajax's vision of the perfect robust woman would come along, and Mary would be one of twins—or even triplets—again.

****

Carmita and I headed back to the Paradox just before dawn. The stars above had already faded, and a thin slice of moon eased across the sky as we made our way through the silent streets. A comfortable walk since the cool of night had not given way to the omnipresent heat of the day.

"Xavier going to fight this week?" Carmita asked.

"Not if I can talk him out of it." Xavier had been working and making love to me, and I liked it when he did. I didn't want him hurt again. "I think Heflin is pushing him into fighting. Customers are paying extra to have the champ guarding them."

"What do you want?"

"Carmita, I want to get on a truck and watch Salvaje disappear behind me.

She chuckled. "That Xavier looks like a bad-ass fucker with that scar. Big man too. Bitch like you could do worse."

Carmita called me a bitch regularly, and by now, I counted it as a compliment.

"Bitch like me has done worse. I wonder—"

My ability to sense weres and vamps had become useless in Salvaje. Six weres in human form poured out of an alley and hit us hard. I didn't have time to draw gun or knife before they relieved me of my weapons and held me tight by my arms. One approached me. I lashed out with my foot. He caught it in his hand. He held then released, as if he didn't want to fight, to harm me. The weres didn't touch the silver knife. They had a human for that. A lean, shifty-eyed scavenger by the look of him, he grinned toothlessly and snatched the blade from its leather sheath.

"Better throw that away, fucker." I snarled at him between clenched teeth. "If I catch you with it, I'll cut your balls off."

The grin faded. He clutched the knife close to his body and scuttled away.

The weres, surprisingly gentle, turned my arms behind my back. Two of them held Carmita. She kicked and cursed in rage as they dragged me away. I didn't want to waste energy fighting a hopeless battle, so I relaxed and let them haul me along. We didn't go far before we headed into Salvaje underground. I'd not been down there yet. All my experiences underground, caves, basements, and such, had come under duress. The weres held me in a firm grip but didn't seem intent on injury.

We moved easily downstairs and through the pitch-black wormhole tunnel. No trouble for them, they could see in the dark. So could I, but I wasn't sure if they knew, so I stumbled and cursed on rough spots to keep up the pretense. They guided with greater care. What the hell?

The tunnel, cool and damp, surprised me. I'd call the odor unpleasant, not choking since I felt a breeze on my face. Only a breath of air, but it moved. I watched and listened and tried to plot my course through the black maze. It didn't take long to realize they were taking me to the Lycos, the main werewolf den.

They stopped when we came to a place where another were waited by a thick wooden door set in the tunnel wall. They opened it and pushed me in, again taking care not to injure me. The door locked with a firm click behind me.

My prison, an empty room, smelled of arid decay. None of the slight breeze from outside entered here. The wall on my right slanted slightly up to a shelf, like it had been part of an original tunnel, then blocked off. Above the shelf, I could see light so faint ordinary human eyes would miss it. Okay, that I could do. I went back as far as could and made a running leap. I scrambled up, caught the rough top, and hauled myself higher—and over. It went down. I clawed at the rock, trying to slow my descent, but crashed into a group of humans, huddling around a lantern. I don't know who scared whom the most, but my tumbling body and cloak snuffed out the light. The participants in the interrupted gathering scrambled away into the dark.

Pain flared in my hands and elbows since I had left a bit of skin behind during my precipitous descent. I lay still for a moment, trying to get my bearings, then climbed to my feet and headed in a direction I hoped would lead me to stairs and into the sun. To my surprise, I passed other humans as I followed the tunnel. They carried tiny lanterns and scurried out of my way as I charged through them.

The sun had risen above, and light seeped through small drainage holes along the way. Heflin had warned us. A minor rain would fill these tunnels with deadly walls of water. Salvaje underground was a midnight highway—or a death trap. For my own sake, it was something I decided I'd better learn more about. If I ever got out.

I trudged on, searching for a place to go up. I heard voices ahead, so I slowed and stopped. A lantern gave the tunnel a faint glow. Peeping around a corner, I saw the ragged thief who'd snagged my knife for the weres. Well, well. *Karma, I most humbly thank you.*

My thief spoke to a tall, broad-shouldered man, one big enough to make the tunnel seem small. Most of us wore the sand color capes, but I'd made conscious note of the subtle differences in individual garments and who wore them. I didn't know this one, but the cape's correct fit on his shoulders and the drape in the front indicated quality tailoring. He had his hand out, and I did see a conspicuous thick gold band with green stones on his wrist. His hood draped over his head, and I couldn't see his face.

The thief's voice whined through the tunnel. "I told you. I got to wait till its time. Any of them see me I'm done. Fucking old witch moves. She hides."

"You were paid." The big cape on the left had a deep baritone voice. I shivered when he spoke. He sounded human, but his voice carried power almost like a vampire's. "Get it or I'll send the dogs after you. I'm not coming down in this sewer again!"

"Yes, sir. Yes, sir." Scruffy bowed. "I'll get it. The old witch…I'll find her sir. I'll catch her and take her down." He flashed my knife in the air.

A thin bony hand gripped my arm. I jerked but kept silent. Elspeth the oracle, who had to be the discussed old witch, stood behind me. I turned just enough to see her. She put a single finger to her mouth.

Elspeth's deeply wrinkled face and wild blue-white eyes did nothing to change the impression of her sanity. Then she proceeded to march around the corner. Giggling the whole time.

What the hell? Crazy old woman. How was I going to defend her? And why did I feel the sudden desperate need to defend her? I had no weapons. The thief forced me to act. He screeched and charged Elspeth, holding my silver knife poised in the air. He'd slaughter a helpless old woman.

I jumped in front of her, lowered my head, and slammed my shoulder into his so fragrant unwashed body. I shoved him back and with brutal purpose, smashed him against the tunnel wall. He collapsed. His breath whooshed out. I grabbed his knife-wielding wrist and twisted his arm out of joint. He released the knife. I caught it before he crumpled to the floor.

I shouted, "Elspeth! Run!"

Of course, she stood there grinning. I whirled to face the greatest and unknown danger. No problem. The tall man had disappeared.

The thief lay on the floor making inarticulate high-pitched noises. Elspeth came up behind me. When I faced her, she had the oddest expression on her face.

"Elspeth. Why didn't you run?"

She shook her head. "No danger." She reached out and touched my face. Her thin small fingers brushed my cheek like feathers. "Poor Angel."

"I'm okay. Who was that man?"

Elspeth didn't answer my question. She fumbled with her multitude of necklaces and separated one from the tangled mess of diamonds, gold, stone, and plastic draped around her neck. I'm sure each had meaning for her. She lifted the chosen necklace over her head. A single stone, a clear two-inch crystal, attached to a steel chain. The ruby Ruelle had given me in New Washington was real. This looked like a cheap thing you would give a kid you knew would lose it. I didn't know whether to accept it or reject it and risk offending her. I reached for it, and when I touched the chain, an odd tingle ran through my fingers. I jerked my hand back.

"Take. Take." Elspeth shoved it toward me. I remembered what Heflin said about trying to placate her if possible. I was running out of time. The weres I'd escaped would be on my trail soon. I opened my vest and turn out an inner pocket.

"Put it in here."

She did as I asked. I secured the pocket.

She grinned and then her eyes…changed. The pale blue-white orbs suddenly cleared and darkened. She grabbed my arm. Her thin bony fingers ended with sharp nails, and they bit into skin. "Keep it. Hide it." She released me and strutted away into the darkness. Her eyes didn't require artificial light either.

I'm not overly superstitious, but I live in a world with shape shifters, blood guzzling leeches, and oracles who saw desperate times ahead. I had a healthy grip on various forms of psychic phenomena myself. I would not ignore those portents, even if I believed they were wrong. I could feel the presence and significance of the stone in my pocket. I checked the clasp again. It wouldn't come open by accident.

I needed to get out of this labyrinth. I didn't kill Scruffy. I wanted to talk to him about the man who left, but I'd have to find him later. I didn't remove his balls either. That would mean touching him. I left him sobbing on the floor.

The silver blade I wedged in my empty shoulder holster. I covered it with the cape. Leather dulled the sensation weres received when they got close. They were super sensitive to silver. That way, if I came on any of them, they'd be less likely to feel the weapon. When I got out, I'd have to find a way to get my guns back. In another minute, I saw stairs leading up and bright daylight streaming down.

Ten feet from freedom, a troop of weres surged out of a side tunnel and surrounded me. One of them was even fuzzy. Shit! They didn't touch me. They stood in a circle around me. There was no way I could escape.

"Come," one said. He was one of the two who locked me in the room from which I'd made my escape. He didn't look happy, but there didn't seem to be any personal animosity.

"Okay." I shrugged. No point in fighting the inevitable. I stared longingly at the stairs and sunlight. My captor sighed and reached for me. "I can walk," I told him. I clamped my arm tight against my body across the knife in the shoulder holster. If I could keep them from sensing the silver, I would have at least one thing to fight with. They formed a cage of bodies around me, but they didn't touch me. I guess they had figured out I could see in the dark and didn't need a guide.

I hadn't come as far as I thought, or the tunnel circled here, because it wasn't long before we went upstairs. They opened a door to a hallway and then into a wider space.

Seeing the bloody werewolf fights at the plaza,

experiencing the combative nature of the city, I understood the significance of standing alone on a sand floored fighting arena. It's a little like having a gun barrel placed at your head. Especially since Anson Sewell sat at the side, turning a small toy truck in his fingers.

Chapter Eight

The situation typified my life's inescapable conflict of coincidence and inevitability. The karma I'd thanked for returning my knife minutes ago had turned on me like a rabid dog. One night twelve years ago, I'd slaughtered a female werewolf who had killed and taken a child from an Ag Commune. That female werewolf had a human man and two werewolf children, a boy and a girl with her. Children changed to werewolves were so rare that I'd only heard of them. I'd never seen one before that night, nor had I seen one since. The man attacked me, I shot him, but he held the female were-child in his arms, so she died too. The little boy werewolf escaped.

I should have guessed it that first night in Salvaje, but too many new things crowded my mind. How did the little boy were-child I'd allowed to escape in Kentucky twelve years ago get to New Mexico? Anson Sewell, the werewolf leader's youthful pretender, had retribution on his mind.

Elspeth's pronouncement that the Angel had arrived had set me up for the perfect disaster. How did he get the little toy truck he'd dropped the night I killed his mother, sister, and father? I'd kept it all these years, a kind of talisman, but as far as I knew, it was with my few personal things stuck in a drawer at the Paradox.

The weres sitting in tiers around the arena had an

unobstructed view of any conflict there. The pungent odor of previous battles, old blood, assaulted my senses. Odd, but the audience had no more enthusiasm for the situation than my reluctant kidnappers had. The sound of hushed conversation carried a rise and fall of displeasure. That didn't mean they'd help me, but I'd learned enough to know that by kidnapping and bringing me here, Anson had deliberately and dangerously violated the intent and application of the Asha, the law.

In my time here, I'd learned that the werewolves did pay homage to the rules. If Anson had issued a formal challenge, there would be laws he'd have to follow. Laws he'd have to obey or become an outcast. Not that it helped me in my current situation.

I approached him, careful to keep the cape over my left shoulder to conceal the silver knife. sheathed in leather. Anson stood. Heavy boned and muscular, clad in leather, an overgrown teenager, he made an impression. Yes, I was afraid. My heart thumped, and every nerve in my body threatened full-blown panic. I locked it down. I'd faced werewolves since the day I had performed a mercy killing of my mother. I squared my shoulders and prepared to fight.

Righteous savagery masked Anson's face.

He shook the hand holding the truck at me. "You killed my mother."

"Yes." No point in denial. Killed her and cut off her clawed hands as proof so I'd get paid.

"I loved her." His wrath filled the room like billowing hell-hot steam. At any moment, he would change shape and tear me apart. I doubted he'd fall prey to the stupidity that overcame some when they changed. I had nowhere to run. My hand slipped under my cape and closed on the knife hilt. The second he started to change shape I'd charge. It would be my only chance. Young, strong... The truth? In this situation, without backup, without my guns, I had no chance at all.

"You loved her?" I spoke softly, knowing every were in the room could hear me. "What about the mother of the little girl she slaughtered that night? Think she loved her child? How long had sweet Mommy been feeding you human flesh?"

The weres around me stirred. Discontented murmurs whisked through them. Weres eating humans was common in the east. The Asha banned it and, according to Jacob, who had made connections with his fellow weres here, they considered it a revolting practice. These were *civilized* werewolves.

Elspeth peeked out from behind Anson's thick body. She sidled close on the tier and stood beside him. She grinned and gave me a friendly wave. What the hell? She gave him the truck? Why? And how had she managed to get in my room in what I know is a secure building? *Meddling witch—a mad prophet trying to create the future of her visions.*

Anson's hands clenched into fists. "You couldn't face her. A rifle. Distance. My mother never had a chance with you, bitch."

No point in telling him my mother never had a chance with the were that ate her alive. He'd dwelled too long on his loss. Younger than me, he'd had time to drown in the misery and longing I'd lived with much of my life. He'd had no Avalon to bring him to the peace I'd found for my past.

"Yes, Anson, I'm a good shot, and I used a long-range rifle and one silver bullet. "Not the best thing to say, but there was no talking that would get me out of here. He was immature and, if I angered him enough, he might make a mistake.

Anson's mouth twisted into an ugly smile. "I want to be fair."

"Okay." I smiled and nodded.

He jerked. Not what he expected. Bet he'd had a speech of heart-rending justification rehearsed. I'd disrupted the plan. He shook the hand clutching the toy truck at me. "I'll give even the Angel of Death a chance."

Elspeth danced a little jig beside him. Still grinning, she waved again.

The sound came from behind me. Feet, massive feet, shuffling through the sand. The odor of carrion wafted through the air. I wanted to keep my focus on Anson, but the immediacy of a werewolf approaching to stand beside me forced me to look. In fur and fang, he topped out at over seven and a half feet, had six inches on Jacob, and was twice Jacob's width.

"This is my champion." Anson seemed to have calmed down a bit. His voice had gone from blazing wrath to bitter chill. He'd had everything in this scene well planned, rehearsed even, I'd bet. A champion? A piss-poor attempt to cover his actions by tossing out a trifling deference to the Asha.

"I don't have claws, Anson." I spoke to the audience, not him.

A grumbling sound came from the tiers around us.

Anson's smug voice offered details. "He's fairly slow, so that should even the odds with the Angel of Death." He held out his hands. "And we all know your skill at killing even the best of us." He wanted support from his peers. They remained silent, neither cheering nor agreeing with him. Even odds. Sure. The werewolf appeared to be one of the dim-witted ones that barely survived that first catastrophic shape change. When Sabrina gave me a lesson on them, she said her pack protected them. Yes, his eyes were dull, but he'd already shifted, so I wouldn't have those seconds in my favor. And I had no idea how Anson defined slow. Mental? Physical? With the size and reach of the arms, he would take me out in one half-assed swipe. He could run me down, too. How weird. He stood unmoving, furry, and smelly, and not seeming inclined to attack anything.

"Anson!" The call came from behind me. I turned to see the female werewolf whose mate I killed on the road the first day in Salvaje. "I claim the right of the Asha," she said. "I will champion the Angel. I will fight for her."

"No." Anson's voice came out as shocked, then his face twisted into a furious scowl. Two more weres called out, offering to be my champion, and again, Anson refused. Taking me like this, breaking the law, his action would fall back on them—or worse. Dumping me in an arena unarmed…what would Xavier do when I went down? I knew him better now. I knew what he could do. Gannett's Butcher. Yes. My death would trigger that drive to slaughter. And Ajax, my demolition man? He wouldn't rest until he'd leveled the city.

I cocked my head and considered the towering werewolf again. With all my body language non-threatening, my posture loose, I stepped back for fighting distance and grasped the knife they fortunately didn't know I had. My furry opponent stood and watched me with mild almost childlike interest, now.

"Anson," I said. "Are you sure—"

"Kill her!" Anson screamed.

The giant werewolf might be dim-witted, but he was not physically slow. Instantly, he obeyed—snarling, flashing, long yellow teeth. He flung his arms up in the classic overhead clawing, killing position. They always did that. I'd seen it so many times over the years. The latest time on the road outside the city. All they did was expose their most vulnerable area. The best way to kill? Keep your distance and use many silver bullets. Not an option here.

Years of experience kicked in. Maat Ferris, the lightning-fast bane of the beasts, was still in her prime. I snatched the silver knife from the sheath just as he lifted his arms, reaching maximum height. One step forward. I plunged it into his heart. I don't think he perceived my move. Silver cut through werewolf flesh and bone easy as stabbing a loaf of bread. I released the hilt and flung myself back, desperate to get out of reach of those long, long arms and massive claws that could still kill me.

The claws slashed down. They caught my cape and snatched me back, smack into his body. He held me against him for seconds until the clasp at my neck broke and my cloak tore loose. I tumbled at his feet. One step…he'd crush me.

I stared up at him. He gazed down, eyes wide, confused uncomprehending. A high-pitched whining noise issued from his mouth. He stood frozen like a stuffed bear. With a great sigh, he slowly crumpled. I'd at least had the sense to roll away. He clutched my cape against him as he fell. My knife? Still in his chest. I surged to my feet.

I stood and stared at the werewolf Anson had set up to kill me. God help me, it was like slaughtering a pet milk cow. Blood pulsed out around the silver blade and soaked into my cloak still clutched in his hands. His frantic heart struggled with the impossible task of healing a silver induced wound. He twisted his head and met my eyes. I know nothing of werewolf emotions, but I knew pain when I saw it. Those pitiful eyes closed. A dead monster lay at my feet.

Stunned silence filled the room. Weaponless, I turned to face Anson.

His change to werewolf began when his hands sprouted brown hair and deadly claws. Elspeth suddenly stepped in front of him. Her thin, bony hands locked on his arms between the elbows and wrists. His shift halted.

"Elspeth wants favor you promised. Wants Angel's life."

"No!" Anson shuddered. He struggled, the effort to escape her grip evident on his face. Stick-like bones, less body mass than a child…she held him. Dear God, what manner of creature was Elspeth to take a werewolf captive and keep him from shape shifting?

"Promised Elspeth," she said, as if speaking to a naughty boy. There was no strain in her voice, nothing to indicate that her actions took more energy than her walk across the plaza my first night in Salvaje.

For long moments, Anson drew deep, ragged breaths, then relaxed and capitulated without a word. I don't think he had a choice. I could see the old witch and young werewolf standing there until they both died of hunger or thirst. Elspeth released him. He dropped to his knees and covered his face with his clawed hands.

Xavier stalked into the arena, gun in hand. Heflin, Jacob, and Carmita, weapons also drawn, followed him. They skirted the dead were and surrounded me. I grabbed Xavier's arm when he turned toward Anson. He wore his fearful killing face. Could I stop him?

"Please don't, please. Xavier. It's over." I spoke softly, but with as much energy as I could gather. He was my man, and he wanted to strike. He stopped. He stood still, terribly still. How amazing. I'd broken through his dreadful rage. He'd surrendered his desire to kill to me, something I never expected.

"Hey, guys. You're late. You okay, Carmita?" I lifted my voice to sound calm while I rubbed the raw, stinging mark on my neck where the clasp on the cape caught and broke.

"Fuckers let me go right after they took you away." Her expression was dark and sullen. I think she wanted an appropriate fight to rescue me.

Anson had broken the Asha's rules for his personal vengeance. That act had made the kidnapping action uncomfortable, so they let her go after her capture, knowing she'd find help. They probably told her where they were taking me. Heflin descended on Anson, spitting out words in rage.

I held Xavier's arm. I still had vivid memories of Arkansas, his face, his disassociation from the Xavier I had known. He gazed into my eyes. He pulled my hand from his arm and lifted it to his lips. Xavier loved me and, for that moment, he was the totality of my world. Even when he released my hand, I could see that calm settle deeper as he relaxed. It would be okay. He would be okay. For now, anyway.

I went and knelt beside the dead were. Silver, guns, and explosives, over the years I'd eradicated them like vermin. No mercy, no regrets either. This monster would have slaughtered me on his master's command had I not acted. I jerked the silver knife from his chest. When I stood, I faced the female were, the one whose mate had attacked me on the road. She had the oddest look on her face. Why had she offered to champion me?

"Is he one of yours, too?" I nodded at the body at my feet.

"A friend. Again, you are not at fault."

"Why did you offer to fight for me?"

She gave a slight shrug. "To honor the law."

She gazed around the arena like someone contemplating a major change in her life. She turned and walked away to join the audience now quietly filing out of the room.

To honor the law. Jacob and I had talked, and he told me something I hadn't thought possible. Werewolves he knew considered themselves to be human, not monsters or beasts, despite their ravaging animal behavior at times. For him, remaining human meant not giving into that savage instinct.

Elspeth wandered around the arena, humming and smiling. I went to her, silver knife in hand. I knew deep in my heart I could spare myself and my people enormous suffering if I killed her. She was not just prophesying events. Somehow, she was creating situations regardless of what failure would mean for those whose lives she so casually manipulated.

"You set me up, Elspeth. You've been playing me since that first night you walked through the plaza. What's your game, old woman? Why did it require that werewolf's life?"

She stopped and stared straight at me. Her fingers wove through the multiple necklaces lying across her chest. Her eyes cleared and suddenly gleamed with sharp intelligence.

"Turn around, little girl. Angel has two faces. Poor Angel." Elspeth howled with laughter and danced in a circle. Then she strutted toward me, hands on her hips. "Elspeth answers to God, not Maat Ferris."

I whirled and stalked away. I deeply desired to run, but even more I wanted to go back and kill her regardless of the consequences. Carmita approached. She handed my guns to me. She didn't speak, but I could see it in her eyes. I'd seen it many times before. Farmers, soldiers, everyone who'd known me professionally. The mixture of admiration followed by the need to distance themselves from a killer. My life, my curse.

****

Heflin offered to file a complaint with the Council, but I told him to let it go. I suspected, from the audience reaction, Anson would get grief from his own kind, and it would be more effective than anything else. I'd watch out for him, but Elspeth's intervention precluded any immediate attack. Heflin agreed with obvious relief.

We returned to the Paradox, and I headed for the women's showers. Xavier went with me and ignored Maureen's girls, who cleaned and oiled their tools of trade, their bodies, and prepared for a day's rest. He wasn't going to let me out of his sight.

While I stripped and washed, I told him the story of the toy truck and my youthful mistakes years ago in Kentucky. We'd spent our Salvaje hours on work, pleasure, and companionship and not had enough time together to speak of much of our past lives.

After I finished and we went to our room I told him my story. "I was hunting a werewolf. One that was killing sheep. But there were kids, Xavier. Werewolf kids. Two in one family. How did that happen? How did they survive the change?" *I know they weren't born that way.* I had never experienced that obscenity before, nor had I seen it since.

Sabrina's harrowing tale of what occurred after a bite, how few survived the trauma of the first change, had the power to move me. For every living werewolf there would be so many infected humans who died during the first change.

The little boy were-child, Anson Sewell, had run to escape my bullets. Now time and the anonymous universe had snatched him from my past and dumped him, full grown, in my path again. And of course, Elspeth's pronouncement of my arrival and today's incident added a wild and new dimension to the strange new game.

"The weirdest thing is how Elspeth got that damned toy truck I'd carried for years out of this locked room." I knew the proficiency of the Paradox's guards. "I grew up, lived, and fought weres all through Virginia or Tennessee. I thought I knew everything. At least until I met you. Now this old woman…"

No doubt Elspeth was an oracle like Christopher. And yes, she followed a predestined path. That being the case, I walked along that path with her, and there would be no escape. Elspeth was insane and Christopher refused to speak which possibility saved him from her illness.

Xavier smiled. "I start training troops next week."

"About time." General Mylona's turf guarding defeated at last. Once Xavier finished here, I knew I could talk him into leaving.

"Yes." He drew me into his arms. "You want to go to Seattle, don't you? See what it's all about. You're at that radio every minute it's on."

"I think about it so often. I'm not sure about Seattle, but I'm ready to be rid of Salvaje. I'm a hunter, not a gladiator."

When I looked at him now, I never saw the scar, only his eyes and wonderful mouth. He sat on the bed, and I straddled his knees, so I could stare directly into his eyes.

"Xavier, do you ever think about that first night at Avalon?"

His hands closed on my waist. "Only when my knee hurts. No, that's not true. I think about…how I hurt you."

I laid my head on his firm shoulder. "When I saw you standing there in the Avalon dining room, despite the danger, I thought about your hands, the way you moved, it's like a picture in my mind. Then of course I tried to kill you."

I laid a hand on his cheek—on the scar. Feverish under my fingers, it seemed a symbol of all his guilt and anger. "So stupid. Down on the fucking floor, couldn't walk, a big strong man towering over me…so what did I do? I attacked with a four-inch knife. Crazy shit…I knew better."

"Crazy? Maybe. You only wanted to save your friend and escape. That's natural. I didn't have to hurt you. I hated you for my weakness."

We engaged in a long, passionate kiss, interrupted by a tap on the door. When I unhappily lifted myself from Xavier's lap and opened it, Maureen entered and closed it behind her. Her concerned expression boded trouble. Extraordinarily little disturbed this woman.

"Maat, I must speak to you." She ignored Xavier as if he did not exist.

The specter of trouble hovered over me again. "Okay, what's wrong?"

"There are two things. First, I understand Elspeth removed private property from this room. She used it to cause you harm. The security of this building is my responsibility. I apologize for my failure of that charge."

"You think you could have stopped her?" I shook my head. "Elspeth says she answers only to God. What if God speaks to her? He wanted her to have the toy?"

"If that is so, we are truly doomed. The second thing. You have a visitor, an important visitor. You should speak with him. I'm sure you'll hate it, and it is not your fault, but you have become a prominent individual in Salvaje. *Beware the Angel of Death.* Elspeth whispers and occasionally shouts that to the entire city. While she does not name you, it's becoming obvious to everyone. I suggest you embrace that role now. Be the Angel. Wear your guns, your knife, always. Show no weakness."

Xavier jerked. "I'll go with you."

I held up a hand. "Please. Only if you hear me shooting."

His mouth tightened, and he stared into my eyes. Then he nodded. And again, he proved his strength and one of the reasons I loved him. He gave me my freedom, even though he'd almost lost me only a few hours ago.

Maureen didn't speak as she led me to a private sitting room on the other side of the building. Her face was a mask as she opened the door and closed it behind me after I entered. The sitting room, from the floors, to furniture, to minor décor, reflected the monotonous beige sameness of this city I grew to hate more every day. No signs of color that spoke to Maureen's decorating here, so I'd bet no one used the space often.

The preponderance of werewolves in Salvaje had muted my ability to sense them at a distance. That didn't happen in this room. All my werewolf detection senses, dulled since I came to Salvaje to live among the beasts, suddenly rose and screamed like an animal caught in a trap.

The werewolf who rose to greet me was silver haired as Lowell, but the resemblance ended at the color. Tall, lean, and ancient, I knew that he had to be among the eldest of his kind. He dressed in the usual sand colored cape, but I'd never seen his polished black leather boots in Salvaje. He bowed his head to me, in a distinctly non-werewolf manner.

"I am Abban Connor, Suriel. I'm honored to meet you."

Connor. The alpha werewolf in Salvaje. Heflin had met him, Jacob had not, a fact that deeply disturbed him for an unexpressed reason. The leader challenged by young Anson Sewell. Such a strange emotion filled me as I stared at him. By the power of the events swirling around me, I'd changed. I'd let go the idea that I had to kill every werewolf in sight without too much kicking and screaming. Abban Connor had not offered me the slightest hint of aggression. So why did I suddenly have a deep burning urge to shoot him? I hadn't even felt that way about Anson, who wanted to do major damage to my person.

"Please call me Maat. What can I do for you?" Polite. I would be polite in Maureen's house.

He studied me for a moment. "Maat. On behalf of my people, I have come to apologize for Anson's behavior. Will you permit me to humble myself?"

"I beg your pardon Sir, but you do not appear

humble. You look about as deadly as anything *I've* ever seen." Connor seemed an alien creature. His human ears tapered to a point, and thick, fur-like hair fell on his shoulders. Shorter fur completely covered the back of his hands. None on his face, but bushy eyebrows stood out over amber wolf eyes.

He smiled. A small smile, but I saw a hint of canines. Despite my body and mind's warning, I went to sit in a hard, wooden chair. The Rudra would be easy to reach. He sat in a more confining upholstered chair opposite me. Not that it mattered. A werewolf this mature could tear me apart in a single breath. He didn't even need to change. I couldn't draw fast enough for a clean kill, so we would probably both die.

But I could ask a question. "Someone once told me weres live three or four hundred years. Or they would if I didn't kill them. That true?"

This time, Connor's smile seemed calculated to fully show his canines. "Age varies, but I was born in Ireland in 1752 and bitten by a werewolf in 1773. I came to the United States in 1912, and to New Mexico in 2010."

I managed to keep my shiver to a tiny shake. *Obscene creature. I so need to kill you, even if I don't know why.* He pretended not to notice.

"It's rare that we live so long, Maat. I was not a part of the movement to show ourselves to the world. We are violent, but before the war, our desire to hide kept that violence in check. I don't know what happened. Then it fell to you and others of your kind to fight back. I harbor no animosity."

"Fight back. That's me. But I didn't want to kill that were today. Someone set me up. I had to defend myself."

Connor sighed. "Yes, Anson has told me the story of his parents many years ago. He knows, rationally, that you had to fulfill your role as hunter. He knows the evil acts his mother committed. But the child remains in him."

"No. Not Anson. *Anson has the right to hate me.* That I understand. But Elspeth? She did the dirty work. Why? Anson's smart enough to have made the connection eventually. She intervened, forced it to happen. She set him—and me—up."

Connor's amber eyes grew bright. "Nevertheless, if you and Anson had met under other circumstances, there would be more than one death. She controlled the outcome of the inevitable. Forgive me, Maat, but that insane old witch is far beyond anyone's control."

"What do you want from me?" I waged a battle to keep speculative hostility at bay.

"I want you to understand." He lifted his hands. His fingernails were short, but obviously permanent claws. "My years have aged me. My appearance is a result. When Heflin, Orion, and I organized the Council of Salvaje with the hope of bringing peace among our races, I knew I might not live to see things through. I've seen enough werewolves in my life to know those who will grow strong, remain intelligent, and not become animals. Anson is one. I accepted him and educated him as a leader. We had a disagreement, and unfortunately many of my people have broken away to follow him—too soon. He'll be a valuable leader someday, but for now, he's too young, too rash, as evidenced by his actions today. A wiser werewolf would have sought you when you were alone and never fabricated a spectacular show."

"How did he get here? I left him running like a weasel through the Kentucky wilderness."

"Luck, good fortune? A pack found him hiding in the woods, and one of the females adopted him." Connor shook his head as if he had trouble believing it happened. "She had family in Salvaje, and she brought him here. I saw the potential in him. I had to get a special exemption for him because of his age.

"I traveled east thirty years ago. About the time you were born, I'd say. I tried to reason with the pack leaders there. They wouldn't listen. They wanted to increase their numbers quickly. Not to just slaughter, but to rule, to create their own world." His hands tightened on the chair arms. "You lived through that fire. Rogues running wild, attacking everything."

Create their own world. Now where had I heard that before. Oh, yes, Ruelle the vampire.

I had more questions and was getting answers, so I went on. "The eastern werewolves, didn't they think we'd fight back? We can breed faster than you can reproduce. It took a while, but once we organized and used the right weapons, you were easy enough to kill. Your only element is surprise, and once a vast number of you change shape, you lose all sense." I thought they were all that way until I met Sabrina. I had to go on. "They call me the Angel of Death. I hunted alone, but I'm sneaky as hell. The militia bands killed far more. Why didn't any the older ones know that would happen?"

"I have no idea. My age sets me apart from them, too."

He had lied to me. He knew what they wanted and would not tell me. Even with my monster sensors dull and overwhelmed, I felt it as I felt his dreadful animal presence. Old didn't necessarily mean wise. He should have given me a simple incomplete answer that wouldn't resonate like a pure lie.

"Now, Maat, I've answered your questions freely. Will you answer one of mine."

"Seems fair." Remembering, of course, that fair was not a word indiscriminately applied to a monster.

"When Maureen opened the door a minute ago, all my senses told me she was alone. I thought you'd declined my request. Then you walked in. I did not sense you, smell you, or hear you coming down the hall with her. I am timeworn, strong, and alpha. That should not happen. So, Angel of Death, tell me why. Tell me how."

And he'd outsmarted me. All he had to do was lure me into talking, asking, and I'd given in to my curiosity about my strange new world. So I gave him an abbreviated tale of my mother and father, my conception before he shifted the first time. I spoke the truth when I said I didn't know why or how. I did not speak of my immunity to werewolf bites. I'd learned my lesson. "It's not perfect, werewolves not sensing or smelling me, but it's been a hell of an advantage. As for me sensing weres? That's useless here in this version of hell. Sorry, but I miss my green mountains."

Connor stood. "I'm sure you do. They're magnificent. Having lived here so many years and watching it decline, I agree. Salvaje is a version of hell. I must go now."

I stood, too.

"Thank you for speaking with me, Maat. I will keep confidence on the matter of your abilities. Perchance we can talk again some time." Connor nodded, then left the room.

I waited until I was sure he was gone before I returned to Xavier. I wasn't sure what the conversation had accomplished. Did he get what he wanted from me? He got more than I wanted to give him. I would admit that while I am clever and smart about many things, I can be manipulated at times. And what was it about him that so disturbed me? Something almost familiar, but just out of reach. I hoped it wouldn't kill me before I discovered what it was.

Chapter Nine

I told Xavier about Connor and then the incident in the underground where I'd almost escaped. He insisted I at least tell Heflin the story of the scruffy thief and the tall substantial man in the tunnel. I described how I retrieved the knife I used in the arena and how he attacked Elspeth. I did not mention the necklace she gave me. Heflin kept nodding the entire time I spoke.

"The man you describe was most likely Galen Moreau. He likes jewelry, big chunks of gold. Moreau runs large cargo convoys like me, mostly to Mexico. He has a house here in Salvaje, but also has a secure compound with guards a few miles outside of town. He comes and goes. He stays out of the way." Heflin sighed, and I heard a bit of envy and regret in his words.

"There are rumors. Say he's a super powerful wizard. Don't believe in that magic stuff myself. I've seen your thief. He's called Buckle. He's as slimy as they come, but good at his trade and way smarter than he acts. He knows the underground. Few do. But to attack Elspeth?" He closed his eyes, shuddered, and stared back at me. Elspeth's mystical image held steady.

I hadn't spoken to anyone except Xavier about how the old witch had stopped Anson's change. I'm sure most would learn eventually. Maureen ruled as the queen of gossip in Salvaje, and her throne was the Paradox. Heflin hadn't asked about Connor's visit. Maureen would inform him, and I'd bet she had a way of listening in this building. Not that I blame her. Living in Salvaje required information.

Elspeth's gift? The necklace. I wasn't sure what to do there. I didn't want to carry it with me. My fingers tingled again when I touched the chain holding the crystal. I also realized, not for the first time, I don't know everything. Occasionally, with great astonishment, I fall prey to caution. I abandon my *jump in without looking first* attitude. I wrapped the crystal in a piece of leather and tucked it in a niche under the stair well going to the practice and exercise room downstairs.

Xavier had, of course, sensed my longing to leave Salvaje. I could go, there was a convoy leaving in a few days. Ty, Cody, Jacob...Xavier. My pack, my family. Thanks to Avalon and blessed Anolia I could accept them. They'd bound me with love. I would stay until they were ready to leave.

****

"You look like a god." Aaron Gannett's face formed a soft adoring smile. He had followed the vampire through the woods to a clear stream. Water gurgled and splashed over rocks as it rushed down a hill toward a great river. Ruelle's ivory skin glowed like polished marble in the full moonlight. The clean water had sluiced human blood and foul fluids from his unimaginably beautiful body.

"And how many gods have you seen, Aaron?" Ruelle stepped gracefully out of the water. He picked up a towel to dry. It and his clean clothing had lain in a pile on the grass.

"I've dreamed of gods." Gannett's eyes never left

the vampire. Warmth coursed through his body as he remembered the fantasies. "Every night I dream Sabrina is a goddess and she loves me again. I dream of you. You're a vengeful god, though."

They all kept the vampire's hours now. They slept by day and traveled through empty land that slid by unseen in the night. Ruelle always left them before daylight, and no one knew where he slept.

Gannett had lost all sense of time and place. He had no idea of where he was or how many days they'd been on the road. He'd had misgivings about the non-military personnel Ruelle collected. The vampire insisted his people travel with them while guarded by the few remaining presidential soldiers. Earlier that evening, when darkness fell, Ruelle found three of Gannett's soldiers who had taken one of the civilian women, beat and raped her, leaving her in a coma. The vampire gave the woman his own blood to help her heal, then staked the men out, broke their bones, and let them scream for hours. After that he tore them apart with his bare hands. He'd then spoken to the remaining soldiers, one by one, to calm them and assert his control. Expressions of fright on the men's faces soon turned to devotion. They'd found a god in the vampire, too. There'd be desertions at sunrise, but only a few.

Gannett reached out a hand but stopped short of touching Ruelle. Ruelle caught Gannett's wrist and laid the hand against his bare chest. The slow, heavy beat of the vampire's heart caused Gannett's own heart to slow in response.

"Your skin is so cold," Gannett whispered.

"I haven't had nourishment in some time." Ruelle drew Gannett closer. "May I?"

Gannett sighed and laid his head on the vampire's shoulder. "You don't need permission."

"Perhaps. But are you not my friend?"

"I don't know what I am, anymore. The men call me Mr. President, but they all hold their breath at sunset, waiting for you. Some a number want to worship you, others are terrified."

"And you?"

"I am among the worshipers. I no longer fear you. You know that don't you?"

The vampire tilted Gannett's chin, and smooth lips murmured against Gannett's throat. A shimmer of pain, and Gannett desired nothing more than to become a part of the creature-being feeding on his lifeblood. He cried out when Ruelle drew away.

"Hush." Ruelle laid a finger on Gannett's lips.

Gannett stilled and closed his eyes. When he opened them again, he found himself in the trailer that served as his presidential mansion on the road. He turned his head and stared out a window at the land he knew passed unseen in the darkness. Slow progress since the roads alternated between smooth and atrocious. Travel after dark was especially dangerous, but Ruelle seemed in no hurry. The whole caravan would stop for a few days and wait for the scouts sent out to check on the path ahead. Oddly, they would stop at specified places for supplies hidden and waiting for them. When he asked...

"I have planned this for a multitude of years, Aaron. I developed plans, hid supplies in the last days of war and disease. There were mishaps and significant changes of course"

Now Gannett fought to remember where they were going, and why. Just when he thought he knew, Ruelle's whisper, a roiling, dark inner voice, swelled and stripped it away. Gannett stopped fighting for the present and surrendered to memory.

Memories came easier now, more vivid and genuine than day-to-day life. He sifted through them and settled on one of the earliest days, when his quick mind had maneuvered him into position as one of the youngest commanders in the Northern Militia. Hard days and terrifying nights, but all entwined with love and laughter. Xavier and Ray Heflin were his good friends. They served under him, and sweet Lilly had agreed to become his wife. Only now, instead of Lilly's dark hair, he more often saw Sabrina's auburn tresses. Ruelle came in sometime during Gannett's fantasies. Gannett thought the vampire would call him from his enchanted world of yesterday, but he only sat and watched as they continued their journey.

Chapter Ten

Three days after my confrontation with Anson, the man whom I had glimpsed with the thief in the tunnel walked into the Paradox. Galen Moreau, Heflin had called him. I was sitting at the bar in late afternoon, enjoying a beer and waiting to see if I would work that evening.

I never saw this man's face underground, but I recognized him easy enough. Tall and exceptionally broad shouldered, he was the biggest man I'd seen in Salvaje. Even coming out of the tight confines of the tunnel he had an impressive body and an equally compelling presence.

Maureen, who had been sitting at a table, instantly rose and went to greet him—or bar his way. Heflin was right about one thing, Maureen was fearless. I tightened up. Fearless or not, she wasn't a fighter. She stood straight and still with her arms crossed barring his way.

"Good afternoon, Mr. Moreau. How may I help you?" Her posture and the sound of her voice said it all. *Okay, Mr. Moreau. I don't like you, but I'm required by an odd and unstated protocol to be moderately friendly. You are not here for alcohol or the girls. State your business, and we can do battle. Or you can leave.*

Moreau stared at her for a moment. Then he gave a slight nod of his head. "I wish to speak to the woman they call the Angel of Death." Ah, that deep baritone voice. Yes, he was the tunnel guy. I'd bet he knew my name, too. I drained my glass and slid off the bar stool. I was incredibly happy that Xavier was out training Salvaje's pitiful army. This felt like a challenge and since it came from a man and not a beast, Xavier's testosterone level would soar to astronomical heights. I would refuse a challenge if possible—my lover would not.

Moreau kept his eyes on me as I approached. He reeked of masculinity. Easily six-seven, his posture marked him an aristocrat, a prince of men. Hair black as a raven's wing fell on broad shoulders. His dark eyes had a slight shine, and he had a mouth almost any woman would beg to kiss.

Maureen introduced him. "Maat, this is Galen Moreau. Mr. Moreau is a Salvaje tradesman like Hef." She nodded at me. "Maat—Ms. Ferris—is one of our guards."

Tradesman? Not this one. Better chances for a rainstorm in Salvaje two days in a row. I think Maureen had claimed me as *ours* because she wanted to prevent a meeting that might turn violent in her élite lair. Or she sought to protect me. Too bad. Maureen's volunteered shield, regardless of her courage, was sheer and thin as a silk curtain. It might work with vamps or weres, but not this one.

Moreau's dark-eyed gaze seemed to be tugging at me, drawing me closer. What the hell? He was calling me like a vampire would, trying to enthrall me. Well, well, I wasn't having any of that. The vampire Emanis taught me I could resist a vampire's call before I killed her. I held steady.

"Ms. Ferris." He gave the briefest nod of his head.

Oh, so polite, a sophisticated man meeting a lowly uneducated hunter. His vampire-like calling ceased.

I'd stopped and stood straight, ready to draw and pull the trigger. My voice had to be perfect for this. It had to carry a challenge—a challenge that said I would fight—but wasn't eager for battle.

"Mr. Moreau. Sir. While I am honored to meet you, it is quite rude of you to add a compulsion to an introduction." Okay, how was that? *I'm polite, but I sent notice that I understood his intent to control me.*

His eyes widened in surprise. Then he laughed, deep and low under his breath. I had amused him. That laughter sounded too much like Ruelle the vampire's teasing.

"My apologies, Ms. Ferris."

Ah, such a pleasant voice. "Your apology is accepted. I am Maat Ferris. I make no claim to the Angel of Death."

"No? But the Mad Prophet of Salvaje named you before vampire, werewolf, and man the very day you arrived." He gave what seemed a genuine smile.

"Sir, what do you want from me?" I knew the answer to that question, but I had to make him say it.

"The crystal Elspeth gave you. It is mine."

"I believe you. The Mad Prophet of Salvaje has taken personal items from me, too." I remembered the tingle in my fingers. I spoke carefully. "Unfortunately, I dropped what you're looking for in the tunnel when the fuzzy were bastards grabbed me again and hustled me off to the Lycos. I'm sure you heard about that little show."

"I heard praises for your bold actions in a deadly situation."." He cocked his head and studied me. The smile never left that beautiful mouth. He knew I was lying about the necklace. He seemed neither surprised nor disturbed.

Those dark eyes focused on me, and I could feel that presence again. Then he spoke in my mind. None of my burgeoning psychic powers even hinted that was even possible. *"There are things in this world far more dangerous than man or monster, even for the Angel of Death. Don't wear that crystal, don't let it touch your skin."*

He turned and oh so gracefully walked out. He'd spoken in my mind. My heart gave one thick, savage, and utterly terrifying thump. I had to shift my feet to keep from falling over. A sour taste like wild cranberries filled my mouth.

Maureen came to stand at my shoulder. "What did he say?" She made her question a demand. Suspicion filled her voice. Not a psychic, but she knew something had passed between me and Moreau. I'd long since realized her power and how she used it on people. Maureen collected words of rumors and idle gossip like picking flowers wild—if wildflowers had existed in Salvaje.

Her, I could lie to. "Just a polite threat—if there is such a thing. Elspeth lifted a piece of junk necklace from him. He thinks I have it."

"Do you?"

"No. She gave it to me, but I gave it back. I'm terrified of anything she's touched." I lie so easily these days. "I told him I lost it because I didn't want him hunting *her* down, hurting her. He'll probably notice, though, if she keeps wearing it around her neck." Having witnessed her control over a werewolf, I had no doubt

Elspeth could stand against Moreau. She did not need me to protect her.

"Who is Moreau?" I asked Maureen, but I suspected *what is he* was a better question.

Maureen stared at the place where he stood. "Moreau runs convoys like Hef, mostly to Mexico. Major convoys that outweigh ours twenty to one." She lowered her voice. "Hef says he's a wizard or sorcerer."

Practical Heflin had spoken of wizards or sorcerers when we discussed Moreau and what happened in the tunnel. I didn't even want to believe magic existed. The very idea terrified me. I had more than enough clear personal psychic shit from my brain in my life without adding another layer.

I dealt with vamps and weres, but they seemed more genuine because they were physically once men. Galen Moreau might be a monster too, only in a different class. Since he'd taken the time to speak privately to me, I'd bet I hadn't seen the last of him.

Chapter Eleven

Pale light painted Salvaje's bland almost featureless buildings a soft pink. The trudge home at dawn wore at my nerves. Such a miserable job. And neither Salvaje nor the Paradox was home. Home would always be the green mountains of Tennessee.

I worked nights for room, board, and considerable gold. I rarely spent money because there was nothing I desired in this place—except a viable way to leave. After the first shock, I averted my eyes at bloody battles and perverted sex. Bloody? I'd lived with violence most of my life, but these weren't desperate, terrifying fights for survival. These people—and creatures—did it for sick amusement. And the orgies? I'd never speak of what I saw there. Battles and sex, all woven into the culture of a walled city in the desert. *Salvaje. Savage. It had earned the designation.*

Xavier worked days training troops and so we saw each other less and less because he said he was often too tired to walk back. I understood. Sort of. But nevertheless, the situation ratcheted my irritable stubborn nature to an explosive level, and I'd bet he was giving his troops hell too.

I'd heard that they had opened the main missile complex, but the deadly vaults housing the launch controls defied Heflin's efforts so far. He had great praise for the way Lowell handled the people involved in the work. He'd taken over that management entirely. Not surprising. Something about the silver-haired former vice president said trust me, follow me. I wondered why he hadn't supplanted Gannett years ago.

****

The night's job had been easy. No orgies. Only a dangerous high stakes poker game. My lucky, or skillful, client started out with a sack of gold coins and finished with so many he had trouble carrying them. I didn't help with the load. I kept weapon in hand and watched for the scum who wanted to save him the trouble of taking all that gold home. Two of the scum tried to jump me from behind. Both ran away carrying silver in their body parts. Silver works on humans too. The cheap bastard I guarded hadn't even offered me the customary tip.

Cody's cry of pain and terror suddenly hit my senses so hard it drove me to my knees. Something cut it off an instant later, but not before I pinpointed its general location—the vampire compound. Cody had told me he'd talked to Orion, the vampire leader, to acknowledge his authority, and Orion accepted him. He offered no other details. He did disappear at night, though, if I didn't need him, which I rarely did. I staggered to my feet. More of his pain seared me. I didn't have enough weapons, and I didn't know how to get to him.

I went through every plan or half-assed plan I had ever devised as I raced through the empty streets. Pitiful, all of them. Worse than taking on the president's army at Avalon. Cody might be dead before I could find help, even if someone was willing. He was mine, damn it, and I'd go for him. More weapons. I needed specialized weapons.

I slowed before I reached the Paradox so the door

guards wouldn't see my panic and alert anyone else. I walked by them, and they silently acknowledged me. There was no one there with the skill or weapons to aid me. Ajax was absent, Xavier was with his troops, and I doubted I could locate Jacob right away. Ty was not an option. Whatever happened, Cody was my responsibility, and I wouldn't involve the others—or place them in danger from a vampire. And the fact is, of all of them, I was best suited to this.

Stand alone Maat, just as you've always done.

I walked softly through the silent house. In the barroom, I hurried to the hall where Ty had taken me and led me downstairs to the wine cellar weeks ago.

I blew out a sigh of relief. The fire stick and hatchet lay on the shelf by the lantern where he'd left them. I flicked the button on the fire starter, and a three-inch blue flame shot from the end. Inventory: Two guns that had negligible impact on a vampire, even with silver bullets. A perfect head shot would work. Not likely I could make that. The silver knife on my arm was better. I'd been carrying the long knife that killed Emanis with me in a sheath on my back. Sharp edge and fire, perfect vampire killers if I could get close enough. If...if...

I stuffed the hatchet and fire starter in a sack I found behind the bar and then headed out. The guards seemed surprised to see me leaving again, but they didn't question me. When I turned the corner out of sight, I headed for the plaza at a dead run.

A few merchants lingered, packing their goods for tomorrow and preparing for a day's rest. I demanded a clay jar of high-grade oil from one and tossed him what copper coins I had without counting them. As usual, none of my plans were worth a shit. I had no idea what I was facing or how to get to it. I did have one gut feeling, though, and I decided to follow intuition.

A number of people drifted out of houses to greet the day, and I asked each of them, "Have you seen Elspeth?" Most ran from me. Elspeth. She'd set me up as a gladiator in a werewolf arena. She owed me.

I had a general idea of the vampire lair's location, but I needed a guide. I needed the witch. I had to get there some way. I located an entrance door and headed down into the tunnels below the streets. A rare and light rain shower had fallen during the night, and the gaping stairway smelled worse than Memphis in July. I eased down, testing each step, allowing my eyes to grow used to the dark, and my senses to pinpoint my direction. I could feel a concentration of vamps down the tunnel to my right, so I headed that way. Twenty feet along, the faint scrape of a foot sent me whirling with the Rudra drawn.

Elspeth giggled.

I holstered my gun when she moved closer.

"Angel thinks Elspeth's not dangerous?" Her beads clicked, and her long, ragged skirt swayed around her ankles. Despite her odd speech pattern, this time she sounded perfectly sane.

"You're dangerous, Elspeth. The favor you demanded of Anson Sewell...if he'd told you no, go to hell..."

"Angel won."

"No. No one won, Elspeth. It was evil." No time for talking. "The Vamps have Cody."

Elspeth giggled. "Will take you there." She danced by me, humming her wordless tune. I followed. I had no choice.

I concentrated on memorizing the path, using the entry point as a base. The line was straight enough. Twice, she stopped, shoved me into a side tunnel, and we waited until someone passed. Finally, we came to a place where the tunnel made a sharp right turn. Elspeth held her finger to her lips. She peeked around the corner, then stepped out and beckoned me. I followed her and came face to face with two vampires standing in front of a large ornate paneled door. Elspeth had apparently brought me to the lair's front entrance. So much for sneaking in. To my right, stairs led to the street above. With brief directions, I could have run down the street and come here on my own.

The two vampire guards stared at me with mild interest.

"Elspeth, what...?"

"Angel go in," Elspeth pointed.

One of the vamps reached for the door and opened it for me. "Suriel," he said softly, "I am honored to greet you."

Oh, God, what had the witch done? I glanced at her, only to see her scurry away down the tunnel behind me. I doubted she'd save me this time.

I walked down the long, wide, carpet-covered hallway. Candles lit the way, casting soft, warm light on ornate scrolled designs painted on the stone walls. The hall dead-ended, and to my right, I could feel the presence of numerous vamps. I followed my senses and came to an open unguarded door. Xavier's image popped into my mind, and I shoved it away. I had to protect my pack.

The room I entered was nearly identical to the werewolves' fighting arena. Seating tiers surrounded an open space with a sand floor. I'd seen many arenas much like it while fulfilling my bodyguard duties. Damn Salvaje, city of constant war.

Time had burned individual battles into my memory, and I'd long since decided that the more you fight, the more you want to fight. Salvaje proved that I was right. The vamps I'd watched for weeks wagered on human and werewolf fights, but they hadn't participated.

The arena's soft light radiated from hundreds of candles hanging from ceiling fixtures and stuck in multi-pronged holders scattered around the room. Unlike the were's bare utilitarian arena, fancy pillows and luxurious drapes decorated the tiers of seats. Vamps lounged amidst the opulence. None of the bloodsuckers seemed to notice my entrance because they focused their attention on the arena's floor.

Orion, vampire Master of Salvaje sat on a lower tier, body relaxed, and his beautiful face unreadable. The vamp standing in front of him had neither grace nor beauty. Short, stocky with long, stringy blond hair, he had to be Gunnar, Cody's former master. He had his booted foot planted on Cody's stomach. Cody twisted and cried in pain.

I wanted to cry too—instead, I looked for and found a killing rage.

"He's mine," Gunnar roared. "I'll punish him as I see fit."

Had Orion objected to Cody's treatment? *What the fuck?* He'd done nothing to stop it either. The door I entered stood in an opening in the tiers. I dropped my cloak, wedged the fire stick in my gun belt, and removed the stopper on the jar of lamp oil.

Suck in a deep breath, focus on only what's before

me—I marched up behind Gunnar. Gunnar didn't hear me coming. Orion or any number of vamps could have warned him, but they didn't. I think Cody saw me because he suddenly began a fresh chorus of cries.

I slung the lamp oil at Gunnar. *Sloppy. Sloppy.* I hit my target with an acceptable spread, but oil also splashed on my hand and coated the leg of my jeans. At least I'd covered his back and shoulders. I dropped the jar, snatched the long knife at my shoulder. I planned to cut off his head as I had Emanis, and then burn him. He whirled to face me. I swung the blade. The bastard leaned back so it barely slashed the skin on his throat. I'd made a deadly mistake. I should have used the fire first.

I slashed at him again. He snatched the blade, and I let go to keep him from dragging me too close. I backpedaled, but he dived toward me and caught my legs. I landed hard on my butt with the Rudra drawn. He raised up and grinned at me. Silver bullets slammed into his chest and body as fast as I could pull the trigger. They couldn't kill him either, only hurt like hell and slow him down. He reared back on his knees, his hands clawing at the bloody holes in his body. He groaned and choked, spit blood at me through his fanged mouth. I kicked him in the gut and twisted away.

Gunner was a clumsy disgrace of a vampire. Ruelle would have had me disarmed and torn apart in the time it had taken this vamp to attack. Unfortunately, in the struggle, I managed to lose both the fire starter and the hatchet. They lay inches out of my reach.

I scrambled and crawled toward them. Not fast enough. Gunnar, recovering way too soon, caught my ankle and twisted the leg I had injured on the Memphis bridge. An incredible cracking sound vibrated through my body when my knee popped out of joint. Waves of unbelievable pain buffeted me. I shrieked. I couldn't move, could barely see.

Gunnar laughed. It sounded like pottery broken and scattered across the floor. He held my leg up, threw his head back, opened his mouth wide, and sank his fangs into my thigh. They tore through cloth and flesh digging for an artery. With the agony in my knee, I barely felt the bite.

To my amazement, he jerked back, wild eyed and choking. He released me and grabbed his throat with both hands. He spit and sprayed blood everywhere—my blood. On his knees, he kept choking and coughing. Blood and saliva spewed from his mouth.

My last chance had arrived. I couldn't get up, but I rolled across the sand and grabbed the firestarter. Gunnar was suddenly on top of me. I didn't think I could be in much more pain.

I was wrong. I flashed the fire starter. The lamp oil on Gunnar burst into flame. So did the oil on my hand and my legs. He jerked away to roll, thrash, and wail in agony. Ruelle, in a moment of weakness, once told me that fire hurts vamps worse than it hurts humans. Once they start burning, they burn—but it wouldn't kill them quickly.

I rolled, too, desperate to snuff my blaze with arena sand. I knew I had a high tolerance for pain... In this case, I'd gone beyond my threshold. At a certain point, the mind goes berserk and overrides the nervous system.

I grabbed the hatchet. Thankfully, it had remained by the fire starter.

The skin where the fire burned me was peeled away from my palm, and white bone glared at me. I couldn't crawl, so I rolled toward a jerking, smoldering, and now moaning Gunnar. I could see his burned skin writhing, healing too soon for me.

With the hatchet handle in both hands, I lifted and brought it down on his neck. Lying on my stomach I had no leverage, no strength. It cut into his shoulder, surprisingly deep. He howled in a high keening sound that soon became a snarl as he healed. Not good enough.

I had to end it soon because the shadows of unconsciousness danced along the edges of my mind. I surged up and buried the hatchet in his thick neck. Not deep enough. I released the hatchet and grabbed my short knife. With my last bit of adrenalin-born strength, I jammed it in Gunner's eye and twisted the blade, stirring Gunnar's brain like a pot of soup. He stopped snarling.

Cody suddenly cradled me in his arms, tears running from his eyes. I wanted to wipe them away but couldn't lift my arm.

Orion, vampire prince of Salvaje, came to hover over me, too. Elspeth stood staring over his shoulder, madness again glowing in her eyes. In my dying brain's imagination, I'd swear she wore a halo around her ragged hair. Agony blotted my senses. Little remained but pain and the stench of my own burned flesh. True to my nature, though, I found words.

"Fucking vampires."

"Oh, yes," Orion spoke. His smile was a thing of beauty. "We are foul creatures indeed, Angel."

Darkness closed around me.

Chapter Twelve

In a restless sea of half sleep, the voices of my dead again stirred memory as they had on the bridge at Memphis. My mother sang a love song while she cooked supper. I sat at the table nearby peeling apples. Uncle Jake's relentless bark urged me to pull the trigger over and over, faster and faster. "You have the courage of a lion," Anolia whispered again. I longed to cry and point out the critical error of her belief, her faith in me. I had utterly failed her in the deadliest of times.

I drew a deep, shuddering breath and awakened to find a vampire sitting by my side. Silky black hair framed his exquisite face. He stared at me with eyes filled with ancient knowledge and fearful power.

"You have returned to us, Suriel." Orion spoke in a flawless voice—the song of a seraph from the mouth of a vampire.

I couldn't speak. My mouth wouldn't work. He gently lifted my head and placed a cup of water to my lips. As he did, I took inventory of my body. It hurt, but nothing like before, and a clean bandage covered my right hand. I refrained from trying to flex my fingers. No pain in the leg either, but I didn't move. I lay naked, wrapped in soft blankets. My guns and knives lay on a small table by the bed, within easy reach.

Orion laughed low under his breath. "Your young

vampire told us you would ask for your weapons first. He gave you his blood, so you would heal. He thought you'd be angry, but he would not let you die. Someone older, stronger, would have been better, but he refused to allow another to bestow you the gift. I've sent for Heflin and your mate to take you home."

I swallowed, my voice caught and stumbled as it formed rough sounds.

"Thank you." I'd never thought of vampire blood as a gift, but at least it had come from one of my own. Cody was right. I didn't want vampire blood to heal, but if I needed it to live, it would be his. And mention of Xavier brought a twinge of guilt. My *mate* was going to be mightily pissed at me.

"Cody has told me much about you, and how he came to belong to you." Orion held up a hand and quickly stifled my protest. "Do not be angry with him. Few can resist me when I question them."

Oh, I believed that. "I'm not angry with him. I don't consider him my property, that's all." I sounded rough but was able to form words.

"He sees the relationship a bit differently. His heart knows you. How else did he call you here to save him? I heard him crying out, just as you did. You've confirmed your sovereignty by killing his former master." Orion held up a thumb-sized, blood red teardrop stone. "What he could not tell me, is where you obtained this."

Another thing hidden in my room at the Paradox. Elspeth must have stolen it and given it to him as she had stolen and given the toy truck to Anson.

"A vampire named Ruelle gave it to me." I could see no reason not to tell him.

At the mention of Ruelle's name, his body stiffened.

"Where is Ruelle?" Orion's voice made me shiver this time.

"Don't know. Not exactly. We escaped and stole his prize, so I'm sure he's on his way here. No one listens to me. It's almost as if they're waiting for him. Which is about the stupidest thing they could do."

Orion laughed softly. A wave of pleasure rolled through me. This vamp had the power to enchant with his voice alone, not just psychic control, and I had no defense against him. He lifted my undamaged left hand and brushed his lips across my fingers. "Yesterday, I'd have thought it ludicrous to believe a human might stand against one of us. Although, many have attempted and paid with their lives. Do you always throw your life at your enemies in such a reckless manner?"

"Only if I can surprise them. Like Emanis. I…"

Orion froze. His face darkened. Oh, shit. Within a few heartbeats, he again relaxed.

He shook his head, and the captivating smile fled. He rubbed my fingers again. "I knew Emanis was dead, but I don't know how it happened. Cody couldn't tell me that. I beg you, will you speak of the matter?"

The Vampire Prince of Salvaje begged me. Why not? A few chains fell away from my life, and I found an odd relief as I told him—not everything—but much of the history of vampires and me. Since I was naked under my blanket, he would know about the chevron pattern decorating my back in an intricate web of scars. I spoke of the nightmare in New York, my time with and odd connection to Ruelle. I told him about killing Emanis in New Washington. The story spilled out in a flood of words. He had reps on the Salvaje Council, so he would know about the nukes.

As I spoke, he stared into the depths of the bloodstone, that perfect ruby, as if seeing another story there. I finished the story. "Before you ask, I have no idea why Ruelle chose to involve himself in my life. I don't know why he saved me in New York or why he's plagued me off and on since then." I shifted, and my knee complained. "Look, I don't want or need jewels. If you want it, please take it."

Orion's hand closed over the stone. "Now here is the mystery. Your life power, your aura, woke me from my sleep when you entered the city at high noon. I felt your presence that night in the plaza. Elspeth stopped my search." His ageless face twisted with a wry smile. I caught a glimpse of fang.

I had a question. "Elspeth. Who is she?"

"I don't know. Not who—or what. She'll answer no questions. Twenty years ago, I woke one evening in a sealed, guarded chamber and found her sitting at my bedside. She comes and goes as she pleases. She seems old, but she doesn't age."

I sighed. "She's stronger than Anson Sewell. She held him like a two-year-old. Did someone tell you that? She held him and stopped his shift to beast. That's impossible, but she did."

He grew still and serious. "She has shown me the extent of her power a few times. Only one in Salvaje is possibly stronger than Elspeth. It is not I."

"Great. And she takes orders only from God."

"She gives orders, too." Orion spoke as if he begrudged her and God the greater power. "She instructed me to tell you the story of this stone."

He grasped my unbandaged hand in his, and his striking face grew calm. "About two thousand years ago, in what is now Central Italy, the prince of a prosperous city married the daughter of a local tribal lord. The Earth Mother's High Priestess blessed the marriage arranged by their parents, and a wedding boat carried the pair to an island for their first night together. The prince and his bride, who had met only the day before, were delighted to find that they were well matched.

"That night, while they lay sleeping in each other's arms, a vampire came creeping out of his tomb. He found them so pleasing he wanted to keep them forever. He shared *eshar*, the blood, and made them like himself. This stone was the bride's wedding gift to her husband."

"Emanis. You were her husband." And I had killed her. What else could happen?

Orion squeezed my hand as if to reassure me. "Yes. Ruelle made Emanis and me like himself. At that time, we were all far different in nature. Time does not age us. We do, however, change. Emanis and I were not murderous by nature. At least not given the age and culture in which we lived. If we killed, we killed criminals who offered us harm. My beloved bride and I walked the world under the moon and stars. As civilizations grew, we studied languages, art, and sciences in a boundless new world. By day, we were faithful lovers, sleeping in each other's arms as we had on our wedding night. We were fearless, invincible.

"Ruelle's inquisitiveness matched ours, but in diverse ways. While we studied things of a human nature, he delved into...others."

The temperature in the room dropped, or at least it seemed to.

Orion smiled a sad smile and continued, "The year would have been about 1000 AD, as time is now measured. Early one evening, Ruelle and Emanis went into the desert to open a tomb they had found. One far older than anything we'd seen before. I had chosen to go another way to speak with a scholar and read scrolls. Ruelle staggered back and collapsed near daylight. Had I not dragged him inside, he would have lain out on the sand and allowed the sun to consume him. Emanis did not return. For three days and nights, Ruelle raged in delirium. I locked him in a vault, and each night I searched for her. I found nothing.

"On the fourth evening, Ruelle grew still and silent. Then he rose to his feet as if nothing had happened and said, 'She's coming.' Emanis returned, but all that remained of the woman I had loved was a memory. He groveled at her feet while I stood aside and mourned the loss of my wife. She was a stranger who had gained great power as a vampire. A tyrant, she acted as if I was a peasant beneath her notice. She never touched me again. Do not trouble yourself on my behalf that you killed her, Angel of Death. My true beloved died long ago. I do not know what they found in that tomb. If any shred of her original soul remained hidden in her, I'm sure she blessed you for ending her vile, pitiful existence."

I would make no guesses about Emanis. I kept my mouth shut, and Orion continued.

"Emanis' power grew quickly. I could not stop her. I followed her one night and found her among humans who worshiped her and fed her their children's blood. She had created new vampire priests as servants. She demanded that I...I don't know if I lost my soul when Ruelle changed me, but there are some acts, some crimes I would not commit for her. I would not kill for her or be her slave. I ran away. I begged Ruelle to come with me, but he refused. The power she had gained fascinated him even though he feared it also.

"Europe became my haven, but in 1872, she found me. I had a young lover. While I was out one night, Ruelle came and took her to Emanis as if she were no more than a stray dog. She had at least a hundred followers by then. I could do nothing, so I ran again. I came to live in the United States. I survived the war here in the desert."

"That's weird. Ruelle told me he was only a thousand years old." *Only? Listen to yourself, Maat.* How many secrets could a vampire carry over time? Did they ever forget? *Not human.* Those two words slid across my mind like the sheen of oil I applied to my dry skin after a shower.

Orion shook his head. "A thousand years? I have no idea why he'd say that. But I haven't seen him in over two hundred years myself."

I'd never talked so casually with a vampire as strong as Orion. When Ruelle spoke to me my heart always filled with bitter anger. "Orion, you've been around a long time, right?"

"Oh, yes." His expression went to eyebrow raising irony and then turned warm as the sunshine he would never see again. Orion might be evil as Ruelle, but he had perfected the charming act. Blissfully soothed, his victim wouldn't know until the trap had sprung.

"What do you know about werewolves? Vampires have hurt me, but weres have torn through my whole life and family like a contagious disease. What are they to you?"

He drew a breath and frowned. His hesitancy to speak meant he was carefully selecting words. It surprised me that someone so articulate would take the time to formulate an answer to my question. But he did go on.

"I did not know werewolves existed until I went to Europe. Our paths rarely crossed. In the present time, their reckless multiplication and ferocity has created an unmitigated disaster. There are reasons we hid from humans. Neither vampires nor werewolves could overcome human determination and breeding capabilities. As for the past, our origins, all I know is a legend. I read ancient scrolls and tablets that spoke of a race of shape changers who lived, not before humans, but before recorded time. They had lost the ability to reproduce, so they experimented with ways to make humans into images of themselves. Foul, evil experiments, creating creatures even more vile than us. Most of those, thank the Goddess, have long since died. Only we vampires and the werewolves remain from that obscenity."

"So, you think you have a common creator? You both can reproduce by giving your blood or saliva to humans."

"There is a kinship. We rarely fight, even if we keep our distance." Orion gave the impression of an emotion halfway between explanation and apology. "I've never permitted humans to follow me like Emanis, Suriel, or made them vampires against their will. I have not tasted human blood in over a hundred years." He stared at the wall then turned back to me.

"Suriel, Angel…"

"Just Maat. Please."

"Maat, I wish you to understand my reluctance to interfere with Cody. Gunnar had a valid claim to him by our law. I would not have allowed severe injury or death. I was trying to think of a way to free him when you burst in upon us. In a magnificent feat of valor, you solved my dilemma."

Praise from a vampire? Oh, how my world had changed. I kept telling myself that a vampire was a vampire no matter how pretty his face. Created by blood and living on blood, they could be nothing else.

Which reminded me. "Why do you have an arena here."

"We have a few…private…contests. Perhaps I'll invite you some night."

This time when he laughed, I shivered. I would decline that invitation. If the regular fights of men and weres I had observed were an indication, vampire battles would be intolerable.

"Your people are here." Orion stood, walked to the door, and swung it open. Ty, Cody, and Xavier rushed in, followed by Jacob. Heflin entered too, but he went to speak to Orion.

Things became a blur then. Xavier holding me, Ty and Jacob touching me to be sure I was alive. Xavier's hands shook. I'd terrified him again. But I'll give him credit, he kept his anger hidden deep. He'd let it go when were alone. Cody soon joined us. When Orion spoke, Cody gazed on him with a worshipful glowing face. How could he do anything else?

One other thing happened. Before we left, Orion stood before us and made an announcement. "Suriel, to my extreme regret, you were injured in my home under my watch. I have sent word through Salvaje that should anyone harm you, I will take it as a personal offense to myself and respond immediately."

I didn't expect that. I'd learned more about Orion's reputation, and his protection was no small gift.

Xavier and Jacob carried me on a stretcher through the streets of Salvaje. Heflin walked beside us. I insisted that we stop downstairs to talk before they put me to bed. I had realized something that they should know, even though it didn't surprise me.

Ruelle the vampire had made us pawns. We were suckers in a hell of a con game. Ruelle had given me Orion's ruby before I left New Washington and headed into the mountains to steal that truck. Oh, he couldn't know that the mission would be successful. He was a gambler and quite willing to wager on human lives. But since he knew me so well, he had known, if I survived, I wouldn't be able to resist the temptation to explore something new. I would go to Salvaje. I'd bet my life that the precious stolen cargo men had died for was exactly where the vampire planned for it to be. He was waiting for the vault to open. Then he'd strike.

I told Heflin. Heflin's dark face turned pale as he listened to me explain how the vampire suckered us into the game. He mumbled something about the Council, tripling the guard, and hurried away.

Fuck the Council. Ruelle would dance past guards as if he were invisible. I had to convince Xavier and the rest of my crew to be on guard.

Later, when everyone left us and we made it to our room, I had to deal with my lover.

"Why didn't you come for me, Maat?" His hand stroked my hair. His whole big body shook.

"I couldn't." I snuggled against him. "Please try to understand. Cody could have been destroyed before I could find you." My leg ached a little, but my hand had healed. Cody's vampire blood had accelerated the growth of new flesh and pink shiny skin across the bone. Unfortunately, the fire had burned away the hard calluses built by years of shooting practice. I'd have to start creating new pads.

Xavier stretched out beside me. "You're afraid I'd get in your way. Still the hunter. Your kill, your triumph." He spoke without animosity or censure, only sadness and resignation of how life battered us at times.

"Living is a triumph, Xavier. Not killing. *No! Wait.* What cliché bullshit did I just spout?" I closed my eyes and drew a deep breath.

He didn't speak, but he wrapped his arm around me and drew me close.

I let my senses touch him and wrap him in my love. Xavier wasn't psychic, but he stirred under that touch. He responded with a love that overwhelmed me.

I fought it for a moment, then let it take us away. Fate or Elspeth and her god might be plotting our path, but we had each other now, and now was all the time in the world.

****

The weeks in Salvaje passed, and I remained miserable I had lizard skin and a nose so dry I spent an hour each day with my head over a bowl of hot water, breathing the billowing steam. I wasn't exactly bored, but I never lost the feeling of being a stranger. The desire in me to leave this hostile battleground remained fierce.

And Ruelle was coming. I didn't know how or when and was unsure of how to prepare for his arrival. It would be different this time. My relationship with him had drastically changed since I killed Emanis.

Jacob brought news one day of a coup in the Lycos.

The weres had chosen Anson to represent them on the Council instead of Abban Connor.

My response? "But he's only a kid."

"I know." Jacob's angular face grew more serious. "Connor's made too many enemies. They don't tell me much because I'm not part of the pack, but Connor tried to increase his power by bringing weres here from the east. Couple of them lost control. Even heard talk about banishing Connor from the city."

Problem was, once Anson became top wolf, he went out of his way to cause me trouble. I'd be working, and Anson would come up to me and start baiting me, calling me names. He told anyone who would stand still long enough to listen that I murdered his mom, dad, and baby sister. He left off how his mother brought home human dinner and how daddy tried to shoot me after I'd agreed to let them go free. The harassment came to a halt though, when I came home one morning to find a slaughtered sheep in my bed. I was lucky I found it before Xavier. I'd always been impulsive and hotheaded, now I worried about my man's shallowly buried killing rage. That's what love will do, I guess.

I had to tell Maureen. I wrapped the poor animal in her sheets and dragged it through the bar room to get rid of it. She went straight to the Lycos. Whatever she said did the trick. Anson confined his animosity to glaring at me from a distance. Maureen's power was her words, not the physical threats the rest of us spread to show how brave we were.

Given the severity of Orion's promise of vengeance, I doubted it would amount to much more than annoyance. Anson would push it though. Young, pumped up on power, he lacked the lessons of survivors like me and my crew.

It didn't affect my work. Heflin said I was in constant demand. Once everyone heard about Orion's pronouncement, they figured it guaranteed safety from attack in my presence. When it came to the *Official Scale of Terrifying Creatures*, vampire threats topped adolescent werewolves' threats every time.

Heflin spent more time away at the missile complex, and guard work slacked off to the point we barely went out one or two nights a week. Parr usually went out to the complex with Heflin. I'd seen little of the former vice president since we entered Salvaje. I missed Ajax, too. He'd left shortly after the brawl in the barroom, and I hadn't seen him since. Mary kept asking about him. It wasn't unusual for him to be out of touch. He had accepted Mary as his woman, and he had an obligation there. I'd take care of her, if necessary, but he usually made better arrangements.

They'd increased the guard out at the complex, Heflin said, and General Mylonas had increased the number of scouting parties. He swore no one would get within fifty miles of Salvaje or the complex without him knowing. I doubted it and steeled myself for the worst outcome. Xavier, Ty, Jacob, and Cody understood that situation. Ruelle was coming and would arrive ready to take over everything.

General Mylonas let his territorial concerns go and accepted Xavier as an equal. Or maybe someone forced him to act. Xavier swore he'd have the troops at least competent within a few months.

I started seeing men and women—and a few werewolves—around town with a familiar symbol on the clasps holding their cloaks. A single black stripe and a white eagle identical to the one Xavier's personal squad wore in New Washington. Only below the eagle was a symbol I didn't recognize. Oh, shit. Xavier was creating his own private army. Unfortunately, he spent more time away from me.

We were in our bedroom, dressing for an evening's work, when I asked about staying away.

"You're gone most of the time. It's not just a job for you. I've seen the clasps on the capes, Xavier. You know every man and woman you train will be loyal to you personally, don't you? Like your black shirts in New Washington. Your nature, your sense of command, won't allow anything else. There won't be any loyalty to Mylonas or even Salvaje. What about the balance of power here?"

"What about it?" Xavier turned away.

"You gonna be a military dictator? Get rid of Mylonas?"

Xavier sighed and looked back at me. "He interferes. I try not to undermine his position."

"Bullshit. You want your own elite force. Men Mylonas can't fuck with, can't control. You'll choose the best, and they'll follow you when we leave. Do we have enough gold to pay them? Or will you have your soldiers terrify Salvaje until it gives you gold to get you and your men out of town."

Xavier laughed softly. "Terrify? No. My men, women, weres, vamps—"

"Vamps? Orion lets you…"

"Who do you think is paying for it? That symbol on the cloak clasps? The one below my eagle, that's his." Xavier grabbed me in a fierce hug and gave me a throat-swabbing kiss.

When he released me, I had to ask, "What about me? Do I get to join?"

Xavier stroked my hair and rubbed his cheek against mine. "Thank you, love of my life, and most excellent monster killer, but no, I don't want you there."

I shoved him away. "I'm not good enough?"

Xavier laid his hands on my shoulders. "Maat, you're a fighter, the best warrior I know. But you lack one important quality of a soldier. You can't—won't—take orders. And you throw yourself into battle like a berserker, without thought, without considering the odds."

He had a point. I knew my own nature. "Okay. You're right. So, you be the general and I'll—"

"Be Maat." His fingers caressed my cheek. "I love you."

"I don't like it. And Orion? What does he want? Something big since he gave you gold. You should never, never, trust a vampire. You could start a civil war. Or worse."

"Yes, but after that there would be some type of order and—"

"Fuck order. "I sat on the bed and glared at him.

He sat beside me. "Chaos follows you like a shadow, Maat. I don't believe you enjoy it, but you thrive. Your uncle trained you, and you are a master of your craft. Others want peace, they want that order. No kids in Salvaje, Hef said. Why? Violence. Vampires and werewolves are a part of our world now. If we can't learn to create a safe place—"

"Safe? Mama said we'd be safe at the Ag commune. And we believed it. I thought I was safe when I joined the Freak Squad, surrounded by soldiers. Illusions. They let you get soft and careless. *Thrive on chaos?* I hate it. But I'm damned good at protection and resolving issues. I don't run away. Is that thriving?"

"But you did run. And I don't blame you. When your life shattered around you after New York, didn't you seek the peace and order of Avalon?"

My hands knotted into fists. I wanted to reject his words. I couldn't. Avalon's peace and order had saved me. But it was never safe. Because I was suffering, I'd allowed myself to become inured to the danger. Otherwise, he and the former vice president wouldn't have captured—and almost killed me—so easily. Since he was talking—such a rare thing—I forged on.

"Okay answer a question. This army you're training. It's not for Salvaje. There are no families here. This so-called city could disappear, become a wayside, a rest stop, and it wouldn't matter. Everyone, human, vamp, or werewolf, could leave, and it wouldn't change the world. So, who are you working for? Yourself? More important, *what* are you working for? I watched them, your personal soldiers. I watched the way they moved, their confidence, trained for aggression, not passive guardians."

"I don't want to change the world. Just my part."

"BS. You, by your nature and the nature of this world, will change things. Look what Gannett did. Or more like what he could have done. The power he held. You know how he did it, don't you? The east is dissolving into chaos without a leader."

He remained silent for a moment. Then, "Maat, could I promise you the answer to that question later? I won't lie. I know I can trust you, but I'm so unsure of things right now. May I ask for time?"

I forced myself to stop frowning and managed not to sigh in frustration. "Yes, I can give you that. I'm not patient, but I'd do most anything for you."

"Except call me when you need me…when you could use help."

"I'll give you patience, time, and love. That's all. Anything beyond that isn't impossible, but it's not likely."

Xavier moved from the bed to kneel before me. I stared into those deep dark eyes that so fascinated from the moment I met him. "You and I are ridden by demons, Xavier." I brushed a strand of hair from his forehead. Tiny strands of silver threaded through the black. "Your demon is blind rage and mine is mindless vengeance. You cage your demon by trying to create an orderly, precise battle plan. I struggle in the chaos. My world has changed so much I no longer know my place. Does this ritualized madness in Salvaje bother you? I know you've seen it at work. For me, fighting is for survival, not rich assholes' games."

Xavier laughed. "Yes, I find Salvaje's rituals degrading to men, vamps, and weres alike. It's truly abhorrent. Oh, my darling hunter. You're a philosopher with a bitch's attitude and silver bullets. I love you anyway. And I'll do my best not to start a civil war."

My mate, my partner, Xavier would stand beside me wherever fate and this savage world carried us. I wonder if the richness of our lives depends on the quality of the people who love us. If that's so, then I'm the wealthiest of human beings on the planet. Xavier and I found a few minutes to make love before we left the room and walked into a dangerous future.

And I doubted we would leave Salvaje any time

soon.

****

I pinned Lowell down one evening when he had briefly returned to Salvaje and pumped him for information. Heflin had told him about Orion and the ruby Ruelle had given me before this whole fiasco began. I did believe it would be best to destroy the equipment, to open the vaults, to hell with the technology inside the complex. The former vice president said he believed the technology was super important, and Heflin had enough guards to repel Ruelle. I gave myself credit that I didn't laugh in his face. It comforted me to know Xavier was out there using his considerable skill to create a credible force, though I doubted he'd have it ready soon.

Ty stopped me as I walked through the barroom early one morning. I hadn't seen him much since Maureen took him into her governance. The last few weeks' physical labor showed on his bare arms and chest. He'd never have Xavier's powerful build, but he looked more like a man—until he grinned. He grabbed me.

"Hey," he said as he nuzzled my throat.

I twisted away from him. "Has Maureen been keeping you out of trouble?"

Ty shrugged. "She keeps me working all night. I don't have much time to—"

One of Maureen's younger girls, a pretty thing with blue eyes and sun-streaked blonde hair, walked in. "Ty, are you…"

Ty grinned at her. "I'll be there in a minute."

She cast adoring eyes on him, smiled, and eased away.

"Ty? Who's that?"

"Jillian. I stay with her some days." Ty's arms circled me again. "Some days I stay with Mira, or Consuela or Maria or…" He buried his face in my hair. "But don't worry, I love you best."

Absolute astonishment froze me in place. "You stopped me just to tell me you were getting laid every day?"

"But I still love you best." He laughed, released me, and sauntered away. I stared after him as he left the room. *Oh, My God.* He was having sex with various prostitutes. I had no problem with the girls, they were surviving and making a living the only way they could. If he wanted a girlfriend among them, fine—but working his way through a brothel like a personal harem? Allowing a handsome young man such liberty right after his eighteenth birthday couldn't be healthy. Oh, hell, did Maureen know? Would the entrepreneur allow a major portion of her income given out for free? Or was she trying to keep her girls from straying from the fold by offering them a delicious young treat? Worse, how was Xavier going to react? He had to find out eventually. I had little standing to object, but Xavier did. He might explode and, since I had firsthand experience in that, I hoped I could calm him down. Especially since he'd started going to church.

Surprised the hell out of me that there was a church in Salvaje—a Catholic Church at that. Aldo Casele, ordained a Catholic Priest in 1912, became a werewolf in 1925 when one of his parishioners bit him during confession. According to Xavier, Casele considered being a were a God-given test of his faith.

Xavier asked me to go to mass with him, but I declined. He didn't pressure me. I figured I prayed enough useless prayers in New York to last a lifetime. Xavier's parents died when he was young and his uncles, both priests, raised him. It seemed important to him, so I had a silver cross and chain made for him. When you live amongst werewolves, you couldn't carry too much silver. I gave it to him early one evening as we rose to get ready for work.

My vision of God was more like Elspeth's all-knowing being, and I'd confessed my sins to Anolia and others at Avalon. I hadn't had time or will to commit any new sins since I left there—at least major sins.

Xavier had held the chain and cross in his fingers. Then he brushed my cheek with the back of his hand. "I love you," he said softly. "Every time I go to mass, I thank God for you."

I couldn't say anything at all.

****

The invitation came in the morning as I finished up my exercise routine downstairs. Soaked in sweat, muscles burning, I gulped down my water to rehydrate. I enjoyed the awesome high of a rhythmic workout. A woman stood at the door. She'd entered from the street, not through the Paradox. Dressed in gray shirt and pants, she wore boots nicer than any I'd seen in Salvaje. She did not wear the standard sand colored cape of the usual Salvaje resident. The patches on her sleeves and chest marked them as a uniform, but none I'd seen before. She wasn't armed, which seemed suicidal in this town.

I remembered the appropriate manners Aunt Nell and Anolia had hammered into me.

"May I help you."

She walked toward me proffering a white envelope. I accepted, and she remained silent while I opened it.

Would you please have dinner with me this evening? I will send a wain for you. 7:00 PM.

A flowing script signature, Galen Moreau, made it personal. He'd chosen a time when he knew Xavier would be, as usual, training troops. Was Moreau afraid of Orion and his threats? I didn't think so, but I didn't know the source or depth of Moreau's power. My curiosity overtook common sense as it had so many times before. Besides, I believed I knew what he wanted.

"You may tell Mister Moreau I would be happy to join him. Ask him to please send the wain to this entrance, not to the Paradox."

She nodded her head.

I had to ask. "You're not armed. Are you safe?"

She seemed surprised but rubbed her hand across her shirt and laid it on a small patch on the shoulder. She turned and left without a word. I got the message. Galen Moreau's uniform was her protection. This could be an interesting evening.

I headed for the clothing room. Some of the clothing Maureen kept there was fancy, but I didn't want to look like one of her girls. I found a pair of expensive looking navy-blue pants that were only a little too big, and a silky, but not sheer blouse printed with delicate flowers. I also located a light jacket the same color as the pants. I had nothing to wear under the blouse. I don't wear a bra because of the scars on my back. My small breasts didn't need one anyway. The shirt should do if I didn't get wet. To my amazement, I found a pair of shoes. I hadn't worn shoes since Anolia coaxed me into a pair as a prisoner in New Washington. They were black oxford lace-ups, so I could run in them if I had to. I couldn't remember a time when I didn't look for places to run, to escape.

I showered and went upstairs. The only mirror I had easy access to was in the clothing room, so I had to go down, pin my hair up, and see check my image appeared before I left. Acceptable. Not fancy, not even attractive, but it would do. I had the jacket, so I left the ubiquitous cape lying across the bed. I wasn't sneaking out, and I wasn't on the job. I passed three of Heflin's guards on the way back to my room.

I wouldn't go anywhere in Salvaje unarmed even with Orion's firm promise of retribution. The jacket had pockets big enough to hold the Aries. I stuck it in one and a couple of silver loaded clips in the other to balance it out. It didn't look too bad. When Anolia had dressed me, she had fixed my hair and painted my face. I wouldn't do the face painting, even if I had supplies. Brushing and pinning my hair up was enough to show I attempted to look classier than a mercenary/thief etc. It would show respect for my host until I knew his game and what he wanted.

Then I had to decide. Should I tell anyone where I was going? If I did and word got to Xavier, I don't know what would happen. I understood. A werewolf and a vampire had seriously injured me since I arrived. He was a man who protected what he loved—even if that woman didn't believe she needed that protection. Heflin hadn't offered any serious warnings. But Heflin didn't know that much about my host either. Wizard he'd said. Wizard my ass. I'd never seen any proof of true magic even in this city with its illusory description. Shape shifting was biological as far as I knew and, despite all the stories, vamps weren't dead

When I went out the door at seven, an open wain stood there, driven by the same silent woman who'd delivered my invitation. It was late enough that people had emerged to tend to their business, so they had to see us slowly pass by. No, my destination wouldn't be a secret.

Galen Moreau's beige single-story home remained true to the pure featureless Salvaje architecture. Except for its more rectangular shape, it held to the tedious conformation of style. Murlex adobe, surely as ubiquitous as the capes most of us wore, allowed few options. No visible windows and a façade punctuated by a single door. More interesting, though, it had a yard filled with cacti and other desert plants blooming with tiny flowers. Oh, not the lavish meadow blooms of my green mountain home, but rare and precious to behold here.

The wain stopped at a sidewalk leading to the door. I stepped out to walk along a path through the dry garden. I did stop to look closer at some of the perfect blooms on the gray-green, barrel shaped stumps. They seemed more like spiked tables than living plants.

The door opened before I reached it, and Galen Moreau greeted me. I rarely saw a man bigger than Xavier. Moreau was taller and equally as broad, but he moved in a smooth, leisurely way. Xavier's cat-like grace, despite his size, always carried the potential for instant violence. Moreau's movements I would call languid—not that I'd take the any low tension for weakness. Any man in Salvaje could turn violent in an instant.

"Welcome, Ms. Ferris."

"Call me Maat, please."

He ushered me inside.

That close to him, I began to feel him as I did vamps

and werewolves, but I couldn't interpret what my senses told me. *I added him to the list of beware the amazing and deadly oddities in Salvaje.*

He held out a hand and gestured toward a room off the entryway. "Come and talk with me a moment before we eat."

He led me into a room of spare blue and gray upholstered furniture and a window the size of a truck. The window looked onto another new sight, this one walled with a lush green garden growing in ceramic pots. One larger pot held an orange tree loaded with fruit. I had to speak. I pointed at the oranges. "That is amazing. So atypical for Salvaje."

"Thank you. I was born in a desert, far from here. But I have, at times, lived in and appreciated more verdant lands. Please sit. I have a bottle of interesting wine."

I sat on a simple, comfortable, but not overly soft sky-blue couch. I could get up fast if necessary. The room seemed set up for comfortable conversation but didn't look like anyone had ever truly lived there. He went to a masterpiece of a cabinet decorated with intricate carvings in the darkest wood. I accepted the glass of wine he offered. He sat in a chair with a low coffee table of the same dark wood as the cabinet between us. The table created a reasonable conversation distance and slight barrier. Was he trying not to crowd me to make me more comfortable? Maybe.

I sipped the red liquid and immediately fell into memory. Avalon. Flowers, the meadow, and the red grapes we picked for Darius our super skilled wine maker. Each year we would open a cask from previous years and celebrate our harvest, our Thanksgiving. We would eat, laugh, sing, and eventually Christopher and I would make love. We were deliciously alive and lost in ourselves. *My eyes popped open.* How stupid, how careless, sitting in a stranger's house, mellow and lost in memory.

I glanced at him. "I'm sorry. Lost my place."

His gaze felt almost tender. "You were living in a pleasant moment, and you smiled. There are few pleasures in this world. It pleases me to give you one."

I didn't know what to say to that. The air suddenly seemed to thicken. Good thing he changed the subject.

"I only returned to Salvaje a few weeks ago. I've heard much about you. All conflicting, but you have a fearsome reputation. Two werewolves and a vampire, slain by hand. Notable since those kills came in single combat, fang to blade. And the strange stories of New York."

"Notable? No. The werewolf on the road outside Salvaje? He seriously injured me. The second was a set-up, a dreadful sacrifice. That vamp I killed crippled me and would have mortally wounded me—except Orion intervened. I've killed hundreds of werewolves with a gun full of silver. I killed vamps in New York. I didn't face them. I buried them under tons of steel and concrete. No pride, no glory, only relief. That's my story if you're interested."

"Oh, I am interested. What would you wish to be different?"

I shook my head. I did wish for one thing, but guilt and sorrow overwhelmed me at the thought of Anolia dying in my arms. I could not yet speak of her death.

I drew the small scrap of leather containing the crystal Elspeth had given me and laid it on the table in front of me. "That's your stone. I didn't ask for it. Anything Elspeth has touched is cursed."

"Thank you. Despite its simple appearance, it is a dangerous object. It is cursed, but not by her."

I couldn't read his expression. He didn't reach for the scrap of leather. He went back to talking about me. "As I understand it, you've been sorely wounded by vampires and werewolves in your life. And yet you came to this place where they walk freely among the population."

I had to laugh at that. "I did what women have been doing for a long time. I followed a man. My supreme goal is to leave Salvaje as soon as possible. But I won't go without him, so I'm still following."

His smile turned warm and generous. I could almost feel the heat of it across the small distance between us. "That's true. Women have followed men through all ages, Maat. From what I hear, this man you follow is worthy of your dedication."

"I believe so" Yes, Xavier was pure until you really, really pissed him off.

"Will you speak to me of your other followers?"

"Followers? You mean my crew? They're individuals, free to come or stay as they will."

"They don't speak of you that way. The werewolf and vampire are especially quick to tell everyone in Salvaje the name of their master. I believe your dedicated humans, even your stalwart soldier, would join you if you were the one to leave. You speak modestly of your own prowess, but Salvaje now sees your group as a single dangerous entity. You're a warlord backed up by a small army."

How amazing. Again, he'd left me speechless. He

broke the silence.

"I have a guard force of 300 men at a facility outside the city. Would your soldier be interested in employment? Though it would be boring after the excitement of Salvaje, I could employ you, too. And you wouldn't have to stay here. You could go south to Texas, Mexico, or even to a few safe places in California."

He picked up the leather wrapped packet and turned it in his fingers.

I shrugged. "I'll tell Xavier to come see you if he's interested.

And where the hell do you go, Mr. Moreau, and what the hell do you do that requires 300 men? More specifically, how would we serve you?

He stood, so I finished my wine and joined him. He gestured to another room and walked behind me. Another expansive window graced his dining room. More blooming cacti and soft western light from a sun that would soon drop below the back wall.

The table, set for two, had something I hadn't seen since I lived with Aunt Nell. A pristine white tablecloth set with crystal and china plates circled with gold filled the table My Aunt Nell taught me many things. She drilled the basics, math, science, history, and English into me as surely and steadily as Uncle Jake worked me with battle skills. She also taught me things I believed were a useless waste of time. She forced me to focus on details other than those in books or guns. I knew to let him pull out my chair and seat me. There was more than one fork, more than one glass, and wonder of wonders, I remembered to place my napkin in my lap. *Thank you, Aunt Nell.*

I'd answered his questions, so I wanted the same

from him. "So, Galen, will you tell me about the places you travel? I'm not an explorer. I prefer familiar ground. Until now, I'd never been west of the Mississippi."

"I go to Mexico and occasionally east. I've been to Seattle where it rains often. The unused buildings are deteriorating, and some days it fills the air with the scent of rot. But when the sun shines and the breeze blows in from the sea, it can be pleasant. Mexico is pleasant too, especially deeper in the mountains. I think you've sampled the coffee I brought to Salvaje. I move goods from one place to another and exchange them for gold or more valuable goods. I've observed many things. I think it's possible to have this country functioning again in...oh, say your lifetime."

Okay, information, please. "Do you know about the fuel facility in Arkansas? Who the owner is?"

"Yes, I know, but I get mine in Mexico. There's a similar facility there. Seattle is now drawing fuel from a place in California."

He hadn't answered my question about who owned the Arkansas refinery. Before I could ask more a man dressed in one of my host's uniforms served us dinner.

Steak. Beef steak. I used the right knife and then bit into the finest piece of meat I'd ever tasted. I had to close my eyes again, this time not in memory but a fine new experience. I opened them to find him smiling at me.

"What? I'm crude and coarse, I know. Am I amusing you?"

"You are neither crude nor coarse, Maat. You're...adaptable. You speak and act according to the situation...according to the requirements for survival. You are different, a mystery. It's my pleasure to have met you."

Okay. He'd read me like he had a character biography. Then he changed the subject and turned serious. "Tell me, Maat, do you know anything about Elspeth? You're new to Salvaje and may not see it, but I observe her affinity with you."

"Affinity? I don't...how did she get your stone?"

Moreau leaned back and sighed. "I entered a room and found her standing there holding the crystal. I'd stored it in a place she should not have been able to enter. And of course, this house is heavily guarded. She ran into another room, I followed, but she was gone.

"I saw the crystal hanging from her neck the next day. She flaunted it. I wanted to snatch her up and tear it off, but this city is important to my trade. I know her reputation. I do not wish to be banned."

"I understand. She's almost gotten me killed, caused me suffering. The scary thing is, I don't know if she's finished with me. I *doubt* she's finished with me. How did you know I had the stone?"

"The lying thief who assured me he could retrieve it saw her give it to you in the tunnel. He came to me later begging for medical assistance from your surprise attack. I aided him since I'd unwisely chosen to use him."

"Well, I am accustomed to making unwise decisions. But so many of the senses, the intuition I relied on all my life, don't work well, or not at all, in Salvaje. Maybe that's what makes me so uncomfortable."

"Please tell me, what do you sense in me?"

I studied him for a moment, then decided on the truth. "I sense a strangeness. A heaviness like a weight on the world. Nothing I've ever felt before. Whatever...sorry. Whomever you are, you have good control. Elspeth is something like that, too. But she's constantly moving. She messes with me. You haven't. So far."

"I assure you I will not trouble you without cause."

I sipped more wine. "That day at the Paradox you spoke in my mind. Are you a telepath?"

"A telepath? No, I do not read minds. However, I am blessed with the ability to speak into minds." He smiled and lifted his glass of wine. "I am able to read surface emotions. Yours this evening have primarily curiosity. I hope I have satisfied that desire."

"Yes, thank you."

"May I ask you…"

"That's fair."

"I'd also heard tales of you and the vampire Orion."

"What kind of tales?" Just what I needed—Xavier hearing lies and jealous of Orion.

"That you are his confidant. His lover. That's gossip of course. Neither seems credible. Although the vampire's warning to take vengeance should harm befall you… I am aware of vampires and their proclivities. Such a vow from a ruling vampire on behalf of a human is the rarest of events."

"It's a little strange. .He spoke of payment for some unexpressed dishonor to his house, but who knows. I get the feeling I affect him like I affect another vampire in my life. I amuse him."

"Perhaps you are confusing amusement with amazement. Truthfully, I feel some of the same."."." He smiled and fell silent. I think he wanted me to ask what he was. I wouldn't. I suddenly knew if I did, and if he answered, it would change my life. I feared that. I drained my wine glass. Then I laughed.

"Thank you, sir, for this pleasant evening. I love

irony. I'm sitting here wearing a prostitute's borrowed clothes eating the best meal I've had in years. The best meal ever." I stood. I had to go. His intensity battered me. "This has been one of the few pleasures I've had since I arrived."

"You're most welcome, Maat."

He followed me silently as I retreated. When I reached the foyer, I saw something I hadn't seen on my way in—or it wasn't there. A sculpture, about a foot tall, in a niche in the wall. I had to stop. A woman, sculpted in cream colored stone, drew me like magnet drew a pin. She stood with arms down, face pointed straight ahead. Detailed, but nothing fine, she was nude and every inch of her projected defiance. Instead of long flowing hair, hers looped across her shoulders in Grecian style curls. I reached out to touch her and then jerked my hand back. I knew better than to touch other people's things.

"Beautiful, isn't she?" Moreau stood close behind me. Too close. "Her name was Satilla, .She was a warrior queen before even Orion's time."

I drew away. "Don't let Elspeth steal her. Please."

"If Elspeth takes that, I will hunt her down and kill her myself."

I believed him.

When I went out the door, the wain and driver waited for me. At the Paradox I met a stony silent Xavier, whom I took to our room where I repeated every word of my conversation with Galen Moreau.

In typical Xavier fashion all he said was, "Three hundred men?"

"Yes."

"What did he want?"

"I have no idea. I felt like I was talking with

someone wise, powerful, who had plans on a level far above my life. Above even Ruelle. I don't think he means me harm. Not yet anyway."

"Okay." He grabbed me. "Want to go down and get a beer?"

So much for stimulating conversation.

Chapter Thirteen

I was sulking. Xavier hadn't been home in three days, sending word by messengers of delays. I wasn't going to embarrass myself by parading my sulk through the Paradox, so I went out. The plaza had two bars open, one full of werewolves and another with a mixed crowd. A mostly human mixed crowd. Guess which one I chose. The place was far smaller than the Paradox, only twenty by sixty feet. The dim light did show me a long wooden bar, tables, a couple of pool tables in the back, and of course, smelled of beer. Expensive beer, however, no rowdy crowd would disturb my sulk. I adjusted my cape and climbed on a stool. I'd never get used to the cape and would rid myself of it as soon—or before—Salvaje disappeared behind me.

I ordered my beer, and when I went to pay the bartender, a gray bearded heavily wrinkled man, shook his head.

"Heflin's people don't pay."

"He owns this place, too?"

He nodded. "Never seen you here before. Thought you stayed at the Paradox."

"Yeah, well, a person—this person—can only breathe so much air of tasteful fornication."

He chuckled. "None of that here. Hef wouldn't allow the competition."

Carmita slid in and plunked her large butt down on the stool next to me. Heflin's other female bodyguard seemed to be…expanding. "Well, well. No work for you tonight, and your man gone and left you all alone." She had a loud voice that swept through the entire room.

"Carmita, why don't you announce your compassion for my situation to the whole bar, woman? Are you looking for a pickup or a fight? You're not getting either from me."

"Why not? You drinking alone? I'm collecting firsthand gossip for tomorrow. Or the week if things don't pick up."

She was right. Salvaje, for all its unusual nature, functioned as a small town where everyone knew everyone's business. The rumormongers performed quite well here. Their queen sat on her throne in the Paradox.

Carmita and I shared a couple of beers, played a few games of pool, and I decided to leave before I got drunk. Yes, I was a well-armed warrior, but the streets were nowhere as bright tonight as they would be on busier nights. Then there were the black alleys. Shadowland indeed. The night had reached the magic hour, when the overpowering heat of the day fled, and the bone gnawing chill of night had not yet descended.

I hated the low ache in my heart caused by longing for Xavier. I'd been in love once before when I was barely more than a child. All that remained were memories of a brief, brilliant time before monster weres tore him away. I'd never had the opportunity or time to long for and miss a living man. My rational mind kept slapping me with words like juvenile behavior and hypocrisy, wanting for myself the freedom I wouldn't grant him. It hurt. And was totally stupid because someone was behind me, too close, before I whirled gun drawn, to face them. Vampire. She stood facing the Aries, calm as a child. She bowed her head.

"Master Orion instructed me to invite you to join him." She had a voice soft as a baby's breath. Her pale blue robe, the silky and shiniest fabric I'd ever seen, draped gracefully over a fine body. Pure luxury and vanity.

"You mean now?"

"Yes. I am to lead you to him."

Vampires are lethal. Despite Orion's projection of principle and benevolence, I couldn't make my mind believe anything else. Even if Salvaje vamps were supposed to be tame and oh so civilized, they required caution. Orion had put the word out that if anyone attacked me, he would punish them. That didn't mean he wouldn't do the deed himself.

I holstered the Aries. "Sure. Why not?"

She bowed her head again and led me away. Not far. Deceptive distances and the convoluted street plan made it easy to get lost. She turned and headed down one of those black alleys. I started to balk, but then drew the Aries and kept it at my side. My night sight kicked in, and I surveyed the empty alley.

When we exited, my vampire guide said, "I would have protected you, Suriel. My Lord Orion would be wroth with me should I allow you to be... inconvenienced." Her soft voice sounded amused. And a little annoyed.

Inconvenienced? Wroth? I holstered the Aries. "Thank you. I'm sure you would have painted the alley walls red with anyone who attacked. You might mess up that pretty robe if they leaked on you, though. Shooting them is easier. And less messy."

That got me an upturned nose and smile of purest arrogance. "I assure you, I have the skill to…not soil my robe."

Vampire. Never, ever, forget.

We came to a two-story building, the same unremarkable beige as every other structure in Salvaje. This one was different though. It had outside stairs built into the structure itself. Almost like a fire escape, but I'm told the adobe didn't burn. We exited onto a spacious roof top deck. It made everything I'd seen here so far, except the Paradox, look shabby.

Low, dim lamps allowed a perfect view of the magnificent night sky of this land. The extraordinary dome glowed so bright the minimal artificial lighting created gentle ambiance. A slight sense of unease winnowed through. Vamps could see in the dark. Why illuminate unless, like me, they needed it to see color.

The scent of pine filled the air and made it difficult to breathe for a few seconds, then thinned with the slight breeze blowing. Tables and chairs draped with cushions and other fabric ringed the deck edge, leaving the center open.

A female vamp with a small harp and a male with a flute played a melody like none I'd ever experienced before. It brushed the ears soft as the down of a newborn chick.

My guide led me to where the exquisite vampire Orion waited. Dark hair, dark eyes, and most desirable, he sat leisurely holding a gold goblet. To my surprise, he stood to greet me. An act of respect performed before his Salvaje servants? He'd told me his age, and I wondered how time had transformed him from the night Ruelle found him and changed him forever. I bet his vampire heart beat, so slow, forcing thick blood through his veins. He had little of the tell-tale hardness I'd come to associate with his kind. How had he appeared as a young vibrant human?

"Thank you for joining me." He sat close, but a small table separated us. I settled in a perfectly cushioned chair. I had a pleasant buzz from my beer earlier, but I didn't refuse a glass of red wine offered. He drank from a solid cup, and I would not ask the contents.

"This is beautiful, Orion. This terrace. I don't know why everyone doesn't have one."

"It was not part of the original city design and required a great deal of manipulation in construction. There was a time when I enjoyed an evening like yours. Drinking with friends, games, but now the intimacy of humans suffocates me. I wish it were not so."

My evening? He'd been watching me, then. I didn't know what to say. *Did the werewolf enjoy the company of the sheep, engage them in merriment before he feeds?* No, not a clever idea to remind a vampire we were his prey. He paused and placed his cup on the table between us, then turned and focused his attention on me. I shivered. I couldn't help it. The attention of a werewolf was a raging fire. A vampire fixated chilled a human like cold on a deep winter night.

"I have a question, Maat. About something you said."

"Drunk said or sober said?"

He ignored my words. "You told a small audience that vampires are monstrous unrepentant killers. That's not an unreasonable statement. But then you said, *I have slept in a vampire's black heart.*"

"I said that? Yep, profoundly ass drunk. I get that way every now and then. Helps me sleep."

"I will not compel you, but I ask as I hope, a friend. What do you know of my black heart? Yes, my kind hurt you. You are not one of us, though, and it seems arrogant and presumptuous for you to speak of such."

A friend? Now that was pushing our acquaintance hard. "Arrogant is my standard, one of my personal defenses. Presumptuous? No."

I'd spoken more of my life in these last few weeks. I had answered Xavier's questions. Only Anolia had received its full terrible burden. Maybe if I let this go, I'd be free of one more nightmare. Maybe I was drunk, too. Orion could forget his vow and tear my heart out, too. "I told you about New York. You saw the scars where they burned me."

"Yes." He leaned forward—way too interested to suit me.

"The New York vamps didn't restrain me during the day when they hid from the sun. I could barely crawl. I wasn't going anywhere. But there were other things. Wolves and big cats wandered the city ruins looking for a meal. They caught my scent. They tried to tear into the building."

The sound of claws raking at the doors would be with me always. And yet it seemed so innocent in a way. Those beasts, creations of a natural world, had to eat, had to live. Let them in, and my greater torment would end. But the will to live is powerful in humans. Then, and forever, I'd fight to my last breath.

Orion didn't move. No indication of what he thought, so I went on.

"Emanis' vamps piled up in a sealed room deep in the basement for the day. After a single night, I refused to go there again. She didn't insist. They slept huddled around her, like a nest of vipers. You frowned. Are you angry?" Any expression, any movement of his required attention.

"Not angry, Maat, trying to understand. Other than the occasional single companion, we are solitary creatures. We each sleep alone. We do not nest. I've never heard of this."

"Maybe my imagination but I saw her…frightened. I think she wanted them close for comfort." I stopped and sipped my wine. Only Anolia had heard the next part of the story. He waited patiently for me to finish. "There were a few other vamps there. Outsiders who weren't part of her elite group. They specifically did not sleep with her. Solitary creatures, yes." I drained my glass, and a vamp immediately appeared with a refill. I wet my dry throat and continued.

The outsiders? Each built his own secure sleeping tomb. Not wanting to be a wildlife banquet if the clawed hunters broke in, I crawled in with any of them who would have me." I stopped speaking when I realized all sound around me had ceased. I had to go on, though. Many times I slept there in a vampire's arms. Emanis forcing her blood down my throat healed me. I'd face the hot iron again when I woke."

And since all were male, they had taken their payment for safety on my body. Sex, no blood. She'd ordered them not to bite me. They feared and obeyed.

I stared into Orion's eyes, black as the end of the universe. He wasn't consciously compelling me. I had no immunity to his voice. I think he wanted a true answer, but he still might kill me for what I knew.

"In New York, while sleeping, something amazing happened. I walked in my companion of the day's mind, his dreams. Those dreams became my own." I kept my eyes on him, that beautiful, lethal creature sitting beside me. "I lived the hunt, Orion. I killed. I reveled when hot blood gushed down my throat. Then, for those brief sated moments, my sleeping host became human. Not human in body, but human with every feeling, every emotion, every sensation of the life they once lived."

The vampire's secret. They slaughtered not only for nourishment. They slaughtered for those precious seconds of illusion that they had regained their lost humanity.

"You're unique, Orion. I agree. But animal blood won't give you the high, the memories you long for. No matter what face you present to the world, eventually, you will hunt."

"And you judge us, Angel? Human? All the same in our desire."

"Yes, I judge. I believe you all share that same hunger, that longing for a few minutes of bogus life. Tell me I'm wrong, and I'll believe you."

He didn't speak. He'd grown still, too rigid. Now he might decide I knew too much and destroy me. Words between us had more power than bullet, fang, or knife.

He chuckled softly. I didn't relax. "Angel of Death, if I asked, would you come to my bed when the sun rises? If I give you my blood, would you share my dreams as you did theirs in New York? Or in Ruelle's arms?"

"No, not by free will. And you don't know, do you. Ruelle doesn't dream. Only once did he allowed me to stay with him during the day. Ruelle is something else—

as I suspect Emanis was. He fulfilled the myth of dead to this world."

Orion made the slightest movement. I'd surprised him. *Ruelle doesn't dream.* He stared across the room, but I knew his focus was inward to memories of ancient times. When he gazed back at me, I saw an expression of curiosity. "So, tell me, fearsome hunter, why have you not yet killed Ruelle? I know, far more than you, of the devastation he's inflicted upon all of us, human, werewolf, vampire, for a thousand years before you were born. Do you pity him? Hate him? Or do you love him, as I do, despite his endless evil."

"I hate him." Easy words. True but... "And yes, I love him. Will I kill him? He's avoided me anytime I had the strength, opportunity, or ability to surprise him. He isn't likely to stand and let me cut his head off."

That didn't answer his question. Would I kill Ruelle? I'd threatened him, but I'd never had the determination to track him down. I kept waiting for him to make another appearance in my life. And another...and another. Were my threats hypocrisy? We'd see. I was as strong or stronger than I'd ever been in my life. And Ruelle was heading my way.

Orion chuckled softly. "And so, here is a mystery. What are you, Angel of Death? You carry Cody, Emanis, and Ruelle's blood. You've lived in a vampire's dreams. Can you still be human?"

"I'm different. Born different. I was different before I went to New York and even more so when I returned. I died in Memphis, and they brought me back. There is nothing in me that does not seem or feel human. I can't define myself. Human with some unique supernatural skills?"

A slight scuffle broke out across the floor. Orion gazed that way. He spoke softly, but I heard a note of danger in the perfect voice.

"Come here, Ava."

The woman who walked toward us hunched over with reluctance and fear. She was a thin waif of a woman with short ash-blonde hair curled around her face. She kept that face averted as she approached. When she stopped before him and gazed up, I could see far more expression than I thought I would ever see in a vamp. Hatred, rage, sorrow—but she obeyed. I suspected no Salvaje vampire would defy Orion.

Orion stared at her but spoke to me. "I have a problem. Will you help me, Angel? I would consider it a great favor." Favor. He'd already given me his protection in Salvaje, but an undefined favor was worth far more.

"I'll try." I shook my head. "But I won't kill for you. I do enough of that on my own."

Orion chuckled. I didn't think it was funny. "Very well, Angel, but hear my story first. Ava came in a convoy last year, and the Council permitted her to stay. Unfortunately, one of my lesser vampires became enamored of her and changed her. I forbid such in my city. I killed him. For security reasons I should have killed her too. Soft hearts persuaded me to be merciful. She sips animal blood, but barely enough to survive. Ava believes we should all burn for her dead lover's deed. Or perhaps burn for killing him."

I shrugged. "I understand vengeance." I stood to face Ava.

Ava glared. She would not exempt me from her scorn, but I'd do what I could. "Ava, is there any way you believe I can help you?"

Ava attacked. How stupid. Not sure why, I thought my words were sympathetic. All she could do was throw herself at me with her pathetic fangs bared and her fingers curled in a feeble attempt to be a real vamp. Young and newly changed, she could no more damage me than Cody. Maybe in a hundred years, but not this night. I stepped aside and thumped the back of her head. A sharp cry of pain sounded as she smacked face down on the floor.

Orion muttered words I couldn't hear. A problem he had called her. He wouldn't tolerate much more before he ended her.

Ava jumped to her feet. When she charged again, I backhanded her hard. She weighed ninety insubstantial pounds, and the blow knocked her sideways and flipped her over the edge of the short wall surrounding the rooftop. Damn! Not my intention, but even a young vampire should withstand a two-story fall.

"Orion?"

"Yes, Suriel."

"Can vampires fly?"

"Only in pre-war romance novels."

I heard her wail as she raced back up the stairs toward me. Ruelle—and Orion—would come up the wall and be at my throat in two seconds. I was ready for Ava. My fist slammed into her face. She flipped back over the wall again. When she returned, Orion stopped her with three words. "Ava. Be still."

She jerked and dropped to her knees. She covered her face with her hands. Oh, the stunning power of Salvaje's premier vampire

I shook my head. All I could offer is pity. "Orion, she's young, and her life has ended too soon. She wants

175

it back. I can't give her that. You can't either."

He nodded in agreement. Ava crawled over to the wall and huddled there. She drew her knees up and wrapped her arms around her legs to make herself as small as possible. I didn't know what I could do, but I went and sat beside her. Misery and fear poured off her in waves. I didn't need to be psychic or an empath to wallow in the flood.

"Ava? I can't help you with what you've lost. I loved a man once years ago. I cried over his grave for a week until my friend, afraid I'd lie there and die, picked me up and carried me away. My friend, he's a rough man but he… Shit. I'm totally screwing this up. He told me I had two choices. I could face my sorrow or end it all. He even offered me a gun. Do you know Cody? He came here with me."

She nodded slightly but didn't look up.

"Cody was fourteen when he was changed. He watched his family die first. But the vampire who made him…"

"You killed him. That vampire. His master. I saw." Her voice sounded as fragile as her elfin body.

"Yes. Have you ever spoken to Cody? Could you ask him—"

"No. He's Orion's. I don't…you don't understand. Rules, there are rules."

Oh, shit. Now what did I say. *Wait. Cody was Orion's now?*

Ava raised her face. She stared at Orion, then back at me. "You killed a bunch of them in New York, didn't you?"

Them. Vampires were *them* to her, not *we*. She remained apart, longing for life.

"Yes. I killed a bunch in New York. Dropped a building on them."

"I wish…" Thankfully she stopped before expressing her wishes.

Orion was not like any vampire I'd known. Could he feel pity? A sense of justice? He killed the vamp that made her for breaking the rules but had spared her.

"Ava, if you could kill every vampire in Salvaje, for you personally, nothing would change. You have choices, like I did. Keep going the way you are, and Orion mercifully kills you, or accept events and go on. He punished your lover, and to keep order in his house, he should have killed you. I guess you could walk out in the sun in the morning if it's that bad."

Orion laughed softly. "I'd rather break her neck. Vampires scream for a long time in the sun. And their bodies…the clean-up." I had amused the Vampire Prince of Salvaje.

He wasn't finished. "This is a most compelling conversation. We must continue it another time. Here is your stalwart lover, Maat. I wondered when he would arrive." He nodded toward the stairs as Xavier stepped into view.

"Ah, Commander. Please sit with us. Do you wish wine or beer?"

"Wine. Thank you." Xavier's eyes widened at me sitting next to the wall close with Ava, but he said nothing. He sat in the chair by Orion that I'd vacated to talk to the fledgling vamp. I had to smile. No matter when or where, all my emotions danced when my lover stepped into view. I spoke to him. "So, I thought you'd be gone all night?"

"I did, too. But a ferocious storm named Maureen

arrived. She explained to me that my priorities were in critical disarray." He smiled at me. My smile. Mine alone. "Maureen was vehement. She reminded me of something I'd foolishly forgotten. To quote the lady... 'Soldiers, arms, and battles are not unique. They're common as flies on the carcass of a dead beast. But some things have no parallel, no equivalent." He shrugged. "Elspeth was standing right behind her."

Of course she was. Foul witch! It amazed me that this man loved me, despite my faults. But... "You knew I was here. Do you have people following me? You locate me with such ease."

"No. People generously, from the kindness of their hearts, inform me when you go somewhere...different. And let me remind you, the two times I didn't know where you were, you managed to run into life-threatening situations."

I glance over at Orion. "What about you? You located me tonight, knew that I was unoccupied, and issued an invitation."

Orion laughed and the expression, *the angels sang,* came into reality. All the vamps on the roof sighed like a delicate breeze in the nonexistent trees. Ava, sitting close, shivered. To my surprise, her thin fingers gripped my arm.

I glanced at Xavier. Oops. Orion's laughter hadn't moved him. Not even an inch. And Orion marked his reaction. Only a flick of an eye, a fraction of a second, but I saw. Dangerous knowledge. Xavier appeared immune to the vampire's voice. Orion would remember.

Orion went on. "No, Maat, I don't have people watch you specifically. However, I do have individuals who watch the city. It is not a vast area to patrol. A small town, really. I know who goes where with whom. Besides, Elspeth, arguably the most eccentric power in Salvaje has taken an intriguing interest in you."

"That's Elspeth. I've suffered from her *intriguing interest.* But why are you interested in me?"

"I'm bored. The years pass slowly. And yet like most living creatures, especially humans, I fear death. I also walk in a separate place. You know it, don't you?"

My stomach tightened. I knew. He was speaking of the psychic world, the dream world of sensation. I'd been there most of my life, but since I died... "And you think that makes me interesting?"

"No, not in itself. But you are a fledging star in that place, shining and ready to blast its way into the universe. And when you do, you will be a new sun bringing a new earth, a new civilization." He turned his face to the star-filled sky and laughed. I could feel the collective consciousness of Salvaje twist in restless sleep. But he had more to say. "Or perhaps the Angel of Death will burn out too soon and go mad like Elspeth."

A fine edge of terror cut through me. I stood. So did Xavier. "Good night, Orion. Thanks for the wine."

As I turned to leave, Orion said, "A moment. Suriel."

Oh, shit. I was the Angel of Death again.

He spoke softly. No need to shout. The entire gathering had kept to that silence they'd held all night. "Ava, come here."

Ava stood where she'd been crouching against the wall. She came, but I could see her whole body shaking. The air around us reeked with her terror. We had, only moments ago, discussed ending her life. She stopped and knelt before him, face down.

"Ava. I don't have time for you. I am no longer your master. I give you to the Angel of Death. Your new master may accept you or turn you out of the city to die in the sun."

Oh, hell and be damned. "I don't have a place or time to care for her, Orion."

"You have the box that Cody slept in. You haven't noticed he's been staying here during the day for some time, have you?"

"No. I don't keep track of him. I told you, I don't own him. I don't want to own Ava."

"Then kill her."

Ava made a small squeaking sound. There wasn't a choice for me.

I sighed and accepted another turn of fate.

"Let's go, Ava. I won't kill you if you behave."

She stood and moved closer to me.

Orion laughed. "You see, Ava, the kind Angel of Death accepts the lost and abused."

Smug bastard. Pious monster. Maat Ferris wouldn't allow that to go unchallenged.

That's bullshit, Orion. Master? Servant? You're truly only one thing. A fucking vampire. A magnificent vampire, yes. Your prey runs to you offering a river of blood. But you're damned. You are still a vampire, body and soul"

Orion stood. His expression frozen in neutral again, and I knew I'd gone too far. Xavier was at my back, and amazingly, Ava relaxed and stepped between me and Orion.

Orion stepped back and laughed out loud. Not the usual soft chuckle, but a true boisterous laugh. "Now look at you, Angel. Your mate stands behind you.

Predictable. But this little mouse...This...t terrified fledging...you have bound her. In mere seconds, she stands willing, knowing she will die for you. The universe has given you a magnificent gift—or a dreadful curse." He reached for me across the psychic connection we'd made when I first met him. "You will be the new sun, Maat. I hope one day to stand in your light and warmth without fear."

Then he was gone, too fast to see.

I slumped, exhausted. Xavier caught me. "Let's go home. Ava, you come too. We'll figure out something for you." I glanced at Xavier. "I didn't ask you. I should ask Maureen too, shouldn't I?"

Xavier hugged me tight. "It's okay. We'll figure something out."

We walked to the Paradox. Dawn approached, and I showed Ava Cody's box. "It's not pleasant, but we had it made during emergency travel. We will do better. I have to talk with Maureen about you."

"Will she let me stay?" She chewed on her fingernails and kept her eyes averted.

"If she doesn't, I'll find something else for you. Ava? The one who made you? Did you love him?"

She raised her face, and I could see all the sorrow in her eyes. "He did not ask. That was wrong. But if he had..."

"You loved him."

She turned away. "You are my master. I will serve you."

I gave up. "There are locks on the inside. Make sure you use them. No accidents."

Xavier and I went to our room, and before we made love, we spoke of the evening. To my surprise he'd read

Orion's nuances as well as I had. Xavier the soldier noticed details. We talked for a long time. What Maureen told him was infinite truth. Violence would come, but we should prize love above all. I told him of my more serious conversation with Orion.

He sighed. "Dreams? Blood as a drug to feel human."

"Orion didn't tell me I was wrong. He did challenge me on comparing him and his vamps to what I found in New York. I can see that."

I did make one other observation. "Orion admits to spies. What does Maureen have? Or did Elspeth corral her for a mission?"

Elspeth. How utterly terrifying.

Chapter Fourteen

Xavier and I walked side by side through empty streets and alleys toward the Paradox. The ubiquitous beige and brown of Murlex adobe buildings that created our path felt more like prison walls. He'd met me as I finished an all-night job. He'd been spending more time with me, I guess to try to keep me out of trouble. I don't resent it too much. I understand his fear, but I'd managed to survive before he came to my rescue.

The brilliant carpet of stars faded as the black sky lightened to pale pink and blue. It promised another sun blasted day. The air remained cool for the moment, so we'd enjoy that.

"How's the troop training going?" I shifted my cloak on my shoulders. It defended me from the night's chill, but now I longed to pull the clasp and let it fall.

"Progress is acceptable."." And occasionally good. I'd accept Xavier's brevity as usual.

"Is Orion happy?" Orion had paid Xavier for unarticulated services. I couldn't think of anything a vampire would need, but I didn't dig too deep on that. I told Xavier everything I thought would affect him, or that deeply affected me. He listened. He didn't reciprocate. But I'd asked for some independence, so I had to give the same.

He gave a relaxed shrug. "Orion has received what

he paid for."

Okay. He still didn't want to talk about it.

I kept working over the pros and cons of Salvaje in my mind. Cons? Parched ground, incredible searing heat, and the constant battles. Vampires. Werewolves. Pros? No cars, a few nice people I'd met, and…nothing. No genius required on that one. I'd roved the mountains and cities of the east as a hunter/killer of werewolves, a thief, and general ne'er-do-well, sowing seeds of discord and rebellion every day. It wasn't the just the violence of Salvaje I hated. It was the ritual and the normalization of hostility as a way of life. It didn't change. No seasons, only hot or cold.

Thankfully, Maureen employed my foundling, Ava. I don't know her exact job, but things seem okay.

One image popped into my mind. Xavier, leading his troops—and they were *his troops*—into battle to open this city to the world. New people, innovative ideas, I could imagine Orion's desire for that.

Xavier slipped his arm around my waist and pulled me close to him. "Maat, the troops are good. Rough, but most of them give me a hundred percent. But if the army comes at us like Memphis, with big guns, this city won't stand a chance. People like Heflin are living in denial." He waved a hand at the buildings surrounding us. "They call it indestructible. That's a salesman's lie."

"Heflin survived the destruction of Memphis with us. That is pure denial." This damned city. The Salvaje werewolves consider it home. They're stubborn. Best to run away, but they'd fight to keep the place. Would Orion and his stated love for Ruelle betray the city? I didn't know.

"Maat, do you consider Orion a gentler version of

Ruelle?" He shook his head, denying knowledge even if he requested an answer.

"Gentler? No, that does not describe Orion. He's old, Xavier. He has a pretty façade. He's still a vampire. All those years, so far from humanity? I'll accept him— or at least the persona he offers here. I won't trust him."

Anyone but me would have taken Orion's subtle offering of friendship and peace as presented. I couldn't. I understood something clearly as he had spoken of Ruelle. Orion loved Ruelle. Of course, he loved Emanis, too, even though he understood why I killed her. Emanis was insane. Ruelle was not. He could destroy the world if we couldn't eventually take him down.

Xavier didn't speak again. We stayed alert as we entered an area frequented by werewolves. He released me so we kept our gun hands free. The dispute between Anson Sewell and Abban Connor's followers had escalated to snarling, clawing dogfights that occasianly spilled out into the streets. Anson now ruled the Lycos, but humans walked cautiously and carried lots of silver. Orion and his vamps ignored the whole thing.

Cody now spent the majority of his free time with his fellow vampires. Ava, my fledgling vamp, had said Cody now belonged to Orion. Cody spoke of Orion in a quiet, worshipful voice. Okay by me, even though I did miss having him around. I couldn't change Cody's physiology. I did hope Orion would not lead him into purest evil.

As we turned the corner a block from the Paradox, we almost walked into a hurried breathless Lowell Parr. Was he running from something? Shocked, Xavier and I reached for our guns, prepared for an attack. Why was he here now? He usually stayed with Heflin out at the missile site. He'd been there weeks.

"Oh, good. I was looking for you two." Parr clapped his hand on Xavier's shoulder. "Need your help with something. Can you spare me an hour?"

I didn't want to spare anything. I wanted to find my bedroom, make love to Xavier, and then sleep. My feelings must have shown on my face.

"I'll go." Xavier relaxed. "Maat needs to rest."

"Oh, no, I need you both." Parr said before I could speak. "It won't take long."

"It's okay," I told them. I'd make sure Xavier didn't get sidetracked. I doubt I needed rest more than he did. "When did you and Hef get back, Lowell?"

Parr laughed. "A few hours ago. We came to report we finally have all the vaults open. Only a matter of hours before we declare victory and change the world's future."

I bit my lip. I wanted to ask why he didn't go ahead and destroy the missile controls, then come home and declare victory, so we could all get drunk and have a party. Hef wanted to kill the missiles, but once they started opening the can, he found some goodies that set him drooling. Progress he called it. "Take a hundred years off the time it'll take to get us back to a pre-war civilization."

"Anybody out there seen Ajax the last couple of weeks?" I asked Parr. Ajax disappeared again, shortly after the incident with Giselle. I wasn't too worried about him, but Mary was losing weight, and it wasn't like him to be out of contact for so long.

"Haven't seen him" Parr frowned. "I thought…no, he hasn't been at the complex."

I decided I'd better see if I could find my demo man

and learn what was going on with him.

To my surprise, Parr led us to a section of the city I'd never visited. This was the oldest before the first Murlex adobe slid into molds. Standard wood board construction, same as the east where they had plenty of trees. Hef had spoken of it, and he said the buildings weren't stable and needed to be torn down. A few nostalgic citizens had objected, so demolition had stopped. Out of ordinary sight, they aged so conveniently forgotten. The two-story buildings stood near one of Salvaje's smaller gates. An interesting sight, an unkept, unoccupied block of buildings, gray weathered instead of the omnipresent adobe beige.

Parr led us to one barely standing building. He stepped onto a concrete porch and shoved a wooden door open. "You'll love this." He seemed happier than I'd seen him since before the weres killed Anolia. My psychic senses gave a jerk, but more a notice than alarm.

Xavier went in first, and I followed him into a wide, empty room. I did sense the muted presence of vamp and were, but it could come from anywhere in this blast furnace town. Morning light found its way through shuttered windows and cut shadows across crumbling interior walls. A wide set of stairs on my left climbed to a sagging balcony landing. The room reeked of neglect and arid decay, but other unfamiliar scents rippled through the air.

"This way," Parr said as he hurried across the floor to a door in the wall to my right. He opened it, walked in—and closed it behind him. *What the hell?*

Wrong! All my senses, psychic and otherwise, screamed warnings. Nothing seemed disturbed—except for the wood-planked floor, where multiple feet had recently rearranged years of dust and sand.

I popped the clasp on my cape and let it fall, .I drew the Rudra. Xavier already had his Aries in hand—which is how, standing back-to-back, we managed to cut down at least ten or twelve of the mass of men who flooded into the room from the stairs and the front door behind us.

No uniforms, but they were obviously trained soldiers. They didn't want to kill us. If they had, they'd have come in the door shooting. Shouts, screams, and the violent concussion of our high-power handguns filled the room before they overwhelmed and disarmed us.

Then I used my hands and feet to damage a few of them, mostly faces and eyes. A scream and the crunch of bones told me Xavier had a more devastating physical effect.

It required three of them, but they finally had me face down on the floor, arms behind my back. Three! Yes, I'd grown stronger since I arrived here. They hauled me to my feet, one man at each arm and the third behind me with his hand locked tight on my shirt. Four had Xavier forced to his knees with his arms twisted behind his back. At least I was standing.

Parr came out the door he exited earlier. He had a pistol in his hand. His eyes widened a bit at the bodies on the floor. Many curled into moaning heaps, and those remaining on their feet grumbled in anger rapidly turning to rage. They had no weapons. Disarmed? Someone didn't trust them not to shoot us. They'd paid a price. One rough looking brute stood in front of me, fists balled, drawing back to swing.

"That's enough," Parr shouted, his voice pitched high with an edge of hysteria. He walked over and pointed the gun at Xavier's head. He caught the soldiers' attention. Theirs—and mine because I noted his shaking gun hand. soldiers stopped grumbling. Killing Xavier might appease them.

I didn't have to ask what was going on. I shoved all emotion, all sense of betrayal, and yes, hurt away. I had to draw his attention from Xavier.

"Lowell?" He turned to me. I sneered at him. "Be incredibly careful. Didn't the vampire give you orders? He told you not to kill us. Didn't he?"

Parr drew back and cringed. No doubts there. Ruelle was in charge. He might let Parr kill Xavier, but not me. If the vampire killed me, he'd do it in person. I laughed and focused on the soldiers, trying to meet a large amount of gazes as I could. "What's the matter, guys? Someone take your guns away? Nobody told you we'd fight back?" I saw it in their eyes. Most were the brown-shirted troops that had made up Parr's special guard back in New Washington. They knew me and Xavier. But they probably hadn't known it was us until after we faced them in battle. It might have been different if they had. They had to respect Xavier, respect his command. He could take charge if given a chance. It would depend on how much they feared the vampire.

Parr's eyes narrowed. His mouth pinched tight as he stalked toward me. Was this the same kind man who comforted me when I was trying to sort things out with Xavier? Who cried for Anolia? I'd liked him, trusted him, and I now knew why my wonderful Anolia died with his name on her lips. She'd learned something and wanted to warn me. Some secret she wouldn't trust to anyone, not even Sabrina.

I took one last look at Xavier's face. He met my eyes

and I saw understanding there. We were both going to die, but I was closest to the still open door. He'd give me the chance, and I'd try to run—warn Heflin and Orion.

Parr pointed the pistol at my chest. "You're not such a tough bitch now, are you? You did your job, though. Xavier did his. Kept each other occupied. So much in love. I didn't expect that. Such a gift. You're both watchful and perceptive, and if you hadn't had each other to focus on, you might have figured things out."

"Anolia...the weres..." I choked. I forced hurt turned to tears, back down.

Parr shook his head. "Killing her wasn't my doing. But if it hadn't happened, she'd have been...removed. You wouldn't have left without her, and Ruelle was adamant you go west. I had no time to plan."

The men had Xavier pinned down on his knees. He heaved himself up and broke free. Parr pivoted toward him. Xavier sailed past him and hit one of the men holding my arms. The impact knocked us all down. I tore loose, scrambled to my feet. I bolted out the thankfully open front door. Outside, I raced down the street at a dead run. A hundred feet, a hundred and fifty. I could stay ahead of them—unless someone found a gun and shot me in the back. Arms clad in white silk seized me and jerked me off my feet.

Ruelle, who hadn't even been in the room, had come into the deadly dawn's light to catch me. Not full daylight, but bright enough it should have been intolerable. He dropped me. A swift flash, and he smashed his way through the boarded window of a derelict building. He had escaped the burning light. The soldiers caught and overwhelmed me.

I'd lost my last chance. I didn't fight them as they

led me back inside. Xavier lay still on the floor. I couldn't tell if they'd killed him or finally beaten him unconscious. I held my fear and sorrow close. Xavier...

They forced me toward Ruelle who now stood in the center of the room. He drew deep breaths, something I'd never seen him do. The blessed sunlight remained a perfect weapon just beyond our reach. He'd had to make his way through walls to get back here. His skin blushed a deep rosy pink. The inflammation slowly faded, but it had to hurt.

The vampire's eyes locked on mine. "Release her."

The soldiers holding me jumped back as if I was the one who burst into flames.

"Hello, suck face." I crossed my arms and tried for my usual banter. I guess I didn't get it right, because he read my emotions as if someone printed them on my forehead.

"Your lover is alive." Ruelle reached out and brushed his fingers across my cheek.

An involuntary sigh of relief escaped, but I covered with an insult. "When did you come slithering in?"

"We took control of the missile complex yesterday." Ruelle cut his eyes to Parr. "Lowell was most helpful. It's amazing the trust he inspires. He simply told the guards to lay down their arms, and they did. Such an actor. He deceived everyone."

Yes, Lowell Parr had played his traitor's role to perfection. The gentle counselor, the mediator of our disagreements, the father figure who kept us together had moved us on.

Two soldiers grabbed Xavier by the arms and dragged him to the door Lowell had wisely used to escape during the attack. Ruelle laid a firm hand on my shoulder and guided me in the same direction. He followed me downstairs into a basement.

Things got worse when I reached the bottom of the stairs.

They'd hung a few lanterns around the room, so the men could see, but shadows cloaked the corners of a basement cut in rock. Anson Sewell, Jacob, and Heflin stared at us from behind silver-coated bars of an expansive cell anchored against floor and wall.

Ty lay outside the cage on the rock floor, ropes binding his hands and arms. A gag in his mouth had silenced him. He struggled against his bonds.

They dragged Xavier to the cell door. As they opened it, a couple men with guns and long silver pointed poles closed in, forcing Heflin and the weres back. Xavier jerked as they dropped him. They didn't have to prompt me to follow.

I knelt beside Xavier and laid my hand on his forehead. The only injuries I could see were cuts and abrasions and a clump of wet bloodied hair at his temple. His eyes were open, but he had a dazed look.

Heflin joined me. "Sorry, Hef, guess you were counting on us."

"It's not your fault." He had a large bruise on his face and blood on his shirt. He cut his eyes at Parr. "I was with the motherfucker every day."

No one spoke as all the soldiers except the two standing over Ty left.

I stood and turned to face Ruelle. "How utterly fearless The sun thing. You wanted me that bad? To take a chance on burning."

Ruelle smiled. The inflammation on his skin had disappeared. "It was important to keep you from spreading news of our arrival and takeover of the missile site. I have worked a number of years on this plan. I can bear a little sunburn."

Anson snarled as Abban Connor hurried down the stairs and joined us.

Aaron Gannett, President and Dictator, shuffled from the shadows. Stained, rumpled clothes draped a thin body, and he hadn't shaved in a while. Gannett's eyes locked on Ruelle. Frenzied eyes—like Elspeth's. Vampire madness. Ruelle had been close to him, feeding on him with the inevitable result.

"Where's Sabrina?" Gannett asked, suddenly staring around the room. His careworn face had sagged and aged, and his voice crackled like crumpled paper. Ruelle laid a gentle hand on his shoulder, and he stilled.

Orion's explanation of what happened in the desert around Babylon a thousand years ago made me understand a little better. Orion had escaped the horror that had touched and changed Ruelle and Emanis.

"What about Anolia, Ruelle?" I asked. "Did she discover your little plot?"

Ruelle shook his head. "Not exactly. Your dear Anolia happened to catch the vice president in the act with one of his young male friends. Horrified her, I fear. He'd kept his preferences secret for so long. Careless of him, especially when we were so close to success. She didn't know the plan, but she knew enough to warn you something was happening."

Others might have missed the disgust in his voice, but I knew Ruelle better. He wasn't disgusted at Parr's preferences, only the carelessness. My stomach knotted. It was all I could do not to glance at Ty, tied and gagged on the floor.

Ruelle moved closer and spoke softly. "I did not order her killed, Maat. I would have simply removed her from the scene, sent her back to her Avalon. You remember I didn't hurt your dark friend Ajax when he challenged me years ago."

Was he trying to placate me? Why?

"And the weres?" I demanded. "The ones at the mountain house...the market where she was..."

"I don't know. They may have originally come from a secret army I'd been trying to build for a number of years." Ruelle shrugged. "Deserters split into separate packs and started recruiting on their own. I hate to admit it, but I lost control of them over ten years ago. I believe the hunter called the Angel of Death killed most of them in the last few years. You understand, you may have been their target at the market."

I lowered my eyes. Yes, I understood. I'd begged Xavier's pardon for his men killed there. I know Anolia would have forgiven me.

"So now there's a bunch of wild werewolves running around New Washington."

Ruelle laughed softly. "No, my love. You, Colonel Xavier, his troops at the market, exterminated almost all of them. I suspect dear Sabrina's pack has already eliminated the rest. They weren't reliable soldiers, anyway."

"Yeah. Unreliable. That's werewolves all right." I pointed at Connor. "Connor knows about unreliable. A good many of his deserted him."

Connor sauntered closer to the cell and glared at Anson. His smile twisted into a malicious smirk. "Anson Sewell, boy king of the Salvaje werewolves." He spit on the floor. Then he turned to Parr and Ruelle. "I'm ready.

Lowell, will you explain things to Anson? I want him to know what's going to happen." He hurried to the stairs and out of the room.

I leaned against the prison bars, each heavily coated with silver. "How long has the old wolf been in your pocket, vampire?"

"Oh, about four years," Ruelle replied. He glanced at the stairs Connor had ascended. "Unlike my recruitment of a werewolf army, this part of the plan has progressed with very few problems."

I stared at Parr. I'd easily marked Abban Connor as evil from the moment I met him. How had I missed Parr?

Parr smiled at us. His handsome face, once warm and congenial, twisted with malignance as he gloated. "We've loaned Connor fifty men equipped with silver bullets and flame throwers," he said. "He's going to take care of Anson's followers, then he's going after the vampires."

Flame throwers. There was no pity, no mercy, in his harsh voice. It echoed off the stone walls and reminded us how Salvaje earned its name in this brutal western land.

"Ruelle? The vampires?" I couldn't contain my shock. "You're going to let him burn Orion? How can you—"

"Stop." He cut me off with a single word. "I have made arrangements."

Arrangements. The full price of my peaceful stay at Avalon. I knew better. I'd disastrously underestimated this vampire. Who and how many spies and servants did he have to carry out this operation across time and distance? What kind of network had he built? A network to rule a world. Could I have stopped Ruelle? I could have by killing him. It would have cost my life, but that's a small thing for humanity *Maat Ferris, braggart queen of denial*.

"I was told you gave Orion the ruby?" Ruelle cocked his head in true interest. "He told you our story?"

"Yeah. He told me."

"Then perhaps you understand."

"Knowledge is not always understanding." Despite my contact, I still understood so little about vampires. Whatever I suspected, whatever bond Orion and Ruelle shared remained intact. Who dominated if they came face to face? Would they fight or fall into each other's arms, delighted to be there after such a long separation?

Behind me, Anson drew a sobbing breath.

"So, what happens next?" I asked Ruelle. I could sense Xavier's presence at my back. He was on his feet now, for all the good it would do.

"For you, for now, nothing," Ruelle said. "You and your companions are going to wait here while we go to the missile complex. The people we brought with us are already programing the first missiles to resolve my problems in Seattle and New Washington. Create a little chaos and give me time to carry out my plans."

"Your plans?"

"Finish the destruction of this civilization and rebuild it my way. I've been power behind a throne a few times, but now it's my turn. It may take a hundred years, maybe longer, to realize the vision." His eyes stared into mine as if he were trying to convey a message.

I grabbed the silver bars with both hands. "Ruelle, you always did make grandiose plans. I won't ask the win-lose details, but what will you have in a hundred years? In a thousand years? Nothing but more time, vampire. More plans, more failures."

"Yes, dear Maat. More time. But I can fill it with such interesting things."

Oh, he could. Since I'd known him, Ruelle had filled his time with carefully planned death and destruction. Suddenly nauseated, I clung to the bars to hold myself up.

"Unfortunately, I need to reward my faithful followers." Ruelle nodded at Anson, Jacob, and Heflin. "Connor wants those three." He glanced over his shoulder at Ty. "I promised Lowell he could play with your pretty boy, but since he's so important to you that you bargained for him in New Washington... Oh, but you failed to keep your part of the bargain, didn't you? I will see you get him back relatively undamaged. Then I'll tell you how you can save his and your lover's lives."

He stepped closer. His fingers brushed mine where they gripped the silver bars. "You won't ever love me." His voice was soft, light, and surprisingly honest.

"I could love you, Ruelle. But every time I get close, your pitch-black vampire soul drives you to a crime I cannot bear." The provocative question, why did he want my love, might forever go unanswered.

Ruelle had once told me he was a thousand years old. Orion said he was far older. No humanity remained in him, but he needed and desired companionship. I'd told Orion of living in a vampire's dreams, how I knew human blood made them feel human for a while. Ruelle couldn't or wouldn't dream. Humans who remained in close contact with him for longer periods of time went crazy like Gannett. All humans except me. Ruelle might eventually destroy me. But God help me, meeting Orion and knowing what Ruelle might have been...

"You plan to kill me or make me a vampire like you." For me, there had always been worse things than death. Being a vampire was among them.

"I don't know," Ruelle said. "So human, and yet you killed Emanis. Lowell told me you dispatched Gunnar, too. You'd make a dangerous vampire."

"Let me out, and I'll show you how I did it."

"We need to go, Ruelle." Parr said, his voice tight with impatience. "Make sure things are ready to roll."

If Parr could have seen Ruelle's face then, he'd have run while it was daylight. No human pushed or hurried this vampire while he was having a personal conversation. Ruelle smiled, the smile that always made me shiver. His eyes never left me as he said, "Yes, Lowell, you're right. We can deal with minor problems later."

"Hear that, Lowell?" I laughed to mock him. "You've been demoted from VP to a minor problem." I reached my hands through the bars. "Ruelle, listen. I'll do what you want. Let Ty go."."

Ruelle shook his head, his face serious now.

I closed my eyes and rested my forehead on the silver bars. Parr got Ty, not as a reward to him, but as my punishment for not going back. For going on to Salvaje instead, even though Ruelle knew perfectly well what I'd do.

Parr gestured at the guards, and they grabbed Ty by the arms and lifted him to his feet. Ty kicked at them. One punched him in the stomach, drawing a sharp cry, even with the gag.

Gannett, who'd been standing quiet like a zombie, jerked at the sound. "What are you doing? Leave him alone. Ty…?" He staggered toward the men dragging Ty away, his hand stretched out to touch him. They stopped. I guess they suddenly remembered Gannett was their president.

Parr's face tightened in rage as he caught Gannett by the shoulder and gave him a savage shove. Gannett spun around, staggered, and fell to his knees. His head turned, searching the room around him, as if he had suddenly awakened in a strange place. Ruelle grasped his elbow and carefully helped him to his feet. The vampire's expression was one I'd never seen before. Concern for another being.

"What's the matter, suck face?" I had to taunt him. "Lost another pet?"

"I'm afraid so," Ruelle replied. I was surprised to hear regret in his voice. "He's deteriorated rapidly since General Borden committed suicide in Memphis."

I frowned at the mention of Borden. "Who sent the army after us? They almost wiped out all your plans crossing the river."

"Yes, that was unfortunate. Aaron ordered Borden to pursue you. And, of course, Memphis Base received word they were coming. The resulting battle was to relieve me of any pressure from the army. Unfortunately, Borden moved much faster than I anticipated. He arrived in Memphis too soon."

"Good cover for me, though." Parr laughed and pointed the pistol at Gannett. "I've waited a long time to see this stupid bastard like this. So much power, and he pissed it away. Shall I ask Ruelle to let me shoot him, Xavier?"

"Why ask me?" Xavier's dead cold voice came from over my shoulder.

Parr moved closer but stopped out of arm's reach.

"He paid Jenks to shoot your wife and start the fire. Killed the baby, too. No werewolves involved. Aaron, your dear friend and commander, let Jenks rape and murder his best soldier's wife. You weren't supposed to run into the fire. And Lilly's accident? You thought Sabrina killed her, didn't you?"

Xavier stood close behind me, and his body trembled. He said nothing, but Ty's gagged moan came from across the room.

"Sabrina?" Gannett shook his head. "I didn't kill her. I shot the wall." He giggled and grinned at Ruelle like a little boy caught plundering in his mother's underwear drawer. "I fooled you, too."

Ruelle nodded. "Why, yes you did," he said in light voice. His expression was grim. I'd bet he planted a command in Gannett's brain to kill Sabrina, but Gannett loved her enough to defy him. Score one for the humans.

"I said take him out," Parr ordered the guards again.

This time they dragged Ty up the stairs and away.

Ruelle led Gannett by the elbow as they moved toward the door. In a rough, jerky movement, Gannett suddenly threw himself at Parr.

Parr raised the pistol. He pulled the trigger. The bullet caught Gannett in the chest. Gannett's eyes popped open, and a red stain immediately bloomed on his shirt. He stood rigid for a second, then slowly crumpled and collapsed to the floor. My ears protested as the shot bounced off the basement walls and echoes filled the room.

The President and Dictator of the United States lay in a spreading crimson pool. Silence filled the air and swelled like a bubble ready to burst into more violence.

Ruelle slowly knelt beside Gannett and laid a gentle

hand on his pale hair.

Until I met Orion, I never considered how lonely it might be to live thousands of years, care for mortals and watch them grow old and die. Or go insane as Ruelle's pets always did. He had told me that when a vampire creates another vampire, he creates a slave or an enemy. Not an act upon someone you love. Ruelle stared at Parr. Such a pale, beautiful face, the blank stillness of marble stone—Lowell would scream for hours before he died.

"What did you expect me to do?" Fear touched Parr's voice. He held the gun up. The barrel trembled. "He attacked me."

"He could not have harmed you." Ruelle's calm, reasonable tone might have soothed some folks. I knew better. Ruelle needed Parr for some reason. Otherwise, he would have torn the man apart right there in the basement. The smooth-talking traitor would get his reward soon—but not soon enough to save Ty.

"I'm sorry," Lowell said. "It was instinctive. He came at me and—"

"We'll speak of it later. It's time to go." Ruelle rose.

I had to have the last word. "Vampire!"

Ruelle stared at me. I grasped the silver bars tight in my fists. "When you're ready to kill Lowell, you hurt him for a long time. Maybe you can even save a little for me."

Ruelle laughed, and he was still laughing as he left the basement to begin the destruction of my world.

Chapter Fifteen

Xavier walked to the back wall of the cell, slid to the floor, put his face in his hands. I went and knelt beside him, but I could think of nothing to comfort him. I turned my attention to finding an escape route. I stood and jerked on all the silver bars. If I could find a loose one...nothing moved.

Heflin sat beside Xavier. Anson and Jacob crouched on the floor, too, in the middle as far from the silver as they could. Still, that amount of the metal hurt them. I closed my eyes and strained to touch the psychic thread binding me to Cody. He slept, unaware of the danger. With all the strength I could muster, I sent a warning, three words, over and over. Danger, Orion, Ruelle. I felt him stir, then wake in alarm. I tried to picture us in a cage. He'd received my message, but I didn't know if he understood.

"What happened, Hef?"

Heflin shrugged. "Lowell surprised me. He knocked me out and locked me up. When the vampire's people came, he ordered everyone to let them in. He'd been acting as a leader for weeks, so it was easy. Less than a minute. A hundred, maybe a hundred and fifty men—and one vampire. We had five weres out there, and they went down fast before they realized they were under attack"

The sound of footsteps came from above us as the men left. There'd be a guard up there. Ruelle wouldn't take any chances.

I whirled at a scraping sound. Elspeth stepped out of a shadowed corner. I'd looked all around the basement when I came in. How did she get in. She pranced on tiptoes toward the cage, her bare feet carefully skirting the bloody pool still spreading from Aaron Gannett's body.

I rushed to the bars. "Elspeth!" Did she walk past the guards upstairs? Had they ignored an old woman? Possibly. They weren't from Salvaje, so they wouldn't know the fear she inspired in the residents. Or was she already here, hiding? Waiting How? Where?

"Elspeth," I whispered. "Help us. Go to Orion. Tell him where we are. Warn the werewolves about Connor. He's going to kill them."

Elspeth giggled. "Nope. Not that way." She crossed her arms, and my hopes faded as I stared into her unfathomable eyes.

"Help us get out, then." I pushed my hands through the bars, pleading. "Can you find a key? Can you—"

Elspeth gave her head a vigorous shake, and beads clicked against one another like dry, rattling bones. She moved closer. "Angel knows what to do." Her mouth turned up in a mocking smile. "Daddy's girl knows what to do."

"Mad bitch," Anson's quivering voice came from behind me.

"Oh." Elspeth mocked and threw her arms wide. "Poor little wolf puppy. Angel took his mommy and daddy."

"Elspeth," I begged. "You may not be sane, but

you're not as crazy as you pretend to be. You think that vampire is going to let a witch like you live?"

"Elspeth dies when God says. Not vampire." Elspeth's eyes suddenly cleared, and her face suddenly became one of an unmerciful judge. "I know what I am, Maat Ferris. I accept my burden. Accept yours."

The moment of sanity faded. Elspeth stared around the room as if she'd never seen it before. She examined the rough blank walls and sang in a rough, grating voice. "Daddy's girl, daddy's girl, poor baby, poor angel."

I turned my back to the bars and slid to the floor.

Xavier's ravaged face stared at me. "Maat, what…?"

"I don't know." I hissed the words through my teeth. My hands curled into fists. What did Elspeth want of me? I thought I knew but I had no miracles in my pocket.

"Maat?" Jacob spoke with pain in his voice. The intensity of silver around us deeply affected him. "Maat? Your father."

Elspeth continued her hateful song. "Daddy's girl…daddy's girl."

I knew where the godawful conversation was heading. I'd discussed the obscenity with Ajax many times. "You think Elspeth is saying I'm one of you? Because I'm immune to werewolf bites. You're huddled like rabbits facing a rattlesnake—I'm sitting here with my skin on silver bars and—"

Elspeth's hands thrust through the bars. Her fingers dug into my shoulders with such force I screamed. She shrieked in my ear. "Do it!"

I won't say I never thought about it. I might be a werewolf because Mama conceived me right after one bit my father and before the change made him sterile. My mother had her fears, too. But nothing happened, and I'd never been anything but human. A human immune to werewolf bites. A human who sensed the monsters she killed from a distance. A human who could creep so close without them sensing her.

Xavier scrambled to me and grabbed Elspeth's hands, trying to loosen them. The instant he touched her, he jerked back. He rolled away, gasping for breath.

"Maat!" Jacob cried out with hopeless longing in his eyes. Anson leaned forward. Desperate, he too sought a miracle to save his werewolves from the fire. *They thought if Maat had a werewolf's strength...she could touch the silver wrapped cage they'd be free.*

Elspeth's fingers dug in like steel clamps. I remembered how she held the powerful young Anson. I twisted frantically to escape the mad woman's excruciating grip.

I screamed. "For God's sake. If I cou—"

Elspeth's fingers tightened. Spikes of agony spread. I couldn't breathe. My fingers clawed and tore at hers with no effect. Shoulder bones would break under the pressure soon.

Xavier crawled back toward me, determination on his face. Elspeth had inconceivable power. She could and would kill him if she believed her God gave the orders.

Ty shrieked in agony. Jacob and Anson's werewolf ears might have heard the actual sound, but Ty's torment, his anguish, stretched across my link to him. It tore through my mind and seared my very soul in a blaze of wildfire.

Elspeth released me.

I wallowed, drowning in the horrific sensation tearing through Ty's body, feeling the agony as my own.

Someone tortured one of my pack and I, his alpha, his protector, couldn't help him. I clawed at the rough, rock floor, tearing fingernails away. My own voice shrieked, mirroring Ty's agony. Over it all, I could hear the mad old woman's raucous voice taunting me. "Daddy's girl...poor little girl."

Werewolves. I'd smelled the stink of a fetid den, a hole reeking of blood-damp fur. I'd dodged razor-sharp claws and teeth. In my dreams I'd charged in for a kill wreathed in magical silver armor. Dreams quickly forgotten or deliberately set aside. Maat Ferris, the premier monster hunter, over 400 kills...I could not be what I had always hated.

"Liar!" Elspeth screamed. Her voice echoed inside my head. "Dreams," she mocked.

Forgotten memories crashed in. *I ran through the woods after the mercy killing of my mother. I ran from the militia. And I wasn't alone. A werewolf carried me, racing away from the cabins, away from certain death. More than one monster, taking turns, they brought me to Uncle Jake and Aunt Eleanor. My father? Perhaps. I had cried for my mother, and tears ran from amber wolf eyes as a long tongue licked my face.*

They'd laid a hot iron across Ty's back, as the vampires in New York had done to me. Fire seared through skin, flesh to the bone, agony so profound I couldn't give it a voice. Blind to everything else, I rolled and thrashed. Jacob suddenly had my arms, and Anson held my legs.

Ty's mind reached for me, called me, begged me for help.

So I went to him. I entered a living dream. I plowed through indeterminate time and space, my only thought of someone who loved me—who needed me. The cage bars gave way under my hands. I clawed, ran, climbed, gunfire. G surrounded me. I paid it no heed. All barriers vanished as I raced toward Ty. Then he was in my arms.

But they weren't my arms because they had fur and claws on the hands. I knew what had happened—and I hated myself. The humiliation of a freak—feared and despised as I had feared and despised. Oh, yes, I remembered my arrogant advice to Ava the vampire who so loathed what she'd become. Accept it or die, I'd told her.

Wrong! Accept it and kill.

A scream of rage and sorrow became a rolling howl as I released Ty, afraid I'd hurt him. I rolled across the floor. Jacob, now in full fur, wrapped me in his arms as great tears appeared on his chest when I lashed out and tore skin. I reached for and found sweet darkness.

Chapter Sixteen

"Maat!" Xavier's voice woke me. Was it time to…my eyes popped open. My whole body lurched. Every muscle twisted and burned in a mighty spasm. I jerked and flopped on a wooden floor that thumped and squeaked under the abuse. Finally, the tremors subsided to a thick vibration under my skin. Shivering, I lay on my back and held up my hands. No claws. Nothing but human fingers coated with a dried russet stain. The stench of the beast remained. My stench.

Xavier appeared over me. He laid a blanket over my trembling body and tried to take me in his arms. I jerked to escape him. I wasn't strong enough. Xavier squeezed tighter.

"Maat, I love you. Please…"

I gasped for breath but managed to sit up. I didn't have time to be weak.

"Ty?" I stared around.

Ty lay on a cot near the wall. A shaft of light from a high window infused the room with gentle amber light, as if struggling to take the edge from the violence inside.

"I'm okay." Ty spoke softly in a voice that told me he was anything but okay. A blanket like the one enfolding me draped his body. Xavier helped me to my feet, and I staggered over to kneel beside Ty.

"Where is everyone?" I asked Xavier.

"Jacob and Anson went to the Lycos to fight," he

said. "Heflin went to get Mylonas and my men. We have to get to the missile complex."

My mind spun. "How long…?"

"It took over two hours for you to change. Jacob and Anson said you were fighting it. Said it happens often during the first change. They held you. You cut them pretty bad. They healed, but…"

"Must have hurt like hell."

"They stayed between you and Hef and me. Kept me from you until you tore out the silver cage bars. If I could have held you, talked to you. They—"

"Saved your life. I'd have torn you to pieces." Memory of my violent dream tried to push in, but I halted it immediately. I did not have time for reflective pondering. No questions. No regrets. Later, I'd do it later. The crux of this journey, of my life, was in motion.

Xavier didn't argue with me. "I'll find some clothes." He left us alone.

I struggled to hold the rough blanket tight and still hug Ty. I kissed him and stroked his cheek and hair. His face carried marks of a beating, and his eyes had a look of dazed wonder—and a deep shadow of pain. Torn skin and welts twisted around his wrists and ankles like obscene bracelets where he'd struggled against his bonds. But his back…oh, God the burns, not as numerous as mine, but the same pattern.

"Parr did this?"

Ty nodded. "He'd seen you. He said he'd make us match."

"Did he…"

"No. He said I was too old for his taste."

If Ruelle didn't kill him, I'd make sure he died as a traitor… He would die in agony for what he'd done to

Ty. Why had he done it, though? Some unknown, complex hatred of Xavier? Or me? Frustration? He couldn't get to a young boy he had wanted. Maybe I'd let him stop screaming long enough to tell me.

Ty almost smiled. "You ripped the door off, your claws—"

"Stop. Don't talk about…stop."

"But they shot you. When you came in. With silver bullets. I saw. Silver. The bullets popped out when you changed back to human. Like magic." A tremor of boyish wonder shaded his voice. He glanced at the corner where a small brazier had tipped and scattered. The stench of smoke from cooling charcoal permeated the room. At least I couldn't smell myself anymore.

"I don't understand, Maat. I liked Lowell." This day had defeated Ty. I was barely hanging on myself. He stuttered over the next words. "Ruelle watched. He…told me he could make me a vampire too."

Ruelle watched because Ruelle liked to see humans suffer. And yes, he'd tell me about it to punish me. "Don't worry, sweetheart. I'm going to take care of the vampire—and the man."

Xavier returned with an assortment of clothing. And my weapons. My sleek Aries, the heavier, powerful impact Rudra, and my blessed silver blade. I stepped outside the room to dress and let Xavier help Ty do the same.

"No blood on these?" I called out to Xavier as I pulled on a pair of large men's pants and jerked the belt tight. I could hear no sound of other people in the building.

"It's a collection from several bodies. You threw one against a wall. Head was messy. Pants okay." Xavier laughed as he said it, his voice way too high-pitched for my soldier. "You took out those silver bars like sticks. You broke some guards…smashed…God, it was so… I love you, Maat."

"That's twice you've said those words in the last few minutes. Are you trying to convince me or yourself?" I went back into the room to help with Ty. I couldn't look him in the eye for fear of what I might see.

Xavier grabbed my shoulders and jerked me toward him. His hands cupped my face. "Let go, Maat. Your ghosts, Anolia and all the others. You're still alive. You think, after all of this, I care what shape your body takes?" His mouth found mine, and he crushed me in a ferocious embrace. *I'd become the thing I hated most in the world. Or I'd become the thing I was born to eventually become. And Xavier loved me.* I didn't hate Sabrina, Jacob, or poor Rachel, who died serving me. Anson Sewell was a pain in the ass, but I couldn't hate him either. If I had never met them…I always swore I'd kill myself if I became a were. I didn't have time. Philosophical musings later. Now I had to act. I had a great deal of killing ahead of me.

Ty was on his feet, but Xavier and I held him up. He could barely walk.

"Ty?" I touched his face, desperate to help him, to fix things.

"I'm fine," he lied to me. "I love you, too."

Yes, I knew. My body splendid. Whatever damage it sustained during the battle had healed. How amazing. I needed time to explore my new self.

"You said I took out the silver bars on the cage?" I asked Xavier as we eased Ty down the stairs.

"You bent them," he replied. "Made a big hole. Big

enough even Jacob got through. It did burn him. He's okay."

"Wish I'd seen that" Ty's voice sounded strained. "When you changed did you—"

"I didn't *do* anything. Not I remember. I'm not sure I could do it again if I tried. I don't want to try. It hurt, I lost all control, I slashed Jacob. If it had been you or Xavier…"

"It wasn't," Xavier said.

"Where's Elspeth?" I stared around but didn't expect to see her.

Xavier sneered. "I don't know. She was sitting in a corner laughing while you changed, but I don't know where she went after you finished and tore out."

A good thing. I had a few choice words for the old witch—and her god. I needed a chunk of quality time .

Before we left the building, we passed bodies of guards. Had I killed all of them? Some torn and bloody, others barely damaged, but dead, nonetheless. Their guns lay scattered around them. Silver bullets? Ty had said they shot me, but the bullets ejected from my body. Well, damn!

I suspect the enormity of what had happened would catch up with me eventually. If I'd seen the signs in my life, I'd rejected them, blinded myself to my nature, and cloaked all emotion with the single-minded intensity of a killer. Had I lived a more sedentary life, one without my Uncle Jake who taught me to kill or Elspeth who forced the change, it might never have happened. How many born werewolves could there be in the world, though? I didn't want to know.

A wain sent by Heflin waited for us outside. We headed to the Paradox. The human citizens of Salvaje had learned something dangerous was happening and wisely stayed indoors.

Heflin's guards stood watch at the Paradox. Maureen herself had to give the order to let us in. Ty wanted to go to his room, but he made us promise to come and get him before we left for the complex. Maureen met us at the door and grabbed him. Maureen's eyes flashed when she realized how much they'd hurt him. She cursed in shock when we told her who was responsible.

Heflin had sent her word to set the guard and not let Parr or Connor in, but he'd given no details. Despite Ty's protests, she sent a guard for a doctor. I left her talking to Xavier and went to wash and change clothes. When I came back down, Maureen stared at me with an odd intensity, so I knew he'd told her.

"Pretty strange, huh?" I waited for her reaction.

Maureen smiled and shrugged. "Perhaps. But this is Salvaje."

Salvaje. Where the bizarre and often unthinkable was part of everyday life. If it weren't so damned dry, I might say it was my kind of town. Might say.

Chapter Seventeen

Jacob met Xavier and me at the main entrance to the Lycos and led us down through a black scorched hall. His grim face told me I should expect the worst, but the hellish stink of burned fur and flesh gagged me. The smell triggered something inside, and I growled—which caused Jacob and Xavier to step back.

"Sorry," I said. I ruthlessly suppressed all emotion.

Heflin came in and headed straight for Xavier. "I've got two big trucks coming. We need to get to the complex fast. Come help me plan." What he meant was *Xavier* come plan for me.

"Come with me." Jacob reached for me with a hand, then stopped and drew it back.

"I'm still Maat, Jacob."

He nodded with a solemn face. Did he believe me? I wasn't so sure myself. Nothing felt different for me. I wondered if he wished to reassure himself of the bond between us, or if he wished to reassure me personally. I also wondered if he was seeing me as some special powerful and dangerous werewolf.

Jacob led me to where Anson knelt on his knees, crying over the charred bodies of at least sixty werewolves. Wails of pain came from down the hall.

"They will heal—eventually. We can from fire if it's not too bad," Jacob said.

Chains rattled, and across the room where Abban

Connor glared at us. They'd taken him alive. Four big weres stood guard where they'd secured him to steel loops in the wall. Connor might be strong enough to break the chains, but it would slow him down and give the guards time to catch him. Two humans had joined the were guards. I'd bet they carried silver.

There was no sign of men or flame-throwers—unless you counted the occasional smear of blood on the scorched floor.

Anson rose and walked to me, wiping his eyes as he came. His stocky body tense, he bared his very human teeth. "You're one of us now."

"Am I?" I wasn't sure what I was, but I damned sure wasn't going to let him define me or my life.

Anson looked away. He wouldn't meet my eyes. "But you can tolerate silver."

"Yeah. I can tolerate silver."

"I still hate you."

"That's okay, Anson. You have your reasons."

Tears formed in Anson's eyes again, and he turned and staggered away.

"Come," Jacob said. He drew me away down a hall and into an empty room and began to strip off his clothes. "You must practice changing. I'll go with you."

Oh, no. I didn't want that. I held out my hands pleading with him. "Jacob, maybe I shouldn't be in such a hurry. It's only been a few hours. I only did it once. And I don't remember exactly how I did it."

"You deny what you are? I know how it feels. You think if you don't ever change, you can have your old life back? It won't happen, Maat. Every one of us prayed for a miracle when we survived the attack that made us. Your father left his family. I left my wife and two children."

Oh, yes. My words to Ava thrown back at my own hypocrisy.

"Learn to control it, Maat, or it will control you. You found that first killing rage after the change yes, but you were selective. There was no werewolf madness in you. You tore out of that cage and headed straight for Ty. That is so extraordinary. Most of us go crazy the first time. We want to kill everything."

Jacob grasped my arms in his hands, and his fingers bit into flesh. He shook his head. "You…it's inside you. It was not something that *happened* to you. You didn't survive brutal wounds. Silver, Maat. You can touch and use silver. Everyone will be afraid of you. If you can't defend yourself, those who fear you will destroy you."

When I first met Cody, he told me werewolf blood tasted too dreadful for vampires to drink. If Ruelle, Emanis, or another vampire had ever bitten me, they would have known. Gunnar bit me and had spit me out like some vile poison. His reaction had given me the break I needed to survive. I never thought about it after that.

I had too much to learn about myself and not enough time. I stripped off my clothes. But how did I change? I closed my eyes and focused on one thing I knew well—werewolf! Those images, those memories were perfection. *The blast of my gun, the claws, roars and screams, mutilated bodies, my mother's half devoured face as she begged me to kill her.*

My heart raced. God, God, I could feel it growing larger, pumping harder, forcing blood through my veins. I'd never been aware of my body as I was at that moment.

I had no words to truly describe the sensation of

shape shifting. How did I endure the searing burn of muscle stretching? And the deeper thick ache of bone reforming into a longer, heavier, and a far denser structure. My body was creating body mass. from…what? My mind stayed clear throughout the process, though. Fur grew on my arms. It itched like hell. I fought the need to claw. Claws. My fingernails thickened to claws.

Above that, though it, t was no wild rage or urge to kill. I'm a volatile human, though, and I suspect I'd be the same as a werewolf. The question remained one of self-control. I'd lived a violent and painful life. Still, I had not prepared me for this transformation.

"That's enough," Jacob stopped me after the fourth change and change back. "You can wear yourself out. But you are amazing. So quick, way better than me."." I spent weeks in the pack's cage so I wouldn't hurt anyone.

We then practiced changing individual body parts. I sucked at the body parts thing. I was marginally effective with head and hands, not so good with anything else. When I did a partial, I had to fight to keep from losing control and making a complete shift.

I wiped the sweat from my forehead. Jacob seemed more worn than I was.

We dressed, but before we started out the door, he clenched his hands into fists and held them against his chest. "You were incredible in werewolf shape. Let's see how you are now as a human. Take my wrists and pull my hands away." The muscles in his forearms knotted. I grasped his wrists and while it took a bit of tugging, I managed to straighten his arms. He sighed.

"You're as strong—no, you're stronger than me.

That's amazing. Be careful until you're accustomed to it. You might hurt the wrong person."

Like Xavier. I'd been growing stronger every day in many ways since Memphis. Had my dying in Memphis been a trigger that began the change to true werewolf form? I doubted I'd ever know.

When we returned to the main hall, the sound of the wounded had faded to a murmur.

Orion approached, followed by Cody. Cody ran to me, and I embraced him.

"Did you lose anyone?" I asked Orion, staring over Cody's head.

"No. Cody woke me. I didn't know what was going on, though, or I might have helped here sooner." He shook his head. "When Jacob arrived and told us, we came through the underground and were able to join the fight." He hesitated but did speak. "I'm told you…how did this happen? I touch you. I knew there was more to you than I could see, but werewolf…never."

I silently shook my head. I couldn't answer his question.

****

The vampires sat in the far back of the long, lightproof truck, and some of the werewolves in human shape sat near the front. Heflin drove and Ty, Xavier, and I sat with the weres. Ty had insisted on coming with us. He'd been forceful, even demanding my Sparks revolver, not one of the newer ones available. He seemed to be stuck in a place halfway between the boy I knew and the man Salvaje had forced him to become. He was recovering too fast. I'd bet he'd received a dose of vampire blood. I hoped it had come from Cody or Orion and not a stranger.

Orion and Anson had brought thirty vampires and fifty werewolves. Giselle's Sergeant Patterson, now Major Patterson, had rounded up Xavier's human army. Heflin only found two trucks fit to make the trip, so they chose the best fighters among them. We left General Mylonas with the remaining troops to secure the city. We had no idea what we would face, but Heflin said we could get inside the complex without detection.

"Every building has a back door," Heflin told me before we left Salvaje. "Military complexes are no different. Once we originally got in, I found a way out. Good thing I hadn't had time to talk to anyone about it."

The unbearable afternoon sun warmed the truck body, and the werewolves and humans passed around water jugs in the dark oven. The vampires ignored the heat.

I needed to learn a few more things, even if it meant a dreaded public display. I sat by Jacob, and we again worked on a partial change. Jacob held out his hands. "Focus and imagine what you want your fingertips to be. Then move through your fingers and draw slowly back to your elbows. I drew a deep breath and called up my monster self. My fingernails thickened and curved. Ah, my fingers. My hands grew heavy as bone density increased. I had to stop there. My human arms weren't strong enough to carry werewolf hands. There had to be something else There was. I regrettably wanted—needed—to learn how to change and blend the were part of my body and human part. At that thought, the creature in me, that was me, tried to surge out. I managed to hold it in check.

I studied my changed hands. Thick pads of flesh covered my palms and fine, brown fur grew across the tops. Too bad the hair on my head wasn't like that. My claws clacked together in a sound I'd heard before. Many a werewolf had alerted me to its presence by that familiar telltale noise. I let go, and my hands were human again. "I need to work more on that."

Jacob frowned. "If you were born, not made. You...I wonder if you could have children."

"That's not possible. I'm a freak. A coincidence." No children. I stared at Xavier. "What would you do if I came up one day with a little werewolf puppy calling you daddy?"

Xavier's eyes narrowed in anger. "I would love your child as I loved my other children—and as I love its bitch of a mother."

I sighed. "Sorry. Not being human is new to me."

Xavier's anger remained. "What makes you so sure you're not human, Maat? You're not a scientist, not an expert in biology."

I leaned back and shut up. Humility wasn't one of my few virtues, and he'd put me in my place.

Ty sat beside Xavier. He caught his father's arm and laid his head on his shoulder. If such a childlike gesture bothered Xavier, he didn't let it show.

"You know what the worst thing in my life was, besides losing Mom and Lilly," Ty said. "I couldn't call you Father out loud. I'd be with Lilly, and you'd be doing something with Aaron, and I'd be so proud. I'd snuggle up and whisper in Lilly's ear, 'That's my daddy.' And she'd grin and say, 'It sure is, sweetie. And don't you forget it.' "

A wave of pain crossed Xavier's face. He sighed. "Stupid, so useless. Lilly didn't have any children. I think she liked to pretend you were her own. If you called me daddy, it might have spoiled her charade." He must have seen speculation in my eyes. "Yes, Maat, I loved Lilly. But she loved Aaron, not me." He sighed. "And he killed her. He killed…" He glanced at Ty and stopped. Ty needed to learn more about his own true mother, but Gannett, who ordered her killed, and Jenks, who carried out the order, were dead.

I needed to move. I crawled to the back of the truck with the vampires. Never in my life had I wanted the power to kill more than I wanted it then. Human or not, I longed to snatch life from Ruelle and Lowell Parr. Guns wouldn't do what I wanted. They'd have been my first choice once. Now I longed for torn flesh and running blood.

I went to Orion.

"May I help you, Sur…Maat?" Orion spoke softly. The truck gave a sharp jerk, and he caught my arm to steady me. I remained unsure of him. He'd shown great kindness a couple of times, but he was a vampire. No matter what happened to me, he remained vampire in nature.

"Orion, will you give me an honest answer to a question?"

"What makes you think I would not?"

"Because vampires lie. Ruelle told me that."

His perfect aristocratic face had an expression of amusement. "We do lie, Maat. For this day, though, I will be honest."

"What did you think of me when I charged into the arena to save Cody."

He drew a breath, then nodded. "When you entered the city, your presence challenged the monotony of time in the desert. Intrigued, I had you watched." His mouth tightened. "And I will admit to some…trepidation."

"Trepidation? Like anxiety? Or fear?"

"Yes, Maat. Fear. The older we are the greater the disquiet. Death stalks humans and werewolves, and they fear the specter. Vampires fear change. We can die. But if we are cautious, death may never find us. Change is far more dangerous."

I realized he'd drawn me dangerously close to him. All my sensory perception screamed *Danger! Vampire!* And here I was spouting life secrets. "I told you before, we don't belong here, Orion. You live, you have a life of sorts, but no purpose. Werewolf? I have no purpose. This world created humans, and they are the only true creators themselves with a form of procreation. Something else made us. Yes, I was born, but my father was, like all others, created. And all we do is kill. We destroy."

Orion smiled. So beautiful, so much expression. He went on. "Then came Anson's bungled challenge at the Lycos and your impressive victory. You were wading through the city, pushing all complacency aside. Your entrance to my arena and willingness to throw yourself into a deadly battle for a young, insignificant vampire astonished me. Did your courage draw Ruelle to you?"

"Big mystery there. I always felt Ruelle kept me around for amusement."

"Perhaps, but I can understand his interest in you. You have changed the dynamic of my city. Now you have changed the way I view werewolves. I am…intrigued."

I blew out a breath. That was too much for me to think about right then. "Listen, I've been practicing changing shape. I'm okay, but I need more. Is there anything you can think of to help me?"

Orion's eyes glowed. "I will try to give you a gift Ruelle and Emanis lost that night when they opened the tomb that should have been left buried deep in the earth. Perhaps with your new…aspect, you can learn."

He grasped my hand and entered my mind. An instant and he was there, just as I had entered the dreams of the vampire I slept beside in New York. Only this time, I walked in a waking dream. Orion allowed me to share his mind. I was no threat to a being of his stature. The New York vamps were puny creatures beside Orion. I was right about one thing. For two thousand years, the deepest of desires could not match his hunger. And yet it did not overwhelm him. It did not rule him. In an incredible shift of reality, we became shadows. The rolling metal walls contained us, but we drifted. Where? I didn't know.

—*I cannot walk into the sun*— Orion whispered in my mind. —*But I can go to this place where no human, no werewolf, can see me. Ruelle cannot find me, nor can any other vampire born to a different life in the last thousand years*—

—*But I am here with you*— I, too, spoke without words. So easy, as if I'd done this all my life.

—*You are, and that is a wonder beyond all wonders. I think you could come here on your* own now *you have discovered its nature. I was so shocked when you told me of walking in a vampire's dreams in New York. Perhaps you are one of the* ancient *dead* races that *created us born again. Forgive me, but I, like Jacob, would wish you to bear children*—

—*And then what would I be? The mother of another race of monsters. The old race died, Orion. I told you, this world belongs to humans.* I've told you several times and my situation has not changed my mind. *I should have never been born to this—*

Orion sighed. *—You are right. We don't belong—*

We came back to the world around us. I had a new sense of my body. Swift and deadly, pure clean knowledge of the werewolf shape skimmed along my nerves.

My ability to sense weres, to move close without detection, was conceivably a natural consequence of my true nature. I'd bet the enormous amount of vampire blood they forced me to swallow in New York had changed me too. Only time would tell how much—and I didn't have time.

I left Orion and climbed back toward Xavier and Ty. Ty, wide-eyed, reached out to touch me.

"What?"

"I saw you." He grinned, and it lifted my spirits. "You faded, were gone, then you came back."

"An illusion, sweetie. Just an illusion." I turned to Xavier. "So, what's the plan? Hope it's better than some of mine."

Xavier wrapped his arms around me. "Oh, I thought we'd make sure we faced overwhelming, insurmountable odds, then charge in fangs and claws sharpened with guns blazing and see what happens."

I laughed. "Well, usually works for me. Except when it doesn't."

Chapter Eighteen

Sabrina cradled the dying child in her arms. Jenny wouldn't make it through the night.

"But why?" Eddie cried.

"It's the werewolf," Sabrina told him. She had seen it many times. "It's a disease. Most of us die when we're first bitten. Others, like me, survive." At least Jenny wasn't in pain. Sabrina laid the sleeping child on the soft bed they'd made for her. She filled a needle with enough morphine to kill a grown human.

"Where did you get…" Eddie asked but stopped before he finished. He'd realized the insignificance of the question. In the brief time they'd been together he'd recognized the aggressiveness of her nature and her need to protect her adopted family. He would fight, but her strength and ferocity dramatically increased their chance of survival.

She answered his question. "The gun dealer, Eddie. He robbed a hospital in Cincinnati. He is…was an addict." Fatigue filled her voice. She'd gone to the dealer's warehouse, killed him and his guards and taken the drug. She had no regrets about the thieving dealer, but his guards caught her, and she had to kill both. Her personal escalation to deadly violence surprised her. It wasn't casual killing. There was no other way. She would protect her own pack.

An enormous ground shaking thunder had startled

them out of sleep two nights ago. A massive explosion had blasted away most of the St. Louis Bridge. No individual or group took credit for the deed. Rumors had circulated of the battle of Memphis and the destruction of the bridge there. That act of violence along with so many others allowed the Mississippi River to run virtually unimpeded from its headwaters in Wisconsin and Minnesota to the Gulf of Mexico.

Jenny woke screaming at the blast. Despite all their efforts, she involuntarily changed shape repeatedly, wearing the life from her small body. She stopped before morning, but by then, she couldn't lift her head. Her screams had given way to woeful cries of pain. Sabrina had seen it before, the end stage of a failed change, the body's final and fatal battle of the werewolf disease.

Jenny woke for a moment when Sabrina injected the morphine. She smiled up at Sabrina. "Mommy."

"Yes, sweetheart." Sabrina stroked her hair. "Mommy loves you."

Joe cried softly. Terrell held him as they huddled on a mattress together, waiting. The morphine calmed Jenny, and she slept.

"How did it happen, Joe? Who made you werewolves?" Eddie laid a hand on the boy's shoulder... "Do you remember? I never asked you because I knew you missed your mom."

"My uncle." Joe's voice quivered. "He came in with some others. Mom sent us to our rooms. I heard her crying. Then my uncle came in with one of them. Said it wouldn't hurt, but it did. Mommy screamed. Me and Jenny too." He sobbed, and Eddie gathered him in his arms. "I thought it would be good after we ran away."

"I'm sorry, Joe. I shouldn't have asked you."

Joe sniffed. "It's okay. They took us…We went to live in the woods. I missed school."

"Did you live in a town before you went into the woods?" Sabrina asked.

"Washington."

"New Washington?"

"Yeah. I liked it there. My dad, he went away. He was in the army. Mom said he would come back for us. I guess he won't be able to find us now." Resignation sounded in his young voice. "We were sick for a while. Then Mom took us, and we ran away."

"Why did your mother run away?" Sabrina asked. She wiped a cloth across Jenny's fevered forehead.

"Oh, she was afraid of the vampire."

"What?" Sabrina jerked and Jenny stirred.

"The vampire," Joe repeated. "The leader, the big one who told all the werewolves what to do."

Sabrina shuddered. "Did you ever see the vampire?" she asked.

"Once," Joe said.

"What did he look like?"

"Like a man…I don't know."

"Did he have long yellow hair? Did it curl on his shoulders?"

"Oh, yes. I remember. And black shiny boots."

"Ruelle." Sabrina spoke softly.

"Yes. That's what my uncle called him."

Jenny coughed, and blood trickled from her mouth. Sabrina wiped it away.

"She's going to…" Joe bit his lip. "Some kids at the farm…they died…will she…will I?" He stared wide eyed at Sabrina.

"No. You seem strong enough,"," Sabrina reassured

him. She wished she had the surety she offered him. He might yet succumb when he reached puberty.

Jenny stopped breathing after midnight. She'd called Sabrina mommy one last time, then fallen into a coma. The next morning, they carried her out of town to a cemetery on a hill, high over the Mississippi River. There was only one stonemason in East St. Louis, and he carved a small simple headstone. He refused their gold when they gave her age.

Like most graveyards, this one had almost gone to wilderness. They found a spot on the green apron of a hill where they could see the river's bright ribbon, winding south. A whiff of a breeze touched them as Eddie dug a resting place for his foster daughter.

"I don't want to leave her here," Joe cried softly.

"She isn't here," Eddie said. His voice carried pain. "She's with your mother."

"In hell," Joe sobbed.

Eddie stopped digging. "Who told you that?" His voice grew cold and tight.

"My uncle." Joe sniffed. "He wasn't one of us. He brought them people for money."

Eddie went back to his work, his body quivering as if he feared he'd break down. Sabrina realized she could love the man. He called up the longing she thought she'd lost long ago. Her awareness of his quiet nature and incredible strength grew each day.

They lowered the pine crate with Jenny's blanket-wrapped body in the hole. After they covered it, Eddie took Joe in his arms, and they knelt beside the stone. Sabrina and Terrell knelt beside them.

Eddie lifted Joe's tearstained face. "Nothing happened to you, Jenny, or your mom was your fault.

Nobody knows better than God. My daddy was a preacher. You know what he told me when my little brother died? He told me all children go to Heaven, because they don't have time to grow up and be bad."

"But we……they made us bad." Joe thin body shivered.

"That's not true. Is Sabrina bad? Was your mom?" Eddie held the sobbing boy in his arms.

"Now," Eddie said as Joe's crying eased. "You pray with me. Our Father, who art in heaven…"

After a few hesitant words, Joe joined him. When they finished, Eddie looked at Terrell.

Terrell nodded. "Dear God, please look after my new sister, Jenny…and her mom."

Sabrina's turn. She had long since given up prayer. Her sorrow had turned to rage. The beast in her rose close to the surface. She drew a deep sobbing breath. "Dear God in heaven, if you love the children of this earth, please help Maat Ferris send that vampire to hell."

Chapter Nineteen

I rode in the lead truck for a while. Heflin led us on a torturous path through the mountains. Dry rock and sand, these were so dreadfully far from the gentle treed slopes I called home. The weres had to get out, change shape, and clear the road of fallen rock several times. Heflin navigated one black hole of an amazingly clear tunnel, too. Our journey ended at fifty-foot high, steel doors neatly set into a stone wall, sheared from a buff and brown-streaked mountainside. Heflin went to a small box set in the door itself.

"This worked before. He alternately cursed and prayed as he pushed buttons inside the panel. Had we come this far, only to have this steel wall deny us entry? That would mean go back fora front door assault. It would kill so many of us And we'd be too late.

My eyes widened as the massive doors suddenly split in the middle and slid back with nothing more than a whisper of metal against metal. Automatic doors were things from another age like the missiles we were determined to destroy.

"Where's the power for this place come from?" I asked Heflin.

"Atomic generator under the vault," he replied. "Run the whole place for at least two hundred years. I was—am—planning to string electrical lines to Salvaje after we destroy the missile controls. There's a lot of stuff in this place that can help us."

I sighed and shook my head. Before the war, atomic generators powered the great cities like New York. No one had thought to bury them in the ground under a secret complex like this one, so they made perfect targets. By 2040 they ceased to exist, and the ground for miles around them poisoned with radioactivity. We entered and unloaded in a hollow, high-ceiling chamber large enough to hold a dozen trucks.

"I'd turn on the lights," Heflin said as he and the others lit the lanterns. "But I don't know what kind of signal it might send. Opening the door might have done it too, but we have to take a chance." Heflin spread a thin printed plan sheet on the back of a truck under a lantern. Xavier immediately focused on what was before him. Uncle Jake had called such things poly-sheets, and there were plenty of them in the arms bunker under our house.

"I found these inside the complex a week ago." Heflin stood. "Sent them home with the supply truck so I could study them later. That bastard Parr's never seen them. Maat, you think there's more than the one vamp in there?"

"Not likely. Ruelle has never trusted another vampire. He's free of Emanis now, so I don't see him hooking up with another. You should ask Orion, not me."

Heflin grunted. "But he does have men, and they probably have silver—or more flame throwers. Don't think he has any werewolves, either. Connor only had a few, and he needed them for the attack on the Lycos."

"He has none from Salvaje," Anson snarled from behind me. "All my people are accounted for—living and dead." He'd avoided me since we spoke in the Lycos. He'd put aside his mourning, and now he stared at me with a smug look on his face.

I understood. I was not immune to suffering myself, but I've survived worse things than being a werewolf. If I had to be a monster, I preferred being a werewolf rather than a vampire. I may have fur and claws, however I could watch the sun rise. I wasn't my usual sarcastic self, but I'd recover—maybe. Then, if we survived, I'd go stomp Anson's arrogant, hairy ass.

Heflin threw his hands up as if to encompass the darkness surrounding us. "This is an evacuation assembly point, in case of an accident. Probably filled with vehicles once."

Xavier spoke, his finger gliding confidently over the poly-sheet. "These lines are escape tunnels leading into the main complex. We're going to use this one. Mostly because it's already open." He grunted. "At least on this end." He rolled the sheet up then unrolled another one. "This is the hub, where the fight will probably be, but this thing has layers down below, and we may have to dig some men out." According to the plans, the missile complex spread out like a wheel, with each separate launch room vault at the end of each spoke.

Heflin pointed out more. "The complex goes deep, layered like bowls stacked on top of one another. The lower levels are mostly storage. That's how we can blow up the missile controls and save the rest. They built these chambers and tunnels to survive a hell of a blast and it's why we needed the equipment to get them open. Couldn't blow a hole in the door. If we'd known about this escape route, it would have saved so much time And lives."

Heflin laid a hand on Xavier's shoulder. "Okay, Colonel, you're soldier in charge now. Get everybody where you want them and give the orders."

"The heaviest arms are on the outside," Xavier said. "Earlier I sent a small force to hide there. At the signal, they'll attack then try to stay alive. That will hopefully draw attention from what's going on inside."

"A diversion." Orion spoke, and we all jumped. He'd been gone for an hour, going inside, scouting our soon to be battleground.

""You are correct. Almost all the armed men are outside," Orion said. "Your escape tunnel opens into an empty room. It will be dangerous. This complex is excessively large but mostly empty, with many hiding spots for ambushes."

Heflin smoothed his hand over the map. "Sure is. The main complex alone could house the population of Salvaje. Looks like the original residents all up and left. Probably plague snuck in, and they tried to outrun the sickness."

"There are armed men inside," Orion said. "They all wear brown uniforms, but there are other men and women who do not look like soldiers."

Heflin sighed. "Technical people I bet. We had some there, too. And our guards. We'll need to find them—if they're alive."

"Did you see Ruelle? Or Parr?" I asked Orion. I had one thing on my mind now. It was not the battle for control of missiles.

"Maat." Xavier grasped my arm. "If you take on Ruelle—"

I jerked away. He shut up.

"I, too, urge you to be cautious," Orion said. "I did not see Ruelle or Parr. If you wait for me, together we—"

I wouldn't argue. "We're losing time. Let's get it over with." I had serious doubts about Orion's resolve to kill Ruelle if he got to him before me. I'd heard his words filled with rare vampire emotion and knew he still loved Ruelle, despite the danger.

Heflin left us, and Xavier studied the plans.

I could see the problem. The narrow escape tunnel would only allow two men to walk side-by-side. Once the fighting started, we might not be able to get our fighters into the battle fast enough. Before Xavier could say anything, Orion spoke up.

"My people and I should go first. We will be your shield. Bullets, even silver, can only incapacitate. And we are swift."

"Bullets can't, but flame throwers can," Xavier pointed out.

"I saw none of those."

Xavier stared down at the plans. Then he said, "Okay, Orion, you and your vamps go out first. Hit them fast, we'll be right behind you. Immediately head for the front door and try to keep the soldiers outside from coming in. That's going to be critical. As soon as I can, I'll send reinforcements. How many do you think it will take to help you hold them back?"

"He won't need many," Heflin said, stepping back into the light. He carried a leather satchel. "I know my way around the place. Give me one hour to get in and work to disable the automatic controls on the doors." He waved a rolled-up poly-sheet at us. "We'll set our watches. If I can shut the front door and lock the troops outside, the smaller doors inside won't close and trap you. Then I'm going to look for our people."

"Not alone." Xavier shook his head. "What if you

run into—"

"I'll go with him," Jacob said.

I understood. The Salvaje weres were under Anson's control, and Jacob belonged to me.

Heflin knew the pecking order. "That okay with you, Maat?"

"Yeah." I grabbed Jacob and hugged him.

Jacob bent his head and whispered in my ear, "I will care for him."

I released him. He'd misunderstood my gesture. It wasn't Heflin I worried about. I worried for him. "Okay, but watch out for yourself, too."

They checked watches, then Heflin and my werewolf faded into the darkness. Before he went, Heflin asked everyone to try not to kill anyone who wasn't armed or immediately surrendered. Xavier agreed they could sort the civilians out later. He gathered us together and described the brown-shirts, Gannett's regular troops, to the Salvaje invasion force. Xavier's personal troops wore his white eagle mark on their shirts.

We stood in the darkness and waited. The soldiers checked their ammo and guns. Xavier walked among them, talking quietly. I'd gone a couple of times and watched him train them. He was as comfortable there as I was comfortable alone in the woods. I was right. They were his men, not Salvaje's. Orion had given him money. What exactly had Orion paid for?

The weres stripped off their clothes. They'd go through the tunnel in human form, but they needed to change fast as they emerged. I had to save shape shifting for a surprise.

I eased up to Xavier, and he put his arm around me.

"I know you're worried, but I have to get Ruelle." I

leaned against him. "I can at least disable him, hurt him." I laid my cheek against his throat to feel his heartbeat.

He held me tight, but he didn't say anything. *He didn't say what we both knew, he might"* Unfortunately, it was a possibility I'd lived with for years.

Ruelle could kill me.

Ty leaned against the truck not far away. He stayed there, deep in thought until Xavier lined us up to go in. He didn't argue when Xavier put him near the end where it would be a little safer.

The vampires entered the tunnel, then staggered sets of men and weres followed led by Xavier. Anson brought up the rear. Xavier didn't give me orders, but I made sure I was in the first wave. Far enough behind him I hoped he wouldn't be thinking of me when he burst into battle. And enough room for me to maneuver if I sensed Ruelle. I'd become used to vamps in Salvaje. This was Ruelle, though. I knew him so well. If I concentrated, possibly I could separate him from Orion's vampires.

The tunnel was a mile long and sloped down, then turned up. Its walls glowed with a soft light, and occasionally the sound of machinery vibrated through the steel tube.

We crowded into a metal-walled room, our attack staging area. The werewolves commenced changing shape, and they produced a whirlpool of energy that almost dragged me with them. I had to fight to stay in human form.

Xavier nodded, and Orion threw open the door. The vampires rushed into the room. Firing began immediately. A few minutes later, I emerged and joined the battle. We entered a massive high-ceiling open space and ran into a squad of troops. They weren't exactly waiting for us, but we must have triggered some warning. Then the clamor of screams and roars added to gunshots made hearing impossible.

I'd seen the plans and understood the pattern of the complex. I could locate the emergency stairs. I'm sure Heflin cut off the elevators. Six corridors led away from the expansive battle room. Gannett's brown-shirts fell back, firing as they went. No silver, so the werewolves led the way and men used them as shields. When bullets hit the living shields, they staggered, but when one fell back another took his place. The vampires had disappeared. It would be a running battle from corridor to corridor, room to room, in a massive place designed to hold thousands of humans.

I wasn't so overwhelmed I couldn't see Xavier's orderly hand in the battle. With his training, men and weres worked together. They'd have the brown-shirts of President Gannett's army under control very soon.

And me? For some inexplicable reason I'd not been in position to fire a single shot. No matter which way I moved, someone, werewolf or human, barred my way. Xavier's doing? We'd have to talk...fight...arguelater. Xavier inspired amazing loyalty, though. His adoring troops might have decided on their own to protect his lover.

At least the few civilians we encountered had the good sense to drop and lie flat on the floor.

The thunder and echoes of gunfire slowed. Xavier shouted orders in the lull, demanding surrender. A sizable number of the brown-shirts threw down their arms. I think they remembered him from New Washington. Still no sign of Ruelle or Parr, but it was a big place. I hadn't expected it to be easy.

All firing in the immediate area ceased, leaving only echoing sounds from the corridors. A single shot. Xavier crouched on the floor. A great splash of red stained his chest.

Memory tore through me.

Thoughts at Avalon while forming my dreadful disastrous rescue plan. I had thought he was big and tough, but one bullet could change that. My words in Fort Smith when I surrendered to him. "I love you. I love you, and I hate it. And yes, sometimes I hate you." Terror seared me like I'd dropped in boiling water. I could not bear that loss.

I raced for Xavier, but another beat me there. A female vampire, one who came with Orion, appeared beside him. On her knees, she had her wrist slashed and forced to his mouth. I knelt beside them. Xavier choked and fought her, but she held one of his arms, and I gripped the other.

"Drink it," I screamed at him.

Ty appeared and straddled Xavier's heaving body. "Drink," he snarled.

Xavier swallowed.

"Orion said I should watch for him," the vampire said in a quiet voice. A few long minutes later, she withdrew her wrist. Xavier licked his lips and breathed deeply. His mouth and throat matched the dark crimson blossom on his shirt. His chest heaved as he gasped for air. Deep gulps told me he would most likely live.

I couldn't stand watching. Too close. My hands shook, my body shook.

"Go," the vampire said to me. "I'll stay with him."

I stood and staggered toward the dwindling sound of battle. My mindreeled from almost losing Xavier—and the knowledge vampire blood couldn't cure everything. If he'd suffered a massive wound, she'd only bought him time. Thinking of him made me careless, and I ran around a corner straight into two brown-shirts. Surprised the hell out of all three of us, and we went down in a heap.

My right hand banged the floor hard. I lost my grip on the Rudra. I grappled with the two men, and one relieved me of the Aries. I had a hand on my knife by then. I sliced them both, and when they released me, I rolled to my feet, and raced away. I had to leave my guns behind.

The crack and ping of bullets hitting metal followed as I turned a corner. I ran on through a door and onto a balcony platform overlooking a darkened room. The room had the feel of a cavern. I hit the rail with my stomach, and momentum carried me over.

Twisting and grabbing, I caught part of the rail, but I had to release my knife and use both hands. I wasn't going to hang there long. The knife clattered to the floor, twenty feet below.

The sound of feet pounded down the hall toward me. Suitable time for practice. I changed to werewolf shape, sucked in a breath of air, howled—and let go.

I hit the floor, feet first. My muscles absorbed the shock as the howl echoed in a dark, hollow, steel cave. Clawed toes scraped the metal floor, and my hands slapped down to keep my balance. Damn I was good. Still a werewolf, but at least a competent werewolf.

I grabbed my silver knife and quickly moved into the shadows, raking off the remains of my clothes as I went. My torn boots had fallen when I changed, and my toe claws ripped them apart. No one followed me. Fangs, claws, and silver would have to do until I retrieved my weapons.

I had only studied the complex's general layout, and this area seemed different. Once I left the balcony area, I entered darker, smaller hallways. I lifted my muzzle and sniffed. Vampire. A particular vampire at that. He'd walked that hall. I didn't need to sense him. With the were shape, my heightened sense of smell allowed me a scent trail. All I had to do was follow—except the odor came through vents along the hallway, and I couldn't pinpoint the source.

I heard voices, and two women in white lab jackets hurried out of a room and almost ran into me. One screamed and fainted. The other froze in terror, body quivering, mouth and eyes wide, she stood and stared.

Good. I changed back to human shape.

"Strip, sweetheart," I said cheerfully to the one who was in shock, but conscious. "I need some clothes. You can keep the coat."

In minutes, I had her shirt and pants, and she wore only the coat. By that time, the other one had come around, and I had her take off her white coat too. "Wave it in front of you,get down tell anyone you meet you're surrendering," I told them. "Tell them Maat said not to hurt you."

The pants and shirt were too big and too short for me, but I needed to stay in human shape. I remembered Orion's physic lesson in the truck. Dangerous because I had no guide as I had then.

I dropped out of the worldas easily as opening a door. It appeared different without Orion there. I could see the room around me, doors, and a set of stairs down the hall. They had faded into a fine mist, though. And there was Ruelle. A steady white flame shining through. I dropped back into reality. I knew the way. I eased down the hallway, up the set of stairs, more hallway, and finally I heard them. Ruelle and Parr. No matter what the outcome of the next few minutes, I knew I could kill Parr. I came to an open door, peeked around the corner, and scanned the room.

Chapter Twenty

Parr and Ruelle stood with their backs to me, watching a wall of screens showing multiple rooms in the vault. I had to resist the urge to stare at the moving pictures. Heflin was right, a lot of splendid stuff in this place.

Desks sat inrows across the room, bolted to the floor, for the men and women who once worked and lived here. I slipped in the open door and behind one desk. I could see a few of the screens from my position.

Heflin's men were herding men and women, the technicians from New Washington, out of the center while the vamps helped disarm the remaining soldiers. I suspect Heflin wanted to persuade some of the techs to stay and bring Salvaje into the future.

"Heflin's setting explosives," Parr said.

"It's too late," Ruelle told him. "The important ones are set, and their vaults resealed." He laughed softly. "Ah, but we have a guest. Maat?"

Shit. I wasn't surprised. If I could feel him, he could feel me. I stood, and then dropped. The bright pain of a bullet slammed into my shoulder. It wasn't silver but dear God it hurt. I rolled and screamed. Another scream sounded. Parr's.

My body began to heal around the bullet wound.

Ruelle hovered over me. "Maat?"

"I'm okay," I told him. "It grazed me. Been shot

worse." I held a hand over the bullet hole in my sleeve. The wound healed itself, but the bloody shirt covered that little wonder.

As Ruelle lifted me to my feet, I saw Parr on his knees, holding his hand close to his body. His wrist bent at a sharp corner angle. Tears ran down his face as he jerked in great silent sobs.

Ruelle relieved me of my knife. He tossed the silver blade to the side of the room.

"I can't say I'm surprised, my darling hunter, but. You are so incredibly resourceful. B how did you do it?"

"Got one of the bars loose." I rubbed my hand across my breasts. "A real tit squeezer though. Once I got Anson and Jacob out, no problems." I needed to keep him off guard without making him suspicious. He wouldn't pay attention to my clothes, but he might notice my bare feet. Ruelle knew my threats and me, so hehad all the confidence in the world that if he were careful, I couldn't kill him.

"Ruelle, you and I have been playing this game for years."I tried to imitate Xavier's *let's be reasonable* tone. "We both know you could kill me anytime—but you haven't."

Ruelle frowned. "No. I want you with me. Beside me. Ihaven't been able to determine how to do it yet. I want your cooperation. I thought keeping your lover and friends hostage…"

"You want me. But you sent me to steal that equipment. I almost died—"

"I knew you wouldn't. An oracle told me about you a thousand years ago. I've waited so long."Ruelle's fingers brushed my cheek.

"Oracle?" My mind went to Brother Christopher and

his horribly correct prophesies.

"The oracle said a queen would stand at my side one day. That could only be you, my wonderful Maat." He laughed. "Would you like to tear Lowell apart? It could take us weeks."

"Sounds good, but we don't have weeks—at least not here." I nodded at the screens. "And it's broad daylight outside."

"Yes but let me show you a bit of pre-war technology." Ruelle led me to a wall where a bulky, man shaped white suit hung on hooks. "I tried it earlier." He lifted the helmet from another hook and rubbed his hand across the tinted faceplate. "It could use a bit more protection here."

We stood there for a moment, and then he replaced the helmet on the hook. "You won't come with me, will you?"

I shook my head.

"What shall I do with you, Maat? I cannot bear to kill you."

"I suggest you put your fancy suit on and run. I can't stop you. Orion might be able to, though. He might be here soon."

Ruelle laughed. "Yes. But he won't kill me. Do you believe that?"

"Yes, Ruelle. I believe."

"He might imprison me though. Very well, I'll go, but you'll see me again. I'd force you, take you with me, but much as I love you, I can't trust you. You may keep Lowell. I'm sure you'll find a suitable way to punish him."

I held my arms at my sides, relaxed, waiting for my moment.

"Do you love me, Ruelle? What's love to you?"

"Some night, when we have more time, I'll explain. You know, though, we've already programmed one missile to fire at Seattle and one for New Washington. We resealed the vaults, so none of Heflin's explosives will touch those controls."

A sick knot settled in my stomach. As Ruelle lived, humans died.

Three steps led up to the bank of screens and I stepped up two steps. That put my head on the same level as his. I crooked my finger at him, and he came closer. I laid my hands on his shoulders, and he wrapped his arms around my waist.

I licked my lips and smiled. "How can you be so beautiful and so evil?"

"It's pleasant to have you look in my eyes, Maat. Hold your breath and let me have one kiss before I go."

"Sure." I drew a deep breath. "Ah...Lowell's trying to pick up the gun."

Ruelle turned his head to look atat Parr.

I changed into a werewolf.

My muzzle hadn't completely changed but was long enough to encircle his neck. I tore out his throat. With all the strength I could muster, I dug my claws into his shoulder joints, trying to tear off his arms. At the same time, I pushed toward him to knock him off balance, and we fell to the floor. With the secondwide bite, I locked down on his spine. Only his death or mine would release my jaws.

Ruelle's hands grabbed at me, trying to tear me loose. My claws had worked their way deep into his shoulder joints, but he wrapped his arms around my back to crush my spine and tear me in half. I bit harder, and my teeth penetrated vertebrae.

One of his hands suddenly came up and caught one of mine at the wrist, then released it and moved above to my head. His fingers stroked my hair, moved over my ear and down my muzzle…a caress. The other hand lay on my back, holding me close against him. He wasn't trying to escape.

Ruelle's spine crunched. I had crushed it with my powerful werewolf jaws. He stopped moving. My enemy and my savior—the vampire was dead.

I pushed up to my hands and knees. Thick sluggish vampire blood ran from his throat and puddled in his tawny curls. The crimson fluid of his incredibly long life soaked my clothes. His eyes had none of Emanis' wide-eyed shock. Had he expected to die that way?

The sound of a clip sliding in the pistol made me look up. Lowell had found his gun. One clip lay at his feet, and I'd bet the one he loaded held silvers. One handed, yeah, but the barrelwas steady, braced in the crook of the arm with the broken wrist.

I threw myself away as he pulled the trigger.

The silver grazed my hip and I howled, but I kept moving. The next shot hit my foot. Then I was behind one of the desks. He followed me, firing two more rounds. Did that model carry seven or eight shots? My hip and foot burned with a powerful intensity—and they were healing. Not as fast as the regular lead bullet had healed, but I'd live if he didn't put one in my heart or brain. I'm not sure I'd survive that.

A bullet smashed into the desk. Five shots. I held my ground. Parr's breath came in gasps, and the pistol's recoil had to be taking a toll on his broken wrist. I ignored everything, jumped out, and rushed at him.

A silver bullet sliced through my side. Parr screamed. Finger bones snapped as I twisted the pistol out of his hand and tossed it over my shoulder. I stood and watched him while my body healed.

Parr stared at the video screens. Did he expect help from anyone out there?

I laughed at the horrified expression on his face when he stared back at me. How did I appear to him? A werewolf where there had been a woman? I'd bet I sounded like a wild animal—or maybe the monster I had become.

The monster closed in. I tossed him around first, like a cat with some small unfortunate creature captured and played with before dinner. I broke his legs, then I shredded his clothes and raked him with my claws, enough to make him bleed. I stood and watched him wallow on the floor, smearing blood, begging, and crying, I searched the rooms around the screen room until I found a locker with clothes. A shirt and pants, too big, but Lowell was wearing a belt he soon wouldn't need. I laid the clothing on one of the desks. It was time. I changed back to human form so I could talk. I went to him and dropped to my knees beside him. "Does it hurt, Lowell?"

He suddenly grew silent. Shock hadn't set in yet, but it wouldn't be long.

"Surprised you, didn't I?" I rubbed my side. It had already healed. "That last one smarted. Look at me. A werewolf that can take silver. How about that? Didn't you guess? You had all the pieces of the puzzle. It's okay, though. I had it inside me, and I didn't know."

"Please." Parr choked on the word.

"Please what?" I had no pity, no mercy for him. Too

many had suffered and died. There wasn't much justice in my world, but this one time...I held up my hands. Claws sprouted, and I stopped the change at my elbows. A moment to savor and I wanted it to be human—or almost human.

He stared up at me heaving and gasping for breath. With one forefinger claw, I tore his shirt's ragged remains aside and opened the skin of his chest. With the utmost patience, I dug and worked my hand under his ribsinside. His shrieks came out as mouse-like squeals.

Just before his eyes glazed over in shock, I grasped his frantic, beating heart in my hand. Then I remembered something. "Brother Christopher warned you, didn't he, Lowell? When he came to New Washington for Anolia. *You'd get your heart's reward*, he told you. Now here it is. You've earned it." Breathing in the smell of blood and terror, the complete change overcame me, and Maat the werewolf, Suriel the Angel of Death, squeezed, twisted, and tore Lowell Parr'sbeating heart from his chest.

Chapter Twenty-One

A small sink by the lockers proved adequate for washing once I changed back to human form. I dressed in my new-found clothes. I wished I felt triumphant. I wished I could gloat. Instead, I went to the vampire who had walked through my life for so many years. Maybe Ruelle had not driven me insane like Gannett and others because I wasn't completely human.

I knelt beside his body. Blood puddled around him where I'd crushed his throat and spine. Yes, I had loved him. Yes, I'd hated him with the blackest hate. I remember how I had to feed lethal drugs to tortured and dying men, women, and children at the farm to give them peace.

I remembered the nights he'd given me blood and comforted me after he brought me, near death, from New York. He would appear and disappear in my life, always causing trouble, but often with incredible tasks for me. Of all the vampires in the world this one I might have called my own. Of all the vampires in the world I wished it could have been different. I brushed a strand of that golden hair from his face.

Then I mourned. I wailed my pain out loud to the uncaring universe until the weight on my soul reduced me to racking sobs. God help me, I wanted him back. I did what I had to do for the sake of those I loved, and I would do it again to save them—but I wanted him back.

Sometime during my mourning my stalwart warriors burst into the room.

Xavier had me in his arms. I glanced over his shoulder and saw Orion. I wanted to say I was sorry, to beg forgiveness. He came to me and laid a hand on my cheek. I heard his voice in my mind.

—Your sorrow is mine. Be at peace, little sister—

There was nothing I could say to that.

Xavier led me out of the room which was fine until I remembered he'd been shot. He'd found a clean shirt somewhere and I pawed at the buttons. "You shouldn't be—"

Xavier caught my wrists. "I wasn't hit, damn it. I threw myself down to avoid a bullet. Next thing I knew I had vampire blood forced down my throat and—"

"But your shirt?" My voice rose.

"Not my blood. I'd helped a wounded man."

"Oh." I sighed. Screw up again.

"Let's go. We'll talk about it later." Xavier released my wrists. "I want to hear the part about how we don't have to take care of each other again."

I didn't. I'd already told him I listed hypocrite as one of my faults. That covered the situation as far as I was concerned.

Ty kept his distance, and Jacob,in werewolf shape, stood with him. I went to them. Ty hugged me, but Jacob dropped to his knees and lifted his face to me, baring his throat to his alpha. I stroked it with my fingers and gave him a soft kiss on his muzzle. His musky, animal scent had me fighting another shape change.

Through the door to the other room, I saw Orion staring at Ruelle's remains. Fair-haired Cody stood at his elbow. Other vampires prepared to move the body.

Orion's face had the same look Ruelle's had the night I killed Emanis. Relief and great loss for a 2,000-year companion. I simply couldn't allow Ruelle to live. He'd already programed missiles with nuclear bombs, for God's sake. Seattle. New Washington. Could we stop them?

Ruelle could have taken me with him, could have killed me before he died. He chose not to. I guess that meant he loved me. But love, without compassion, without empathy, has no power. If beautiful Ruelle, with his cunning mind and sharp intellect, ever had those qualities, then the world lost something precious in Babylon those thousands of years ago.

Heflin arrived. "We need to get everyone out of here. The charges are set. I don't want to take any chances. We will come back later and get the things we need, but for safety, I want it completely emptied now." He wouldn't meet my eyes. "Maat..."

"I know. One missile. Set for Seattle is in a sealed vault. One for New Washington. Ruelle told me."

Heflin sighed. "I've set charges outside the vault doors. Maybe it will work."

"Maybe." I doubted it. The control hidden in this mountain vault was sending out the launch countdown to missile silos somewhere far from here. All we could do was hope entropy had damaged the missiles and they would fail.

I turned to go, and I saw Xavier and Ty standing over Parr's body.

"I don't know, you ask her," Xavier said.

Ty considered me, an odd expression on his face. "There's a hole in his chest."

I walked over to him. Lowell's dead eyes stared at

the ceiling. His gaping mouth framed his final scream.

"Yep," I said. "Looks like a hole to me."

"Well?" Ty planted his hands on his hips.

"Well, what?"

"Where's his heart?"

I shrugged. "Well…I think maybe I ate it." My voice went up a notch. "Maybe."

I wasn't sure what to make of the look that passed between Ty and Xavier. I hadn't planned to eat the damned thing. When I tore it out, the smell of blood and fresh meat in my claws overwhelmed me. It was the first raw meat I'd eaten since the change. Tasted fine, but it was a tough bastard.

We hurried through the center toward the waiting vehicles. Orion wasn't with us. I turned to go back for him when he came toward us at a quick pace.

"I am returning the way we came with the light proof trucks." He smiled at me and hurried away.

Ty sidled up beside me. He handed me the Rudra and the Aries. "We found them in a hall. Ah…did you really…you know…eat his heart?"

I turned to him. Was this going to be a problem?

I hedged. "I got caught up in the moment."

Jacob laughed softly from behind me. He'd changed back to human form and located some clothes. The pants wereblood stained. I turned and planted my fists on my hips. "Your face is as fuzzy as mine, smart ass. What's the first thing you ate?"

"A rabbit." He grinned.

"A rabbit? That's pitiful. Pathetic. A little bunny." I slipped my arm in Ty's. "Some weres don't know how to live."

I wiped my hand across my face. Were those tears?

For whom? Maybe I cried for Maat Ferris the monster killer, the Angel of Death, whoate a human heart. The sharp pain in my stomach made me gag, but I didn't throw up.

Jacob reached out and drew me too him. He spoke softly in my ear. "It's okay, Maat. To cry. I cried too when it happened. We endure."

****

It took longer than I expected to load up and go. Heflin had to do a double check to be sure we left no one behind. Finally, we were out of the command center and driving toward Salvaje. There were plenty of trucks at the complex, and Heflin made sure that everything that would roll went away. The vamps, men, and werewolves were on their way back to Salvaje with the prisoners.

Heflin, Xavier, and I rode in a Turtle, and we stopped on a high hill about five miles from the complex. Shadows stretch eastward across the arid land as the sun set on the strangest day of my life.

"I mag locked all the doors," Heflin said. "That should keep the blast local at the two vaults. Should keep that atomic generator intact, too."

"Will we be able to see the missile?" I asked. "I mean if it...flies."

"Should," Heflin said. "Silo's probably within a hundred miles." He glanced at his watch. "Ten minutes."

What was there to see? Confirmation that Seattle, the shining star of the new world, would die because of greedy men and a vampire? That New Washington, so close to my green mountains, would cease to exist. Knowledge that I failed, even as I succeeded. I wanted to know that Anolia and so many others on this journey hadn't died in vain. It was of negligible comfort to say that three deadly missiles would never leave their silos. They would sit there for all eternity until entropy crushed them in their earthen graves.

Fools like the Salvaje warriors and I could always hope someone learned a lesson. Then there'd probably be humans, vampires, or werewolves to laugh at us and show us how wrong we were. And we were going to lose Seattle.

"I'm sorry, Maat." Heflin shook his head. "I...what's that?" He pointed toward the mountains.

A Turtle raced toward us, sending a trail of dust like a billowing brown fan behind the vehicle. We checked our guns and waited. We relaxed when we recognized Ajax.

The Turtle skidded to a halt, and Ajax stuck his head out the window. "We need to move back some, boys and girls." His laughter rumbled across at us. He raced away leaving us to follow his dust trail. I got a glimpse of the woman sitting next to him. She seemed a bit Asian, lush, but not to his usual substantial standards.

If Ajax said run, we should run. We followed him at a dangerous speed, given the terrain. Six more miles, down a hill and up another, we made it to a rocky plateau. Ajax had stopped, and he and his lady friend stood waiting when we arrived.

"Don't want to be too close," Ajax said. He had his arm wrapped around the woman's neck. She didn't look so happy. "This here's Susie." Ajax squeezed Susie with a bit more force than I thought necessary. "Susie came from New Washington. Didn't you, baby?"

Susie nodded. Her eyes darted back and forth and if he released her, I thought she might run.

"Where you been, Ajax?" I asked. "You missed all

the fun. We had a hell of a fight."

"Nah. Fun's just startin' babe. Hef told me about all the old tunnels and lines around that place, so I checked it out. I was about to leave when Susie's crew arrived. I hung around real quiet for a while, till I saw that fucking vampire and figured out what they were up to.

"They had the original plans for that hellhole with them. So, I went to borrow a set, and Susie happened to come in during the borrowing. I persuaded her to join me. Didn't I, sweetheart?" He squeezed Susie again.

"Don't worry, Susie," I said. "No one's going to hurt you. You can let her go, Ajax."

"I was nice to her." Now Ajax sounded offended. He released Susie. "I didn't…"

"I'm fine," Susie said. Her voice was soft and cultured. "The vice president—"

"Is dead," Heflin told her. "So is the president. All the control rooms have explosives. Except the most important, the ones they relocked. But they are programmed to launch a missile toward Seattle and one to New Washington in—"he glanced at his watch"—"two minutes."

Ajax's laughter echoed across the plateau, and I resisted the urge to slug him. He reached into the Turtle and drew out a small metal box. Blinking red numbers flashed on one side. Counting down…thirty…twenty-nine…twenty-eight.

"Guys that built the thing in that mountain weren't no fools," Ajax said. His loud laughter sounded like it had in New York before he realized he'd made a mistake and created Pink Guys. "Knew one thing though. Might have to make a big boom to keep it out of enemy hands. What you call it, Susie babe?"

"A fail-safe." Susie replied. She sighed. "It's beautiful."

"Yeah. Fail-safe. Anyway, Susie and me went looking for the fail-safe. Found it, too."

The numbers on the counter worked their way down. Fifteen…fourteen…thirteen.

Ajax stared at the counter. "We'll see how it works in a few seconds."

Nine…eight…seven……six.

We turned our faces toward the mountain. Three…two…one. Nothing happened until…my werewolf senses picked it up first.

"Oh shit," I said.

"What is it?" Xavier slipped his arm around me.

"The ground." Deep in her heart, mother earth moaned. Then she roared.

"Shit, Ajax." I screamed at him. "What the fuck was this fail-safe?

Ajax grinned, his eyes bright. "Tell 'em, Susie."

"The device is a five-megaton hydrogen bomb," Susie said, as if she informed us what we were having for dinner. "But really rather small as they go. And it's quite deep, so it should be okay."

"Who armed it?" Xavier asked. The shocked look on his face mirrored Heflin's—and mine.

"I did." Susie crossed her arms.

"Ajax wouldn't have made you…"

"No. He couldn't." Susie cast a speculative eye on my demo man. "But I will say he does have a certain charm about him. And he was most eloquent in explaining the situation."

Ajax suddenly had a suspicious look on his face.

We all moved away from the vehicles, praying the

plateau would hold under us.

"We're too close," Susie shouted as the ground danced. "Need cover."

We ran for what we hoped was a solid rock gully, as the land shivered under our feet. We dropped down and huddled against the trembling earth as a dry rain of pebbles and sand sifted down on us. The larger rocks vibrated and hummed as the geological spasm rumbled, until it broke out in a blast that sucked air from my lungs and hammered through me, into me, and forced me into werewolf form. Force is way different from voluntary. I rolled and clawed the earth, howling my agony to the sky, finally finding peace only when darkness flowed over me.

Chapter Twenty-Two

I opened my eyes to a smear of brown fur. Oops. I lifted my head. They'd found a blanket to lay me on. Susie sat not far away, watching me with curious, but not fearful, eyes. Okay, let her watch. I changed back to human form.

Susie eased closer. "Does it hurt? To change?"

"It hurt the first time. Not so bad now."

Susie nodded. "They said you killed the vampire. I'm glad. He fed on us." She turned, and I saw the healing fang marks on her throat.

"Help me find some clothes." I forced myself to sit up. "I've *got* to learn to control this."

Susie brought me a shirt and pair of pants, obviously hers. After I dressed, I approached my men. Ajax's face was so neutral I immediately became suspicious. He didn'task about me being a were. "Did you know? Asshole. Don't you lie to me."

Ajax blew out a breath and shrugged. "After the vamp brought you to me from New York, you were crazy, confused…you sort of changed one night. Not all the way. Never told you. Only happened once. Guess I hoped it wouldn't happen again. Guess I didn't want it to. Remembered you saying you'd kill yourself if you got bit."

Sweat gleamed on his dark skin. I had to go hug him. No matter what, he was still Ajax, and I loved him.

We weren't about to go back and see what happened. A dirty copper colored cloud churned in the sky above the area of the missile complex. At least the wind was blowing away from us. Susie said the blast was underground and the dust shouldn't be radioactive. Then she amended her words to only *mildly radioactive*.

"Wow," I said. "That had to be Ajax's biggest boom of all."

Susie shook her head. "Not bad." She grinned. "The builders designed it to destroy only the facility. .".."They miscalculated. A little. Susie frowned. "Heflin says they're going to send all the people who came with me back to New Washington. He said it's not our fault. Will everyone feel that way? I saw them shooting the guards from Salvaje when we came in."

"Stick close to Ajax. He'll take care of you."

"Come on, Maat," Heflin called from the Turtle. "Let's go check on Seattle. We'll have to wait on news from New Washington." He stared at the dust cloud for a moment. "Damn. I had plans for that atomic generator."

****

We returned to find Salvaje in chaos. The bomb's detonation had caused a mild earthquake and sent people running into the streets. Water and gas lines held, and the Murlex adobe fulfilled its promise to flex and not break. Not so, the buildings interiors. They were like dollhouses, picked up and shaken by a child's temper tantrum. We rushed into the Paradox to find Maureen sitting with Mary amid the ruins of her main barroom, drinking beer.

Heflin eyed her.

"Yes, my love," Maureen said. She rolled her words

a bit. "Beer." She held up her glass. "Beer is in barrels. There is not a single unbroken bottle of wine in Salvaje." She sighed. I saw tears of relief in her eyes, though. She knew where he'd been.

Heflin wrapped his arms around her shoulders. "Don't worry, darling. I'll get more." He kissed her cheek. "Right now, we need to find the radio."

Maureen nodded agreeably and sipped her beer.

Mary's eyes had narrowed down on Susie. Ajax motioned for us to go on. Mary got along with the quiet, good-natured Giselle, but God knew how she'd take Susie, who was far more intelligent and had a much stronger personality.

Heflin, Xavier, and I left them there. Now we'd see if it went off or if we destroyed the controls in time. He found the radio. We had a couple of tense moments when it wouldn't work, then came the sound we wanted to hear—Radio Free Seattle. Hopefully, New Washington was the same. Would Seattle's residents ever know how death and destruction had missed them by only minutes, thanks to the courage of the monsters, vampires, and humans of Salvaje—and the ingenuity and luck of Ajax, a man who believed bigger was always better.

Xavier and I went down to the showers. At least there was warm water. We left our bloody clothes in the trash and walked to our room wrapped in towels.

Ty wasn't in his room when we passed by. "Should we find him?" I asked.

"No. He'll come if he needs us."

Ava had slept in her box through everything. Orion didn't want her with us. He—and I—still considered her a bit volatile.

Xavier made me sit on the bed and then he knelt

beside me. He gathered my hands in his own and kissed my fingers. "Will you marry me?"

Marry? That's a word I'd never thought to hear. I grasped his face in my hands and stared into those beautiful dark eyes—eyes that so captivated meat Avalon. Avalon, how long ago? Mere months in actual time—but ages in our lives. I loved him.

"Xavier. I'm a werewolf. One of the monsters."

"We can add your promise not to eat me to the vows. Marry me, Maat."

I laughed and kissed him. "I'll marry you."

Xavier's breath hissed between his teeth. "When?"

"After we decide what we're going to do next."

He grinned. "Seattle."

"Seattle. That's where Sable took my money, anyway."

"So that's why we had to save Seattle. Hard to spend radioactive gold."

"You bet." I'd thought about Sable, but the gold never crossed my mind. I eased away from him, stretched on the bed, and tossed away my towels.

Xavier lay down beside me. I guess we intended to make love, but we both fell asleep within seconds. I dreamed of my mother, and she spoke of the father I'd never known. For some reason, I dreamed of Ruelle and Orion, standing side by side, smiling at me.

****

Each day that passed after the destruction of the missile complex brought a change.

I witnessed the execution of Abban Connor. Tension was high, but older and wiser weres made Anson understand the wisdom of a clean death for him. Connor retained a few devoted followers, and rather than risk a civil war, Anson offered them amnesty for peace. He wouldn't let Connor live. Orion wouldn't have allowed it either. There had been a couple of flame-throwers in the missile complex, and he'd lost two of his vamps. If Orion and Anson had their way, they'd have tied Connor to a stake over a slow fire.

Heflin accepted the loathsome duty of executioner. A single silver bullet to the head and it was over. Connor died with his eyes locked on mine. I wanted to look away, but I didn't.

I'd accepted responsibility for one new vampire, Ava, but I lost Cody to Orion. "I want you to be happy." I said as I held Cody tight in my arms. My young vampire cried when he asked me to release him. I'd miss him, but I knew Orion could protect him better than I could, until he grew older and stronger. Yes, I worried about the darkness, the hunger, but there was nothing I could do.

"Will you send word from Seattle?" Orion asked. "Tell us what it's like."

"Sure. Thinking of relocating?"

"Perhaps. I've been here a long time." His voice carried bit of longing. "You're the most interesting thing that's happened in years. I expect excitement will follow you like a shadow."

"I'll send word." For the first time in my life, I'd had enough excitement.

Orion turned to Cody. "Will you leave us for a minute?"

Cody eased out of my arms and out the door. Orion came close—too close.

"Orion, I thought…"

"I am not going to seduce you, wolf, much as I would like to. I have a gift for you."

He slid one arm around my waist and drew me close. "Let me into your mind," he said softly. His voice beguiled me but did not compel. I'd have fought that. I relaxed and let him into my senses as I had when he taught me to walk in the place of mist.

Vampire. I shivered. Not Ruelle's foulness, but the frigid wind of death and darkness rose from the depths of time. And the ever-present hunger.

"Change your hands." Orion brushed my cheek with his fingers.

I did as he asked.

Orion held out a wrist. "Make a cut...here."

I laid one claw on the inside of his wrist. "Are you sure?"

"Do it."

My claw gouged out a rough trough in his flesh. Deep garnet liquid gushed out and dripped to the floor. "Drink, I beg you." He spoke quietly but with firm resolve.

My first meal as a werewolf had been a human heart. As much as I hated vampire blood, despite the times it had saved my life, I lifted his arm, placed my mouth on the wound and drank. I suddenly became something I didn't want to be—a part of him. Not like the place of mist, not like a dream, but pure reality.

Ages and ages, time weighed upon him. Memory lifted the burden a bit. Lovers, human and turned in Orion's arms, and enemies lay dead and torn at his feet. I touched on a power of such a magnitude it seemed impossible that his body could contain it.

I gasped. I drew my mouth away from the wound and it healed.

"You are so much more. The New York vampires

are…"

"Inconsequential. Emanis and Ruelle stopped… maturing. I did not. I can tell you, there is something flowing into this world. Magic, some psychic phenomena, or something new after thousands of years. I don't know its source. I don't know what to call it. I do know you, with your peculiar mixed blood, would do well to examine it. Control it if you can. I think it will make us, the descendants of the old race greater—or it will destroy us. Now tell me, what do you hear?"

"Hear?"

Orion's mouth hovered close to my ear. "Will you come to my bed if I call you? Will you lie down and spread your legs for me, or bare your throat if I sing to you?"

I pulled away from him. "No, I told you. I…" Something had changed. "Your voice."

"In New York, they gave you immunity to our will. I give you immunity to our voice.

Chapter Twenty-Three

My body rebelled against changing back to a regular sleep at night, wake up at dawn pattern. The darkness outside called to me as it never had before. We would be leaving before daylight the next day. I'd finished packing when Xavier walked into the bedroom. I sat on the edge of the bed, wrapped my arms around his legs, and rubbed my face against him.

"I have a problem," I said.

"And that problem is…?" Xavier pried me loose and lifted me to stare into my eyes.

"I'm a werewolf now."

"And?"

"You don't have to be so careful with me. Until I get used to being stronger, I have to be incredibly careful with you."

Xavier studied me for a moment and then lifted my shirt. He sank his teeth into my nipple and bit down hard. Still holding tight, he tugged. I shuddered and almost came.

"Like that?" he said as he released me and forced me down on the bed.

I sat there speechless, drawing deep breaths. He none too gently stripped my clothes off and, when his mouth and teeth went between my legs, I did come. He entered me, and from his moan of pleasure, I knew everything was okay between us. I rubbed his powerful muscled back with my hands.

"I love you," he whispered as he released himself into me. Xavier loved Maat, the foul-mouthed hunter. He loved Maat, the werewolf. He loved me.

My lover, my husband to be, fell asleep. So, did I. A werewolf's dreams are not human dreams. I ran wild under a new moon, across a desert landscape. Somewhere, across the sand, I heard someone call. I should know that voice, but I couldn't remember.

****

One other interesting event occurred before we left. A messenger arrived carrying a box and refused to give it to anyone but me. Xavier, Heflin, Maureen, and I were sitting at a table in the downstairs work room drinking coffee.

"Well, this is a surprise. Xavier?"

He shook his head.

"Your birthday?" Maureen clapped her hands.

"No. But let's see." The second layer of wrapping paper held an envelope with a card.

I recognized the flowing handwriting. I'd seen it once before.

I think you should have this. Call it a reward for returning my property. I will see you again. Perhaps Seattle. I laid the card on the table for the others to see. They all knew of my strange dinner with Galen Moreau.

The box opened easily. I plundered through packing tissue and lifted out the sculpture.

Satilla. The image of the warrior who lived before Orion's time.

"Oh, my God. This is…" I held it close. "I saw this in his house. It's priceless. I can't own priceless things. I break too much. I'm not good enough." I set it on the table for them to see.

Maureen reached out to touch it, then drew her hand back much as I had in Moreau's house. We all stared. Then Maureen gasped. "Oh, oh. Don't you see. Maat, it's you. The thing is you. Look at the face, the body."

"Come on, Maureen. That's ridiculous."

She shook her head.

Xavier did reach out and carefully grasped the statue in his hands. "She's right. Look, look at it. Why do you believe you are not worthy of something priceless, Maat?"

"Come on, Xavier. I'm a typical were hunter, rude and crude. Now I'm a fucking goddammed werewolf like the ones that destroyed my life. I'm the thing I've hated most in the world. That statue is not anything like me. It's graceful and...pure."

He carefully returned it to the table. I grasped the precious object. "If I ever see him again, I'll give it back." But I was standing there holding it tight against my heart. And God damn it, tears were running down my face. I don't cry. Really, I don't. I sat down, embracing my gift.

Xavier lifted me from my chair and led me upstairs. He brought the box with him and set it on the chest that held our few clothes. He made me sit down and sat beside me.

"Maat, I don't know what to say. I wish I could help. All I can do is love you."

"That's all I want, Xavier. I don't think I'll ever come to terms with the werewolf in me. Galen Moreau is so unbelievably strange. He's not human. He talked about magic and other weird things. Why did he send me that sculpture?"

"I don't know why, but you can deny it all you want. That statue is you."

He drew a breath, started to speak, then stopped.

"What?" Now that wasn't going to work.

He gave in. "Were you in love with Ruelle?"

I didn't have to think on that one. "I loved him, yes. I was never in love with him. Is that enough?"

"Yes, my darling. It is enough."

Chapter Twenty-Four

We were to leave before dawn. There were no safe roads going straight north from Salvaje. Moreau had spoken of a route, but he had three-hundred men to guard him on what he admitted was a dangerous path. We had to go over a thousand miles back east to St. Louis and catch a convoy to Seattle from there. Heflin was our wagon master again.

"I am on a life-or-death mission to obtain more wine," he had said. "By God's grace, I found ten unbroken bottles in the basement, but they won't last long."

The trucks lined up according to Wagon Master Heflin's instructions. A hundred and fifty of Xavier's trainee troops chose to go with him. That required more supplies and four more trucks. Xavier and I had almost no money when we entered Salvaje. Even with well-paid work we couldn't afford the required funds. Now he had troops, trucks, supplies. I didn't ask who paid for them.

"Could you be careful, asshole? That's my bedroom you're kicking around." Oh, shit. That was Ava. She stood watching them load the box in which Cody had slept on his journey here. I offered to get her a new one, but she declined. She'd taken control of one aspect of her life and filled the box with fine cushions and other pads. To my surprise Orion had given her gold, so she bought a few of the nicest clothes Salvaje offered. She didn't speak to me but handed me a folded note from Orion.

I've instructed Ava to obey you, but once away from here, you may have to discipline her. Or kill her if she's too much trouble. She is no longer human, but the human concept of having a master is grating on her. If you meet other vampires, it will become critical. She may betray you. Good journey to you, Maat Ferris.

Ava climbed up in the truck and then into the box.

"Ava? Let me know if you need anything."

She shrugged and pulled the lid down to shut out the light. She had been calm since she'd joined us, but I could see the anger and resentment at her situation returning. She had read Orion's note, and I was sure she'd challenge me before long. Half an hour later, as the sky lightened, we rolled away from Salvaje. I didn't look back.

Xavier had purchased an almost new, large-cab truck for us. It would hold all the supplies we'd need for the trip, however we had to obtain those supplies in either West Memphis or St. Louis. The bomb earthquake left Salvaje short of everything. Ajax, Mary, and Susie followed in his truck, still carrying hisvolatile pulp and powder explosive. He'd managed to hide it away after he found out about the nuke under the complex. Mary and Susie tolerated each other, and I'd swear Susie had gained thirty pounds since I first met her.

I told Jacob he could remain in Salvaje if he wished, but he declined. "I think I'll have more fun with the Angel of Death."

The road remained smooth. Ty sat in the seat behind me with his eyes closed and his head rolling to one side. Jacob sat beside him.

"Is he alive?" Xavier asked after a while.

I glanced back. "He breathes occasionally."

All of Maureen's ladies insisted on saying goodbye to him before he left. As I had predicted, Xavier had found out about the boy's brothel adventures and was livid. *Turning him into a whore* was one of the nicest things he said to Maureen. He dragged Ty away to lecture him. I didn't hear that one, but Ty wouldn't talk for a couple of days. I'd hear more if Xavier learned I knew about it and didn't tell him.

Heflin wasn't the only one who required supplies for Salvaje, and the convoy stretched too long. Hard to defend if attacked. Word had come that they'd repaired the bridge at St. Louis, and trucks were crossing again, but everyone had abandoned East Memphis.

Our trip wasn't leisurely—no journey through the wilderness can be fun. We drove in shifts for two days, then found a defensible place to stop. That's when I saw Elspeth facing off with Ava. Elspeth carried a ragged bag, had a sand-colored Salvaje cape draped across her shoulders, and a pair of the soft boots the vampires usually wore on her feet—only one was brown and the other black. I would be responsible for her, of course.

Elspeth's eyes and strings of cheap beads and diamonds remained unchanged. The old witch was going to do whatever she wanted anyway. She must have been riding in one of the other trucks. Ava broke off and stalked away when I approached.

"Is something wrong?" I asked but didn't want an answer.

Elspeth shrugged her shoulders. "Vampire." She spoke as if that one word covered everything.

I sighed. "Have you eaten?"

She shook her head. "Come on, I'll help you get food."

I led the way to the food prep area. We passed several unhappy people. They made signs to ward off an evil witch and grumbled. The cook, on the other hand, greeted her. I remembered Heflin saying Maureen had told her kitchen people to feed Elspeth when she came by. He fixed us plates, and I found a place for us to sit. She ate everything. Her thin stick arm worked steadily to get it in her mouth.

I stood to meet Heflin when he came storming up. "Where the hell did she come from?" His expression seemed like a mix of fear and fury.

"I don't know. She had to have been in one of the trucks."

"I have to get rid of her. She's a nightmare."

"So, you plan to abandon her here in the desert?"

He shook his head and glared at her. "Will you look after her?"

"I suppose, but no one can control her."

I sat back down where Elspeth was licking her plate. She sighed when she finished.

"Elspeth? Can you understand me this morning?"

"Yes." A single word with multiple invisible *buts* hanging on the end.

"Will you try to control yourself for a while? I know you're smarter than you pretend to be. I'll be in serious trouble if you do something weird."

"Elspeth be good."

"I hate that. I know you can talk as well as I can. This speaking in third person is annoying. And you better not steal anything of mine."

Elspeth raised her face to me. She raised a hand and

touched my cheek. She said one word. "*Satilla.*" Then she giggled, her whole body shaking.

Why did I have the feeling that a woman, a goddess, a thousand or more years in her grave, would eventually be a problem? Worse, Moreau's crystal hung around Elspeth's neck amid the diamonds and stones. She'd taken it again. And I would have to find a way to cover the diamonds or dull them to look like fakes. She'd make a great target. I made her a bed on the back seat of our truck. Xavier and I had a small tent.

When we left the next morning, Jacob went back to one of the troop trucks and left his place for her. I glanced back and saw her curled up on the seat, sleeping, but holding Ty's hand.

Ty smiled. "She's okay. Is she ours now?"

"Unfortunately, yes"

"And Ajax?"

"Yes. He swore he'd never leave me again because I got in too much trouble."

"I miss Cody." Ty appeared to have genuine regret for the boy vampire.

"So do I, but he's safer with Orion."

He didn't mention Ava. At my request, Jacob had taken Ava out to hunt and help her learn to take care of herself. Orion had supplied her with blood. That was gone now. She avoided all of us, except to occasionally and quite sarcastically ask if I wanted something from her. She was lovely, and a few of the men approached her. She sent them away by displaying her fangs.

Elspeth earned her way when she suddenly warned us of bandits ahead. Heflin, Xavier, and I had seen enough that we believed her. Xavier led a band of men and me to attack in force. Those thieves would trouble convoys no more.

Chapter Twenty-Five

When we arrived in West Memphis, we found only partial truth to the rumors. The river's east side did sit in total ruins, but West Memphis had grown, and repairs on the bridge progressed enough Heflin decided to leave us and head farther east. I know he was curious about what was taking place in New Washington. Our blast at the complex took out its missile too.

Other rumors ran rampant. Dictator Gannett had disappeared...in hiding...in Atlanta...forming a new army. Radio broadcasts were coming from New Washington, exhorting people to be calm. Congress was reforming and there would be elections soon. What frightened me were the calls for Gannett's army officers and security personnel to surrender on charges of treason.

"We've already talked about that," Heflin said. "The Salvaje radio station will be broadcasting within weeks. It probably won't make it to New Washington, but it will reach Seattle. We're going to tell the world what happened."

When he left us, we made promises, but the odds were good we'd never see him again. His generous parting gift was two fully loaded fuel carriers. He said the city of Salvaje treasury paid for those.

We'd have to alternate driving and riding. Elspeth

would ride with whoever could stand her. We'd have to switch off on that one. She'd joined the pack, though I could feel no real connection with her.

West St. Louis rumbled and squawked like a midwestern boomtown. The last convoys of the season were forming to head for Salt Lake City and on to Seattle. If they didn't cross the mountains before the first snow, they'd be stuck until spring.

Finding the right convoy became a problem. Most were already full, and no wagon master wanted too many trucks. We had eight with the addition of the fuel haulers. I knew a couple of the wagon masters, and they wanted me as a guard, but when they found out about my fellow travelers, including Xavier's small army, they refused. Having too many people was a liability, just like having too few.

Finally, Xavier went out one day and came back with a bearded, rough looking wagon master, one who was familiar with Seattle and its werewolf and vampire populace.

"I told you," the wagon master grumbled, "I need trucks, but I got guards with guns."

"Can they see and hunt in the dark?" Xavier asked. I thought he was referring to me, but he nodded at Jacob. "Show him."

Jacob held out one hand, flexed his arm, and his claws popped out.

The wagon master stepped back, and his eyes narrowed. He studied the claws, then sighed. "Okay. You can keep him under control? I'm from Seattle. Sometimes—

"He'll be fine." Xavier's voice carried an angry note. The wagon master had spoken of Jacob as if he were a guard dog.

The wagon master nodded. "Okay. Fee is twenty gold per truck. Make sure you got your own food and fuel."

Wow. A small fortune. Xavier simply shrugged.

****

Two days before we were to leave, Xavier talked with the convoy's mechanic.

"Good vehicles, all of them," the mechanic said. He closed the hood. He was a sturdy looking man who smiled often and with ease.

Xavier paid him his fee. The wagon master required that the convoy's mechanic check out the trucks—at the truck owner's expense. The mechanic would be traveling with us, so he could repair vehicles on the road if necessary—at the truck owner's expense.

Ajax and Ty faced off on a patch of grass not far away, with Susie, Mary, and Elspeth cheering them on. Ajax spent some time teaching Ty his own special type of hand-to-hand fighting, and Ty made a credible student. He'd grown taller and slimmer than Xavier over the summer, but he'd inherited his father's swift, devastating speed. The boy had become a man, physically as well as emotionally. He wore only a leather vest and jeans, and his bare muscular arms complemented powerful legs. Ty lashed out with one foot, caught Ajax behind the knee, and took him down.

Ajax started to rise, then fell back, arms and legs askew. "I give up," he said.

Ty knelt beside him, which was a mistake. Ajax immediately grabbed him, flipped, and rolled him over. They tussled for a few minutes, then, laughing, separated, and allowed Mary and Susie to help them to their feet.

Ty threw an arm around Mary's shoulder. "Sweetheart, why don't you be my girl? You're too fine a woman for..." Ty's voice trailed off, and he stared.

A woman walked toward us, accompanied by two boys, one about twelve, the other younger, maybe seven. At a distance, she looked ordinary from her pants and shirt to the green scarf covering her hair.

Ty suddenly roared with laughter. He released Mary, ran to the approaching woman, wrapped his arms around her thighs, lifted her in the air, and spun around. Her scarf came loose, and glorious auburn hair whipped like a flag in the late summer sun.

"Hey," the mechanic growled. He picked up a long, heavy wrench.

Xavier caught his arm. "It's okay, he's a friend of hers."

"Put me down, Ty." Sabrina shouted and pounded on his shoulders with her hands.

He set her down but didn't release her. Not that he could have anyway. She had her arms around him, and I could hear her sobbing something about him being alive. Finally, she pushed away from him. "You've grown up," she said.

Ty nodded. Something like sadness flickered across his face. "Things have happened." He nodded at Xavier and me.

Sabrina slowly approached us. Xavier and I stood side-by-side, but not touching. She said, "You're...together. That's lovely."

Xavier stepped closer to her.

The mechanic and his wrench moved in. Sabrina gave him a dazzling smile. "It's okay, Eddie. These are friends. I never thought I'd see them again."

Eddie stopped. He accepted her words, but he remained on guard. I saw the love in his eyes. He'd die for her—and she belonged to him.

"I owe you an apology, Sabrina," Xavier said. "I was wrong. Wrong about many things."

Sabrina accepted his apology with a graceful nod of her head.

"I heard…" Sabrina swallowed. "Aaron's dead?"

"Yes." Xavier glanced around. No one within hearing distance except Eddie, Ty, and me. Eddie appeared a little confused, so I guessed she hadn't told him who she was—or had been.

"Tell me," Sabrina said.

"He died…" Xavier stopped, and then lied so smoothly it scared me. "They were going to hurt Ty. Aaron tried to do the right thing in the end. He tried to help us. Parr killed him."

"Lowell? We trusted…Oh, God. Anolia." Sabrina closed her eyes and hung her head.

I started to go to her, but I remembered my silver. I drew my blade, removed the wolf pendant she had given me what seemed like so long ago and handed them to Xavier. Sabrina jerked as I took her in my arms, and she realized what I was. I stared straight into her eyes. "You and I have so much to talk about. It's a long way to Seattle, sister wolf."

A word about the author...

Lee Roland is a writer of urban fantasy and paranormal romance. She lives in Florida with her family. http://leeroland.com

Other books from TWRP by Lee are...

Huntress Rising ~*~ Book 1- Angel of Death Series
Bone Dance ~*~ Book 1- Bone Dance Series
Blade of Redemption ~*~ Book 1- Guardians of the Blades

Thank you for purchasing
this publication of The Wild Rose Press, Inc.

For questions or more information
contact us at
info@thewildrosepress.com.

The Wild Rose Press, Inc.
www.thewildrosepress.com